Eric Wilder

Krewe of Illusion

Edmond, Oklahoma

Other books by Eric Wilder

Gondwana Press
1802 Canyon Park Cir. Ste C
Edmond, OK 73013

Front Cover by Gondwana Graphics

ISBN: 978-1-946576-19-4

for Marilyn

Krewe of Illusion

A novel by
Eric Wilder

Chapter 1

A glorious spring had arrived in New Orleans. Jazz Fest had just concluded as I sat at the bar of Bertram Picou's mostly empty drinking establishment on Chartres Street in the French Quarter. Someone entered the bar that I recognized. Seeing me, he smiled and walked over. It was Frankie Castellano, looking wealthy in thousand-dollar shoes and a suit worth more than most people make in a year.

Frankie was one of the most powerful mob bosses in the South and was often referred to as 'Don of the Bayou.' He had dark hair and eyes and a receding hairline. His bulldog-like face made him look angry even when he was smiling.

"How you doing, Wyatt?"

"I'm good, Frankie. How about you?"

"Me too," Frankie said. "May I join you?"

"Pull up a stool," I said.

Frankie said, "Where's Bertram?"

He laughed when I said, "Probably on his way to the bank since he made so much money during Jazz Fest."

"Me, Adele, and Toni just caught the last act of Jazz Fest."

"Are Adele and Toni with you?" I asked.

"Over on Royal Street window shopping."

I ducked under the bar and said, "Then you probably need a drink. Scotch?"

When Frankie saw the bottle I poured from, he said. "Good memory. Monkey Shoulder is my favorite brand."

I handed him the scotch and said, "You're here for more than a drink and to test my memory. How can I help you?"

"A little problem I need someone to look into."

"Glad to help, though you usually call Tony on such matters," I said.

Former N.O.P.D. homicide detective Tony Nicosia had retired from the force under duress and was now, like me, a private investigator. I'd worked for Frankie in the past, though always alongside Tony Nicosia.

"Tony and Lil are on vacation in Italy," he said.

"I just finished my last case a few hours ago, and my dance card is open," I said. "Tell me how I can help?"

"Locate a missing person."

"I can do that. Who do you want me to find?"

"My sister."

"I've known you for a long time, Frankie. I didn't know you had a sister."

"Neither did I until a few days ago."

"Maybe you'd better explain," I said.

2

"This past Mardi Gras, I was king of the Krewe of Illusion. You familiar with it?"

The Krewe of Illusion was one of the oldest and most exclusive carnival clubs in New Orleans. It was rumored that only the city's richest and most powerful men ever ruled as King of Illusion, and then only after donating a cool million bucks. Frankie's question made me smile.

"Of course. My grandfather was King of Illusion once."

It was Frankie's turn to smile. "I keep forgetting your granddad was governor and the most powerful man in Louisiana."

"Unfortunately, none of it rubbed off on me."

"It sometimes doesn't pay to keep a high profile," Frankie said.

I understood what Frankie was insinuating. My grandfather was indeed powerful and had paid for his power by being assassinated in the capitol rotunda. I skipped over Frankie's reference.

"Sorry I interrupted. Please continue your story," I said.

"The Krewe has specific rules, and having Adele as my queen wasn't an option. The committee chose Harper Devereaux to serve as queen. You know who I'm talking about?"

"Me and everyone else in New Orleans," I said.

Harper Devereaux was a quintessential New Orleans socialite, a young woman as gorgeous as she was wealthy. The Devereaux family was among the wealthiest and most powerful families in New Orleans.

"Trust me when I tell you the amount of time Harper and I had to spend together didn't endear me with Adele."

"I can imagine." When Frankie killed his scotch, I said, "Another?"

"Please."

I stood across from him on the other side of the bar and refilled his glass straight from the bottle.

"Was Miss Devereaux the one who informed you about your sister?" I asked.

"Yes."

"Please explain how she knew about her."

"Harper is a philanthropist who does extensive charity work and is on the Louisiana Office of Behavioral Health board. One of the mental health facilities is the Pinebridge Mental Hospital. Heard of it?"

"I had an aunt who spent some time there," I said.

"And?"

I poured Frankie more scotch. "The hospital doesn't have a stellar reputation," I said. "Maybe things have changed, but patients were once treated like inmates. Beatings, mental deprivation, and maybe even torture occurred. Want to hear more?"

"Your aunt?"

"She survived," I said. "I remember some of her stories. Was your sister at Pinebridge?"

Frankie nodded. "Apparently," he said.

"A patient?" I asked.

"My father wasn't a very savory person."

"I understand," I said. "You just want to know the truth."

Frankie nodded again. "Can you help me?"

"Do you know your sister's name," I asked.

"Bella Donna Castellano."

"Any idea when she was born?" I asked.

"No clue," he said. "Right now, you know as much about my sister as I do."

I grabbed my cell phone and said, "I'll check my database."

"You have a database?"

4

"We P.I.s can't tap into the database used by law enforcement. There are several extensive informational databases available for the rest of us."

After a minute, Frankie said, "Well?"

"Your family has no birth record of a female named Bella Donna Castellano," I said.

"Impossible," he said. "What database are you accessing?"

"It's called Tracker, a comprehensive database for P.I.s," I said.

Frankie smirked and said, "Maybe you'd better trade it in for one that works."

"Bella Donna is your half-sister," I said.

"That's crazy," Frankie said. "My parents never divorced."

"You and Bella Donna have the same father but different mothers."

"Let me see that," he said.

When I handed him my phone and showed him Bella Donna Castellano's birth certificate, he stared at it.

"What's this supposed to mean?" he asked.

"Your dad had a mistress named Hattie Depoy. She was black and lived in the Lower Ninth Ward. Bella Donna was born in 1952. Your dad was only seventeen then and hadn't married your mother yet."

"What happened to Bella Donna?" Frankie asked.

"Hattie was from Arkansas and moved back there, taking Bella Donna with her."

"Then how did she end up in the Pinebridge Mental Hospital?"

Frankie was agitated, and I topped up his glass.

"Don't know," I said.

"Is Bella Donna still alive?" Frankie asked.

I shook my head and said, "I can find no death certificate."

Frankie downed his scotch and said, "I want you to go to Pinebridge and find out what my half-sister was doing there."

"Because you think your father is somehow involved?"

"Paco was a mean old bastard," Frankie said. "I know how bad he treated Mama and me."

"Bella Donna could be dead," I said. "Pinebridge has a bad reputation. Many of their patients were never accounted for, and some say they were buried in unmarked graves."

I nodded when Frankie said, "Pinebridge was that bad?"

"There are all sorts of unconfirmed allegations of rape, bondage, torture, and even murder," I said.

"How the hell did they get away with that?" Frankie asked.

"Mental illness, until recently, has been a taboo subject. Therapeutical treatments such as full-frontal lobotomies were green-lighted because not even medical professionals knew for sure what they were doing. Bad things were swept under the rug, and no one wanted to take responsibility."

"If Bella Donna is alive, I want you to find her. She's my sister, even if she is half-black."

"I'd like to interview Harper Devereaux. Can you arrange the meeting for me?"

"Why do you need to talk to her?"

"She's on the board of directors and can give us access to the Pinebridge facility without questions."

Frankie grabbed his cell phone. After a short conversation, he said, "Harper will speak with you. Can you go now?"

"Of course," I said.

Frankie clutched my wrist. "You're a former lawyer, and I know this goes without saying. . ."

"Whatever I learn, I won't share it with anyone other than you. You have my word."

"Thanks," Frankie said. He pulled out his checkbook, wrote me a check, and handed it to me. "This is only a retainer. Feel free to bill me for any expenses you may incur."

Frankie smiled when I said, "I've worked for you before, and you've always been more than generous. Give me Ms. Devereaux's address, and I'll head her way."

"Wonderful," he said. "Can you pour me one more scotch before you go?"

"I'll go you one better," I said as I sat the Monkey Shoulder bottle on the counter before him. "Help yourself."

The value of houses in the Quarter ranges from expensive to don't ask. Miss Devereaux's domicile was, 'You won't believe me if I tell you.'

I found Harper Devereaux's home near the corner of Ursulines Avenue and Royal Street. It was a stately mansion with a stucco-over-brick façade the color of buttercream. Tall shuttered windows opened onto a wrap-around balcony overlooking Ursulines.

I rang the doorbell, half expecting a butler to answer. Instead, Harper Devereaux, dressed like a runway model, appeared at the door, and I had to catch my breath.

"I'm Wyatt Thomas," I said. "Frankie Castellano just called about me."

Harper Devereaux was stunningly beautiful. I'd seen her pictures on society pages, but they did her no justice. Long auburn hair draped her shapely shoulders and brown designer low-cut sheath. Her smile told me she understood her appearance's effect on me.

"Come in, Mr. Thomas. We can talk in the den."

The parquet floors, wicker furniture, and hanging ferns in the foyer were perfect. Harper Devereaux smiled again when she saw me looking.

"Your house is beautiful," I said.

"Circa 1810 Creole cottage," she said. "I picked the property up for a song and did extensive renovations."

"I can see you have. Impressive."

I followed her to her den, which looked out into a courtyard through a floor-to-ceiling picture window. The door to the courtyard was ajar, and the babbling fountain filled the room with soothing vibes.

"The den is my favorite room," she said. "It's my haven from stress and life's chaos."

"I see why."

A large white couch dominated the room, and the white cat lying on it didn't move when Harper Devereaux sat beside it. I took a comfortable rocker near the couch.

"Now, Mr. Thomas, how can I help you?"

"Please, call me Wyatt," I said.

"Absolutely, and you can call me Harper. How do you know Frankie?"

"Frankie's wife Adele and her father Pancho owned an Italian restaurant in Metairie I frequented. I knew Adele and Pancho before I met him."

"I see," she said. "Can I get you a drink?"

"I'm an alcoholic," I said.

Harper smiled when she said, "A French Quarter P.I. who doesn't drink? How tragic. Do you mind if I mix something for myself?"

"Absolutely not."

Harper was young, probably in her late twenties or early thirties, though she moved across the room like an A-list actress. She wheeled her antique liquor cart to the couch and mixed us each a lime and soda water.

"Cheers," she said.

"You have an eclectic selection of liquor," I said.

"Everyone in my family drinks, and they all have expensive tastes. When they visit, I try to accommodate their favorites. What was your favorite alcohol before you gave up drinking?"

"I'd degenerated to the stage that I would drink almost anything short of battery acid, but my favorite alcohol was scotch."

She showed me a bottle in the cart. "Have you ever tried Monkey Shoulder?"

"Never did," I said. "Is it good?"

"I don't drink scotch," she said. "You're not here to talk about alcoholic beverages."

"Frankie Castellano's like a bulldog when he wants something. You ignited his fuse when you told him he has a sister he knew nothing about."

"I probably should have kept the information to myself," Harper said.

"Frankie hired me to investigate. He'll never be happy until he knows."

"Pinebridge is a medical facility. I'm on the board, and there are HIPAA rules I have to follow."

"Frankie's family and he has a right to know," I said.

"Probably so," she said. "Where do I begin?"

"His sister's name, for starters."

"Bella Donna Castellano."

"How did you learn Bella Donna was a patient at Pinebridge?"

"The Administrator of the facility is a close friend of mine. She told me."

"What's your friend's name?" I asked.

"Celeste Gauthier," Harper said.

"I'd like to interview her," I said. "Can you arrange it?"

"Pinebridge is a day's drive from here in Central Louisiana."

"Been there," I said. "My aunt was a patient at the hospital for a while."

"Then you know the facility has a bad reputation," she said.

I nodded. "Mental illness is a social stigma. At least we've advanced beyond referring to mental health facilities as insane asylums."

"Amen to that," she said.

Chapter 2

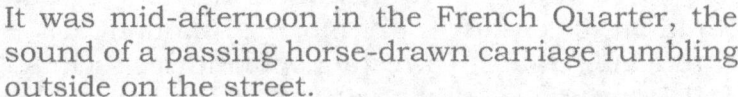

It was mid-afternoon in the French Quarter, the sound of a passing horse-drawn carriage rumbling outside on the street.

"I've been planning a trip to Pinebridge. You can ride with me if you like."

"Wonderful," I said. "Living in the Quarter, I don't need a car much."

"When we get to Pinebridge, I'll take you wherever you need. If you stay longer than me, you can rent a car."

"That'll work," I said.

"When did you want to go?" she asked.

"Soon as possible. I'll need to pack and see to my cat."

"You have a cat?"

She smiled when I said, "Just like every intelligent person I know."

"Bring her with you. She and Silky will get along famously."

"You sure?"

Harper put Silky into a cat carrier and said, "My car's parked in the back."

"Aren't you going to pack?" I asked.

"I own a house in Pinebridge," she said. "I have clothes there."

Harper's car was a Range Rover with all the expensive amenities. I could only imagine how much she'd paid for the vehicle. I didn't ask.

"Where to, Wyatt?" she said.

"Bertram's bar on Chartres Street. I have an apartment on the second floor."

Bertram's wasn't far from Harper's house on Ursulines. When we arrived, she parked on the street and exited the big SUV.

"Aren't you afraid you'll be towed?" I asked.

"I'm a Devereaux," she said. "It'll be here when we return."

I drew a deep breath, wondering how anyone could be so confident. Her money, I thought as we entered Bertram's. The establishment was rocking, and Bertram was mixing drinks at the bar. When he saw Harper and me enter the front door, he motioned for us to join him.

"Where you been?" he said. "And who is this gorgeous woman with you?"

"Harper Devereaux, meet Bertram Picou, the owner of this illustrious establishment."

Bertram had a way of disarming his customers with his charm, Harper no exception. She smiled and offered her hand. Having seen his performance many times, I shook my head and smiled.

"Frankie hired me to do a job for him. I must pack a few clothes because I will be out of town for a few days."

"Want me to take care of that mangy cat of yours?"

"I know you don't like her," I said.

"Quit your whining! You know me and Lady will take good care of her. "What did Frankie hire you to do?" Bertram asked.

"Confidential, Mr. Nosy," I said.

"You can tell old Bertram. It won't get farther than this bar," he said.

"Frankie swore me to secrecy and would kill us both if he knew I'd told you anything."

"Whoa! I don't need to know that bad. Can I get you something to drink, pretty lady?"

"Ginger ale," she said. "Wyatt and I have a lot of miles to cover, and I don't drink and drive."

"Can you put it in a go-cup?" I asked. "It's getting late, and I need to pack."

Bertram poured Harper a ginger ale and a lemonade for me.

"How long you going to be gone?" he asked.

"Until I solve Frankie's mystery," I said.

I nodded when he said, "Then keep me posted."

Harper followed me upstairs to my apartment on the second floor. Compared to her stately mansion, mine was little more than one room comprising a bedroom and a kitchenette. My cat Kisses was asleep on the bed.

"Oh, what a beautiful cat," Harper said. "What's her name?"

"Kisses."

"What happened to her tail?" she asked.

"Born that way. Guess she's probably part-Manx."

"Love your little apartment," she said.

"It's comfortable and all I need. Kisses loves the balcony and so do I."

"Don't apologize," she said. "People would kill to live in the heart of the French Quarter and have such a stunning view."

Cars passed on the street below, rowdy college students shouting obscenities at the pigeons.

"Thanks," I said. "How far is it to Pinebridge?"

"Two hundred miles, about three hours of driving time for most people, less than that for me."

"Should I increase my insurance before we go?"

"You'll be fine," she said with a grin. "I'm a good driver."

"Then I'd better hurry. Fast or slow, it'll be dark when we get there."

When Harper and I descended the stairs with my suitcase, Bertram's bar was filled with new customers.

Bertram waved and nodded when I said, "See you when I see you."

Harper's expensive Range Rover was waiting for us in one piece, an N.O.P.D. cop standing beside it on the sidewalk making sure of it. He smiled, saluted, and opened the door for her.

"I'm impressed," I said.

"Comes with the territory," she said.

After helping me load my bag, she drove away and headed for I-10. We were soon on our way to Baton Rouge, the swampy lowlands characterizing the Bonnet Carre Spillway prevalent on both sides of the highway.

"We'll head north after reaching Opelousas," she said. "Relax. We're a long way from there."

Relaxing wasn't difficult in Harper's opulent Range Rover. Unlike Kisses, Silkie liked traveling in a car and was asleep in the backseat.

I had questions for Harper, though I refrained from asking her. Frankie didn't want me to discuss the case with anyone, and I thought I knew why. Despite Harper and Frankie's forty-year age difference, I had a hunch they'd had an affair, maybe even an ongoing affair. It would explain the bottle of Monkey Shoulders Harper kept in her den.

Affairs are very personal and most often secretive for apparent reasons. It seemed to me Harper had shared her affair with Frankie with Celeste Gauthier, the administrator of the Pinebridge Mental Hospital. If not, how did Ms.

Gauthier even know about Frankie Castellano to the extent she told Harper about her discovery?

The reason might have been that Harper and Frankie had been the king and queen of the Krewe of Illusion. Maybe. I decided to ask her when the time was right.

My thoughts were shattered when Harper asked, "Don't you ever speak?"

"Sorry," I said. "Years of single living ruined me for small talk."

"How did you become a private investigator?"

"I was a French Quarter lawyer, though years of alcohol abuse ended my marriage and legal practice. I was disbarred. When Bertram finally fished me out of the gutter, dried me out, and gave me a place to stay, I needed a job. P.I. work came easy for me."

"You never tried to get your license back?"

"I think about it from time to time," I said.

"And?"

I smiled and said, "Thinking about it is all it has ever come to. What about you?"

"What about me?" she said.

"You seem happy living alone. Have you ever been married?"

When Harper answered my question, I could tell by her voice that she hadn't taken offense.

"The right person has never come along," she said. "Besides, I have Silky, and we're happy."

"What prompted Celeste to tell you about Frankie's sister?"

My question surprised Harper, and I could tell she was displeased that I had put her on the spot.

"Celeste knew that Frankie and I had been king and Queen of Illusion. She thought I would be interested. I was."

"Mardi Gras ended in February. You and Frankie are still friends?"

"Except for my father, Frankie's the most powerful man I've ever met," she said. "He's an extraordinary human being, and it's an honor for me to call him a friend."

Harper smiled when I said, "Frankie told me his wife was jealous of you."

"Did he now? I can see why. We spent lots of time together, sometimes until late at night."

"Did you and Frankie have an affair?" I asked.

"Inappropriate question," she said.

I decided not to pursue the subject. "What's Pinebridge like?"

"Hilly with lots of pine trees. There's not much there except for the hospital and the college. The parish was dry until a year ago. Now, they have a café in the square called Raven's Roost that Celeste and I like. It has a bar and shaded seating on the patio."

"Then you and Celeste are more than just business associates."

"You called Bertram nosy. That's like the pot calling the kettle black," she said.

"Sorry," I said. "It's a P.I.'s lot in life to ask questions."

"It's okay. Celeste cares for the house I own in Pinebridge. She lives there, and we're roommates when I visit."

I had fallen asleep sometime after we'd turned north at Opelousas. I opened my eyes when Harper awakened me with a shake of my knee. It was dark.

"Wake up, sleepy head. We're here," she said.

"Sorry I fell asleep on you," I said.

"No problem. There are motels ahead. Name your poison."

"Is there someplace closer to the center of town? I like to walk when I can."

"There's an old two-storied hotel downtown near the hospital and the college," Harper said. "It's family-owned and anything but modern."

"Sounds like it's right up my alley," I said.

"I'll drop you at the front door and wait until you check in, and then we can visit the hospital," she said.

She laughed when I said, "Celeste works this late?"

"She's a workaholic."

Dark streets typical of a small Louisiana town marked the outskirts of Pinebridge. On our way to the town center, we passed motels, fast-food establishments, used car lots, and appliance stores. The town square was different, with a historic courthouse near its center. The little town was old and dominated mainly by two-story buildings. Harper pulled the Range Rover into the entrance to the Beaufoy Hotel.

"I'll wait in the car while you check in," she said.

When I entered, Beaufoy's had a welcoming waiting room and a smiling woman behind the counter.

"Help you?" she said.

"I need a room. I don't know for how long. Can I keep the check-out date open?"

"You bet," she said. "Seventy dollars a night. We have a complimentary breakfast beginning at six in the morning."

"Wonderful," I said.

She handed me a key and said, "Room 201 on the second floor. The best view in the hotel."

"Great," I said.

The room was small though clean and serviceable. The single window looked out over the town square. I closed the curtain, sat my suitcase on the bed, and went downstairs.

When I opened the door to Harper's Range Rover, she said, "How's the room?"

"Good," I said.

"I called Celeste. She's waiting for us at the hospital."

"Great," I said.

"Let's stop by my house first and drop off my cat. Silky has spent lots of time there, has the run of the place, and loves it."

Harper's little house was anything but. The single-story Louisiana ranch-style house stood alone on a bluff overlooking the Red River.

She grinned when I said, "Little?"

"I had a local architect design it based on Louisiana delta homes," Harper said. "You won't believe the deck that overlooks the river."

Harper pulled the Range Rover into the house's three-car garage. She turned on the lights when we took the cat carrier into the den. Silky exchanged nose rubs with Celeste's big Persian when we opened the doors to their carriers.

"Your house is awesome. If I owned it, I would never leave," I said.

Harper checked the water and food in the bowls beside the oversized fireplace.

"They'll be fine. Let's go to the hospital."

The Pinebridge Mental Hospital was nearby, and Harper parked in the lot in front. The modern façade was an addition to a much older facility. The person at the front desk recognized Harper, smiled, and gave us the high sign. I followed her down a darkened hallway to Celeste's office. When we opened the door without knocking, Celeste got out of her chair and embraced Harper.

Celeste proved as attractive as Harper, only older. Her long hair was darker, and I guessed her age to be forty-something. She was dressed in faded jeans and a pale blue sweater. From the

18

duration of the embrace, I was aware that the two women truly liked each other.

"Celeste, this is Wyatt Thomas. He's a private investigator from New Orleans."

When Celeste shook my hand, I said, "Pleased to meet you."

Celeste's office seemed more like that of a corporate bigwig than a Louisiana public servant. She sat behind her big oak desk as Harper and I took seats in two of the spacious office's expensive chairs.

"I'm so glad you made it in one piece," Celeste said. "I worry every time Harper is on the road."

"You're not my mother," Harper said. "I'm a great driver."

"I can attest to that," I said. "This facility is awesome, and my spine tingled when we walked down the hall. I hope you don't have to spend much time here after dark."

"It comes with the territory," she said. "I'm used to the ghosts."

Celeste's words had barely died away when we heard an unearthly wail through the cracked window in her office.

"More than ghosts," I said. "That sounded like a big cat."

Chapter 3

Celeste hurried to the window and slammed it shut with more force than was probably necessary.

"We aren't far from the Kisatchie National Forest. Swamps and woodlands thick with pines surround Pinebridge. Some people call it the pine curtain. If you let yourself get caught up in the sounds of the night, it'll drive you nuts."

"This place is noticeably old," I said. "Can you fill in its history for me?"

"The facility, originally called the Louisiana Hospital of the Insane, has a sordid history. Suffering people were sent here because there was nowhere else to put them. Medical treatments were either non-existent or bordering on the medieval."

"We've come a long way," Harper said.

"Thank God for that," Celeste said. "This facility has less than a hundred patients and is a mere shadow of its former self. During its heyday, it had hundreds of patients from every part of the state. It was self-sufficient with a dairy, a hundred-sixty-acre farm, a cathedral, and a cemetery."

"Can you arrange a tour for me?" I asked.

"Of course," Celeste said. "Most old outbuildings are no longer in use and lying in disarray. It isn't a place you want to visit after dark."

Before I could reply, someone began banging on the door. Sensing something neither Harper nor I did, Celeste flung it open. A dark-haired young man dressed in jeans and a tee shirt stood in the doorway, obviously shaken from his distressed expression.

"Billy, what's the matter?" Celeste said.

"Trouble," the young man said.

Celeste was tall but stood six inches shorter than Billy. Grabbing his arms, she shook him until he stopped stammering.

"It's okay. What's wrong?"

"Mr. Marshall," Billy said. "He's bleeding."

"What happened?" Celeste asked.

"Something terrible," Billy said.

"Where is he?"

"The cemetery," Billy said.

Billy became even more nervous when Celeste asked, "What were you doing in the cemetery?"

"Noises," he said.

"You mean like the noises our patients make at night?"

Billy shook his head. "More like the scream of a woman."

"Take me to him," Celeste said. "Harper, there's a flashlight on my desk."

Harper grabbed the flashlight, and we followed Celeste and Billy out the door. We'd gone no more than ten feet when Celeste halted.

"We're taking a shortcut through the psych ward, and you need to be warned. In this confined space, even the faintest sounds echo off the walls. Haunting noises punctuate the silence, each more unnerving than the last. Sometimes, it's enough to scare the hell out of you."

When Celeste entered a combination on a keypad to open a heavy metal door, it took less than a minute to understand the reason for her ominous warning. Even in the dimly lit corridor, it was impossible not to see the faces of the tormented souls peering from behind the tiny barred windows of their padded cells.

The plaintive cries of patients lost in the labyrinth of their minds wailed a heart-wrenching chorus of anguish reverberating off sterile walls, a chorus that lingered like a mournful lament. Some voices were barely more than whispers, fragile echoes of fractured souls, their pain palpable. Harper clutched my hand and squeezed.

"I hate the sounds they make," she said. "I don't know how Celeste tolerates it."

Frenzied screams shattered the uneasy calm, signaling a moment of crisis. Footsteps echoed down another hallway, and the metallic clinking of restraints and the rhythmic thud of heavy doors being locked. Whispers of fragmented conversations and delusional laughter, devoid of joy, were a chilling reminder of the thin line between sanity and madness.

Harper released my hand when Celeste used the keypad to open the psych ward's exit door. I could still hear the cacophony of the tortured souls even after the metal door shut behind us with a dull thud.

As Celeste, Billy, Harper, and I emerged from the dilapidated rear of the old mental institution, the air hung heavy with the oppressive weight of the night. The moon, obscured by thick clouds, cast an eerie glow upon the desolate landscape, cloaking the abandoned outbuildings and gnarled pine trees in shadows.

We traversed an old cobbled path, our footsteps muffled by the damp earth and shrouded in a mist that seemed to rise from the very soul of the forsaken grounds. A chorus of chirping crickets and the flickering dance of lightning bugs provided the only semblance of life amid the graveyard silence.

With each step, the sense of foreboding deepened, amplified by the whispered legends of the institution's tormented past that echoed through the wind-swept corridors of memory.

We followed Billy through the murky darkness, our nerves taut. Every rustle of leaves and the distant howl of a nocturnal creature sent shivers down our spines.

We reached an old cemetery, a somber testament to the forgotten souls who had once wandered these hallowed grounds in search of sanctuary. Amongst the weathered headstones, a chilling sight awaited us: a man's lifeless body slumped against a moss-covered monument, the jagged wounds upon his flesh a grotesque tableau of savage brutality.

The moon broke free from its cloud-shrouded prison, casting its pallid light upon the scene, illuminating the man's twisted visage in stark relief. His eyes, frozen in a silent scream, bore witness to the horrors he had endured in his final moments, while the zigzag lacerations that marred his skin spoke of a violence born from the depths of primal instinct.

As we stood there, transfixed by the grisly spectacle, a sense of dread enveloped us like a suffocating cloak. At that moment, amid the desolation of the abandoned cemetery, I realized that we weren't alone. The darkness held secrets far more sinister than I dared to imagine.

I touched the man's carotid artery.

"There's nothing we can do for him," I said. "He's dead."

Celeste's hand went to her mouth. "Oh, my God! Are you sure?"

She embraced Billy, and they both began to cry when I nodded and said, "I'm sorry."

What killed him?" Harper asked.

"Don't know," I said. "Call the police."

Within minutes of Harper's 9-1-1 call, we heard the sirens.

"What now?" she said.

"This is a crime scene," I said. "Don't touch anything."

We waited in the darkness, none of us speaking until the lights of police cars stopped in the parking lot of the old cemetery. Officers with flashlights soon appeared through the mist that continued to rise from the ground.

When a man in blue pants, a khaki shirt, and a dark blue windbreaker with a Rapides Parish Sheriff's office insignia approached us, he said, "I'm Detective Willoughby. Where's the body?"

Celeste pointed the flashlight to the headstone the body was propped against. As police officers began spreading out, a black woman dressed the same as Detective Willoughby motioned us to follow her. We stopped when we reached her white SUV police vehicle with the flashing lights.

"I'm Detective Henstooth," she said. "Give me your names and tell me what happened here."

The name sewn on the windbreaker read Det. Maya Henstooth. Her short hair was swept back enough to reveal blue zircon earrings and a diamond ear piercing at the top of her ear. Except for her watch, the earrings and the piercing were the only jewelry she wore. Detective Henstooth took notes when we told her who we were.

"Do you know the victim's name?" she asked.

"Oliver Marshall," Celeste said. "He was a nighttime attendant."

"A nurse?" Detective Henstooth asked.

"No," Celeste said.

"How long had he worked for the hospital?" Detective Henstooth asked.

"Many of our most severe patients are capable of harming themselves and others. The attendants make sure that doesn't happen."

"So, they're like jailers?" Detective Henstooth asked.

Celeste didn't like Henstooth's insinuation and let her know it by the anger in her voice when she answered.

"They are certainly not jailers," she said.

"Do they have medical training of any kind?" Detective Henstooth asked.

"We train them here to perform their needed tasks," Celeste said.

"How long has Mr. Marshall worked here?" Detective Willoughby asked.

"Ten years," Celeste said. "He was here when I became Administrator."

"Who discovered the body?" Willoughby asked.

"Billy came to my office about thirty minutes ago and told us about finding Mr. Marshall's body," Celeste said.

Billy was even more anxious, shaking when Celeste nudged him toward Detective Henstooth.

"What were you doing in the cemetery?" she asked.

Billy stuttered when he said, "I heard a noise. I went to see what it was."

"Billy is the hospital's caretaker. He lives in one of the unused hospital buildings," Celeste said.

"I was outside my door watching the fireflies," Billy said.

"Did you know the deceased?"

Billy nodded and said, "I know everyone who works here."

Detective Willoughby moved away from us and motioned Detective Henstooth to join him. Following a brief conversation, they returned to the SUV.

"What killed Mr. Marshall?" Celeste asked.

"We'll know more after the coroner has time to examine the body," Willoughby said. "You are free to go, though Detective Henstooth and I may have more questions for you later." When we started to leave, he said, "Not you, Mr. Thomas."

"We'll wait for you in Celeste's office," Harper said.

When they were gone, Willoughby said, "You're not from around here."

I showed him my P.I. badge and license, and he donned reading glasses for a better view.

"I'm here on assignment," I said.

"Mind telling us what for?" Detective Henstooth said.

"I'm looking for a missing person who may have been a patient here years ago," I said.

Willoughby handed my badge and license back to me. "I don't know how far along on your assignment you are, but don't leave the area without checking first with us."

I nodded and started to leave when Detective Henstooth said, "One more thing, Mr. Thomas. You're an experienced investigator. Did you see or hear anything else that might be of interest?"

"We were in Ms. Gauthier's office. The window was open, and we heard what sounded like a large cat."

"A tom cat?" Willoughby said.

"Bigger. More like a panther," I said. "I only got a brief look at the body, but it seemed to me like a big animal, possibly a cougar or some other large predator, attacked and killed him."

Detectives Henstooth and Willoughby exchanged glances and then handed me their business cards.

"We'll be in touch," Willoughby said.

The back door to the hospital was locked, so I took a long walk back to the front door. Celeste and Harper were waiting for me in the lobby.

"Celeste and I are going to the Raven's Roost in town for dinner and drinks. Come with us. When we finish eating, I'll take you to your room."

"Wonderful," I said.

Celeste unlocked the door to a black BMW and said, "Meet you there."

I climbed into the passenger seat of Harper's Range Rover, neither of us speaking until she pulled into the parking lot of the little café.

"You won't have to take me to my hotel," I said. "It's just across the street, and I can walk."

She grinned and said, "You may need me to hold your hand."

"Maybe," I said.

The Raven's Roost was an old building renovated into a modern café and bar. A pretty young waitress greeted us at the door.

"I'm Kayla," she said. "I'll be waiting on you."

Kayla led us to a corner table where hanging ferns and large potted plants blocked our view from the rest of the establishment. The bistro was ominously dark, and when Kayla seated us, I learned why.

"Most of our clientele are college students," she said. "Pinebridge College is Baptist, and the administration doesn't allow drinking hard liquor."

"How shortsighted of them."

Harper and Celeste ordered martinis. I requested a glass of lemonade.

"Wus!" Harper said.

"Sorry," I said. "I have no tolerance for alcohol. I'd be dancing naked in the streets."

"I'd pay to see that happen," Harper said. "Celeste and I will take care of you."

"Until the police show up and throw us all in jail," I said.

"Do you have an opinion about who or what caused Mr. Marshall's death," Celeste said.

Kayla, our pretty waitress, appeared at our table without drinks before I could answer.

"Are we eating tonight?"

"Yes," Celeste said. "What's your special?"

"Crawfish Étouffée," Kayla said.

"Not me," Harper said. "What else do you have?"

"Eight-ounce filet mignon and baked potato," Kayla said.

"The rarer, the better," Harper said.

"Me too," Celeste said.

"Étouffée for me," I said.

"And another round of martinis," Harper said.

When our dinners arrived, Harper was on her third martini. I was starved, and so was Celeste. Harper seemed more interested in getting a buzz on and not losing it by eating. Having been guilty of the same thing when I was drinking, I recognized the syndrome. She left most of her steak on the plate and ordered another martini when Kayla arrived to clear the table.

Harper's words were slurred when she said, "This town is fucked up."

"How so?" I asked.

"Everyone is so uptight and afraid they will shame themselves or their families if they follow their hearts."

"A different ideology," Celeste said. "Every place in Louisiana can't be the same as New Orleans."

"Right about that," Harper said. "Downtown Pinebridge isn't exactly Bourbon Street."

In an attempt to change the topic of discussion, Celeste looked at me and said, "You haven't told us what you think of the death."

"At first glance, it looked like a big cat had killed him," I said.

"Crazy talk," Celeste said.

"Don't say that," Harper said. Wyatt is an experienced investigator, and he's so handsome."

Harper spilled her martini on me when she crawled into my lap. I glanced at Celeste and saw her staring a hole through me. Getting out of her chair, she grabbed Harper's hand and pulled her out of my lap.

"I'm taking you home," she said. "You can get your car tomorrow."

Kayla was at the table when Celeste led Harper out the door.

"Another lemonade?" she said.

"Please," I said.

When she brought my lemonade, she said, "Those two are here a lot. They argue like an old married couple."

She nodded when I said, "Is that what they are?"

"Why are you in town, Mr. Thomas?"

"It's Wyatt," I said. "I'm a private investigator looking for someone who spent time at Pinebridge Mental Hospital. My job is finding answers to questions my clients have."

"Celeste is the Administrator. "She'll know."

"Maybe," I said.

"You sound suspicious of her," Kayla said.

"Should I be?"

"If you hang around until I finish my shift, I'll tell you what I know."

"You got it," I said.

Kayla wasn't smiling when she returned to the table. "Guess we'll have to make it some other night."

"What's up?" I asked.

"The crowd has picked up, and the manager has asked me to stay late. Just as well because my mom just walked in the door, and we don't have an open table."

"She can take mine," I said.

"Mom's not next in line," Kayla said.

"Then have her join me. I'd love the company and need to pad my expense account."

"You mean it?"

"I wouldn't have offered if I didn't."

Chapter 4

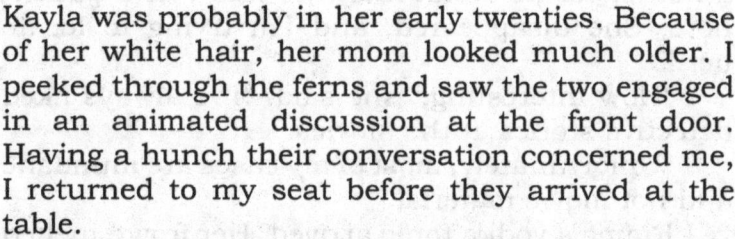

Kayla was probably in her early twenties. Because of her white hair, her mom looked much older. I peeked through the ferns and saw the two engaged in an animated discussion at the front door. Having a hunch their conversation concerned me, I returned to my seat before they arrived at the table.

Kayla's mom was as attractive as her young daughter, her long white hair hanging almost to her waist. Though turquoise jewelry draped her from earlobe to neck, her features and deep blue eyes didn't look Native American. Her dress was faux buckskin with cutouts and sewn-in shades of blue.

"My daughter is insisting I horn in on your dinner," she said.

"On the contrary," I said. "I'm from New Orleans and only know a few people in Pinebridge. I relish a bit of company."

"Kayla said you offered to buy my dinner," she said. "You don't need to do that."

I smiled and extended my hand. "I'm Wyatt Thomas, and I apologize for seeming to disrespect you. It wasn't my intention."

"Emma Duhon," she said. "No offense taken."

"Your daughter is gorgeous, and now I know why. Are you from Pinebridge?"

"Lived here all my life, Mr. Thomas," she said.

"Wyatt. I'm an alcoholic and don't drink, though I'd like nothing better than to buy one for you. Please, join me."

Kayla smiled when Emma Duhon sat and asked for a vodka tonic.

"Be right back," she said.

"Kayla said that you're a private investigator. Something to do with the hospital?"

"Good guess," I said. "A client of mine learned a half-sister he didn't know he had was a patient here. She disappeared, and I'm trying to locate her."

"How interesting," she said. "I've always liked detective stories at the movies."

"Unfortunately, most of my cases are mundane and not movie material."

Emma's vodka tonic arrived. Her frown melted away, replaced with a smile when she sipped the drink.

"I'll bet you have many interesting stories to tell, and I'd love to hear them."

"It's your story I want to hear. You're out late without a date, and I don't see a wedding ring on your finger."

"Are you hitting on me? Please don't say no because it's been a while since I had any masculine attention."

"You're so attractive, I imagine your phone never stops ringing."

Emma smiled and said, "You're trying to get into my pants. Don't stop. I love it."

"Sorry," I said. "I can't help myself."

"You're closer to Kayla's age than you are to me."

"Nonsense. You two could pass as sisters."

"You're a liar, Wyatt. If you keep it up, I'll embarrass Kayla and take you home."

Kayla arrived with Emma's dinner before I could comment.

"First time I've seen that smile in days," Kayla said. "Guess I need to keep the vodka tonics coming."

"Good idea," I said.

Kayla returned to the kitchen, and I waited silently as Emma ate her steak and baked potato and started on her next martini.

"Guess you're wondering why I'm so much older than Kayla," Emma said.

"The thought never crossed my mind," I said.

"Liar," she said. "Felix, my husband, was almost old enough to be my father when I met him. He wasn't too old to get me pregnant."

"Felix is Kayla's father?" Emma shook her head when I said, "Is he deceased?"

"My marriage was an ongoing abusive relationship. He beat me and forced me to have sex with him, even when I was bleeding. I stayed with him because he was a good provider, and people around town knew and respected him. They didn't know what I had to endure. I did it because Felix was rich, and nothing was too good for me and Kayla."

"There's nothing good about abusive relationships. There's never a happy ending. How did you find the courage to get out of it?"

"Kayla," she said. "When I learned Felix was abusing her, I could take it no longer."

"She told you?"

"Kayla was too traumatized to speak. I'm not even sure how much she remembers. We moved to West Monroe until she graduated high school before returning to Pinebridge."

"So sorry for your ordeal, though happy things turned out okay."

"Felix has a twin brother and the bond between twins is almost unbreakable. Do you know what I mean?"

"The former love of my life had a twin sister," I said. "I know exactly what you mean."

Emma was slurring her words when Kayla arrived to bus the table.

"Mom, you're drunk. I better take you home before you get us both in trouble," she said.

Emma wobbled when Kayla helped her out of the chair.

"Thanks, Wyatt," she said. "You can't imagine how much you raised my self-esteem."

"My pleasure," I said.

Emma returned to my table briefly when Kayla went into the kitchen.

She touched my shoulder and said, "I could tell you much more about my marriage. For Kayla's sake, I'll keep it to myself."

"Be safe, and I hope to see you again," I said.

"Thanks, sweet talker. You were just what the doctor ordered."

Kayla appeared alone and with a smile, along with my invoice. I paid in cash and gave her a hefty tip.

"Thank you for babysitting Mom," she said.

"I enjoyed every minute of it."

"You were my last customer. I'm taking her to the house and putting her to bed. See you here tomorrow night?"

"Wouldn't miss it," I said.

When I walked across the street to my room in the Beaufoy Hotel, it was dark, and a neon light flashed through the open window. It was times like this when I missed alcohol. If I'd had a bottle in the room, I would have been tempted to drink. Instead,

34

I took a cold shower, turned out the lights, and crawled under the sheets. I had barely closed my eyes when my cell phone rang. It was Frankie Castellano.

"What you got for me?" he asked.

"Nothing much," I said. "There was a murder at the hospital, though it has nothing to do with your sister."

"Sure about that?" he said.

He laughed when I said, "Frankie, you're a suspicious man."

"Comes with the territory. I called Harper, who told me she and Celeste had dinner with you. She was drunk and could hardly pronounce her words."

"Not my fault, boss," I said. "She was on a tear, though I don't know why."

"What can you tell me about Celeste?"

"She's intelligent. I understand why the powers-that-be hired her."

"What does she look like?"

"Very proper and presentable," I said.

"You don't have to be politically correct with me," he said. "Does she have a nice ass?"

"She's drop-dead gorgeous, her ass included," I said.

"How old is she?"

"Mid-forties or early fifties," I said. "Just a guess. Old enough to get you in a lot of trouble with Adele."

"I thought we weren't going to mention Adele," Frankie said.

"You're my boss; Adele's my friend," I said. "I love your money, but there's a line I won't cross."

"Wouldn't have it any other way," he said. "That's what I like about you and Tony. Got to go. If you have any info for me, call me anytime."

I had known Adele, Frankie's wife, longer than I had known Frankie. He had always been a family man, and I'd never detected the least bit of him desiring sex with someone other than his wife.

Knowing about Frankie's affair with Harper, I felt complicit in the deception. I'd justified taking the job by convincing myself Frankie's affair was little more than a fleeting dalliance. Tonight's conversation told me otherwise.

Frankie had tasted the sweetness of the forbidden fruit and was hungry for another bite. I was considering calling and telling him so when someone knocked on my door. I got out of bed and went to the door dressed only in my boxer shorts.

"Who is it?" I asked.

"Harper."

I opened the door and pulled her inside. "You're wasted. What are you doing here?"

"I have a few things to get off my chest," she said.

"Can't it wait until tomorrow?" Harper began to sob. "Come in and tell me what's so important."

The room was lighted only by the neon flashes pulsating through the open window.

"It's dark in here. Can you turn on a light?"

I closed the curtain and flipped on the sidelight on the stand beside my bed.

"You could have gotten a D.U.I. driving here," I said.

"No, I couldn't. I'm a Devereaux. Remember?"

"I thought that only held for New Orleans."

"The police have looked after me since I ran away from home at thirteen," she said.

"Why did you run away?"

Harper didn't answer me. Instead, she began removing her blouse.

"I can't go back to Celeste's," she said. "At least not tonight."

36

"Take the bed," I said. "I'll sleep on the recliner."

Harper clasped my hand. "No, I need someone to hold me. Squeeze me tightly in their arms. Convince me to keep living for at least another day."

"You're scaring me," I said. "You aren't contemplating suicide, are you?"

"About a thousand times," she said.

"I'm not a psychiatrist, though it sounds like you need one," I said.

"I don't need a psychiatrist. I need a warm-blooded man. Are you that man?"

By now, Harper had stripped down to her panties and bra. As I watched, she undid her bra and tossed it on the floor.

She smiled for the first time when I said, "You're putting me at a disadvantage. I'm an addict, and that goes for sex as well."

"I want to show you something," she said.

When Harper turned her back to me, I could see the faint crisscross scarring.

"Who did that to you?" I asked.

"My father," she said.

She nodded when I said, "Axel Devereaux?"

"I was nowhere near puberty when he started holding me in his lap and fondling me. At first, we were clothed. Before long, I was naked. Later, so was he."

"Good God Almighty!" I said. "Your father was molesting you? Wasn't your mother around to protect you?"

"My father divorced her and got custody. There was no one to protect me. He had a leather whip. When he was angry, he beat me."

"I'm so sorry," I said. "How long did the abuse continue?"

"It's still going on," she said. "Please don't tell me to file charges. You know how powerful my father is. I can't escape him."

"Is that why you had an affair with Frankie?"

"He's the only man I know whose power is even remotely close to my father's."

Harper nodded when I said, "Let me guess. You told your father about your affair with Frankie."

"Yes," she said.

"What did he do?"

"Vowed to kill him."

"You believe him?"

"Yes," she said. "Right now, I need you."

"You're playing me," I said. "You know your power over men very well, even though you don't like them."

"You aren't hiding your attraction for me," she said. "Even in dim light, I can see you're responding."

I got off the bed and went into the bathroom, returning in a terrycloth robe.

"Maybe this will help," I said.

Harper laughed and said, "Not much."

I watched as she removed her panties and dropped them on the floor. With a grin, she pulled the robe off my shoulders and then wrestled my boxer shorts off, tossing them to the floor beside her panties.

"You need to be as naked as I am," she said.

"I'm trying to resist you," I said. "I'm not having any luck."

"I'm spending the night with you and not taking no for an answer."

"I don't want to pass as your father," I said.

"I'm no longer a child," she said. "I want to have sex with you, and it's my choice."

Harper turned out the side lamp and pulled me beneath the sheets. I was beating myself up for having no mental resolve, though not for long.

Chapter 5

I awoke to someone banging on my door. It took me a moment after opening my eyes to remember I was at the Beaufoy Hotel in Pinebridge and not in my little apartment over Bertram's bar in New Orleans. Harper was gone, and I got out of bed and pulled on my pants.

"Don't knock the door down," I said. "I'm coming."

Homicide detective Maya Henstooth was waiting at the door. She wasn't smiling.

"Did I wake you?" she asked.

"The sun's barely up," I said. "What time do Alexandria cops start work?"

I could almost hear her fatigue when she said, "I haven't been to sleep yet."

"Come in. I'll make you a cup of coffee."

The Beaufoy Hotel was old and timeworn, though a two-cup coffee pot and complimentary coffee on the cabinet were some of the freebies. I put the coffee pod in the tray and flipped the on switch.

"Not much furniture in my little hotel room, but you're welcome to sit on the bed or in the recliner," I said.

Detective Henstooth was staring at something on the floor. I saw my boxer shorts and Harper's panties when I glanced down and quickly kicked them under the bed, relieved when she acted as if she didn't notice. Detective Henstooth sat on the bed, and we soon enjoyed coffee from plastic cups.

"Thanks," she said. "I have questions."

"This cup of plastic coffee tastes like hell," I said. "Let me put on a shirt, and maybe we can find a place that offers the real stuff. I'll answer your questions there."

"There's a café down the street," she said.

"Mind if I brush my teeth first?" I asked.

"Knock yourself out," she said.

Maya finished her coffee while waiting for me to brush my teeth and put on a clean shirt. I felt almost human as we walked downstairs and exited the old hotel. Abner's Diner was down the street. We grabbed a booth and were soon drinking coffee from real mugs.

Detective Henstooth smiled when I said, "You look pretty good for someone who was up all night."

"Used to it," she said.

"No one at home waiting on you?"

"I'm asking the questions, Mr. Thomas," she said.

"Wyatt," I said. "What's your name?"

"Detective Henstooth."

"Your first name."

"You're ballsy," she said.

"I want to know."

"Maya," she said.

"Did your mother name you after the poet?"

Maya smiled and said, "I was sixteen when Obama was elected. My mother adored Maya Angelou years before she recited the inaugural poem."

"Good for her," I said.

"Are you a Democrat, Wyatt?"

"Apolitical," I said. "I have friends on both sides of the aisle. What about you?"

"Same here. My Dad's a Republican, and my mom a Democrat."

She smiled when I said, "You're lucky you were born. Why were you up all night, and where is your partner?"

"Rapides is a big parish, and we're stretched a little thin right now. Detective Willoughby was assigned to another case."

"I didn't realize there was that much crime in central Louisiana."

"We have gangs and professional criminals and everything in between," she said.

"Sounds serious," I said.

"Rapides has more crime per capita than New Orleans Parish."

"Then you are stretched thin. I'm hungry, and I'll bet you are too. Have time for breakfast?" I asked.

"I could eat something," she said.

We were soon drinking more coffee and eating bacon and eggs.

"Nothing like a country breakfast," I said as I daubed the remainder of my egg yolk with a slice of buttered toast. "I feel halfway human and ready to answer your questions."

"I ran a background check on you, Mr. Thomas."

"I thought we had agreed on first names. Mine is Wyatt," I said.

"One thing stuck out to me."

"Only one?"

"Your knowledge of voodoo."

"Everyone in Louisiana knows something about voodoo," I said.

"In New Orleans, maybe. Not here in central Louisiana."

"What does voodoo have to do with this investigation?" I asked.

"Billy Williams, the man who found him, had a voodoo symbol tattooed on his wrist," Maya said.

"It's more likely that Marshall was killed by some creature of the night than a victim of voodoo. I find both explanations hard to believe."

"It's true he had strange lacerations that suggested an animal attack. Those cuts weren't what killed Mr. Marshall."

"What did?"

"Someone cut his throat."

"What about the claw marks?" I asked.

"Someone worked him over after he was dead," I said. "Maybe with artificial claws."

"How do you know that?" I asked.

"There was no blood associated with the claw wounds, which implies Marshall was dead for some time before the clawing occurred."

"To cover up his real cause of death," I said. "What made the lacerations on the victim?"

"Our killer," Maya said. "Our only suspect is Billy Williams, though we found no evidence to link him to the murder."

"How can I help?"

Maya punched a picture on her cell phone and showed me the tattoo on Billy Williams's wrist.

"Can you tell me anything about this?" she said.

"I can tell you it isn't a voodoo veve."

"What's a veve?" she asked.

"A symbol of a particular voodoo deity."

"If it isn't a voodoo symbol, what is it?"

"A witch marking," I said.

"What the hell is that?"

"Also known as apotropaic marks, they are ritual symbols etched into buildings, furniture, gravestones, and other objects to protect them from evil. They are often found in drafty areas like windows, doorways, and fireplaces."

"How do you know so much about witches?"

"Voodoo isn't the only thing practiced in Louisiana. We have lots of witches."

"Get out of here!" Maya said. "What does the mark on Billy Williams's arm mean?"

"It means a witch put it there to protect him from something."

"Like what?"

"Don't know. You'll have to ask Billy."

"Thanks," she said.

"I have a problem as well. Maybe you can help me with it," I said.

"Maybe. What's your problem?"

"As I mentioned last night, my client has hired me to find his half-sister. She was a patient at Pinebridge. I found no death certificate, release papers, or anything about her. It's as if she dropped off the face of the earth."

"What's her name?" Maya asked.

"Bella Donna Castellano."

"I'll run her I.D.," Maya said. "There's a rumor about a mass grave where Pinebridge disposed of the bodies of the patients that died there without explanation," Maya said.

"Do you believe it?"

"I have a poli-sci degree from USL. I'm a practicing Baptist. Still, the hospital has a bad reputation, and I couldn't help but feel the spirits of the lost souls in the cemetery last night," she said.

She smiled again when I said, "I should have known you're a Ragin' Cajun."

Maya grinned and said, "Just a simple Rapides Parish girl."

"I've never known a Ragin' Cajun who wasn't crazy as hell," I said.

"I'll take the fifth on that one," Maya said.

I let the subject drop and said, "There's something unexplained still going on here, and it possibly holds the answers to your murder and my missing person. Maybe we can work together on this."

Maya glanced at her watch and said, "Maybe. Right now, I have to go. Thanks for the breakfast. I'll be in touch."

"Wait," I said. "How far is it to the Pinebridge Mental Hospital?"

"About a mile," she said. "I'll give you a ride."

Maya's patrol car was a brand-new white Buick SUV with red lights on the roof.

"Nice wheels," I said. "You must rank high in the hierarchy of the sheriff's department."

"The sheriff's brother-in-law owns the Buick dealership."

Maya nodded when I said, "Sweet."

"I'm not bitching," she said.

"Neither would I," I said. "No one has ever supplied me with a free car."

"Squad car," Maya said. "I only use it for work."

"I believe you," I said.

Maya dropped me off at the hospital's front door and gave me one of her cards.

"Call me if you come on to something," she said.

"Will do. Thank you,"

I watched Maya's cruiser disappear into the distance before turning my attention to the modern entrance of the creepy old mental hospital. I found Celeste alone in her office, and she smiled when I joined her.

"You're up early," she said.

"So are you."

"Duty calls."

"Where's Harper?"

"You kidding? The princess doesn't get out of bed before noon."

"Must be nice," I said.

"She was out late. You wouldn't know anything about it, would you?"

"I went to bed early. What's going on with the murder?"

"The cemetery is swarming with police looking for clues. They took Billy to Alexandria for questioning."

"Did they book him?"

Celeste shook her head. "He's already back at work."

"Did anyone you know of have a motive to kill Mr. Marshall?" I asked.

"He had no enemies that I know of."

"He had at least one," I said.

Celeste handed me a Manila folder. "Here's everything I have on Bella Donna Castellano."

"Thanks," I said.

"I have a comfortable chair. You're welcome to read it here and then ask me any questions you may have."

"Thanks again."

"There's a coffee bar outside the door," she said.

"Don't mind if I do."

With a hot cup of coffee, I relaxed in Celeste's comfortable chair and dived into the file on Bella Donna Castellano. Much of what I read was disturbing. An hour had passed when Celeste spoke, breaking my concentration.

"You look shocked," she said.

"Bella Donna accused her father of sexual abuse. The details are graphic. Does sexual abuse lead to mental illness?"

"Adult psychiatric disorders resulting from CSA and other forms of maltreatment range from depression, PTSD, panic disorder, and substance abuse to schizophrenia and antisocial personality disorder."

"What's CSA?" I asked.

"Childhood sexual abuse. I doubt Mr. Castellano will be happy learning his father was a child abuser."

Talk of childhood sexual abuse more than jogged my memory of my talks with Harper and Kayla's mother concerning the subject. Celeste was an expert on CSA, and I considered asking her about Kayla and Harper. I thought better of it.

"Frankie's father was a murderer, one of many evil traits of which Frankie is well aware. I have little doubt his father abused him, though the abuse was probably verbal and not sexual."

"Words often cause more mental damage than fists ever do," Celeste said. "What now?"

"What happened to Bella Donna? There's no record she ever left here."

"She was gone before I became Administrator. What you see in the file is all we have on record for her."

I returned the file to Celeste, and she thumbed through it.

"She seems to have disappeared from the system," she said.

"Is that normal?"

"You know it isn't," she said.

"What's your explanation?"

"Many unexplained things happened at Pinebridge before I got here," Celeste said.

"Detective Henstooth informed me there is a mass grave somewhere on the grounds. Is that where she is?"

"This place is notorious, though you can't believe everything you hear," Celeste said.

"I'd like to take that tour when you have the time."

"My appointment calendar is open. Are you ready?" she asked.

I left the comfortable chair and said, "Right behind you."

The grounds of the Pinebridge Mental Hospital were immense, more than one-hundred-sixty acres. Instead of the shortcut we'd taken the previous night, we took the long way to the backdoor.

"I've never visited a mental hospital," I said. "Our detour last night was eye-opening."

"Sleep resets the brain, and people with severe mental health problems rarely sleep," Celeste said. "The patients you heard and saw last night have descended into their own brands of madness; their conditions are irreversible. There is little we can do to help them."

"Is that the reason for the attendants?"

"Exactly," she said. "Like I told the police, their job is to keep our most severe patients from harming themselves or others."

"Must drive you crazy," I said.

Celeste smiled and said, "Crazy isn't a word we use here."

"Sorry," I said.

"It's okay. Few people understand the breadth of mental illness. Come with me. It's a beautiful day, and the grounds are glorious."

Unlike last night, the sunny day provided a wonderful view of the facility. Like much of central Louisiana, the terrain was hilly. A cobblestone pathway led from the back of the hospital down a hill through a tranquil park with giant oaks and flower gardens. The path ended at the entrance to the cemetery.

Beyond the cemetery were the many abandoned outbuildings. Patients in blue gowns were wandering the manicured grounds. Billy Williams was on his hands and knees, pruning the bushes in a rose garden.

"It looks like Billy isn't the worst for wear," I said. "Is gardening his normal job?"

"He's the caretaker for the grounds and tends the flowers, among other things."

"This place is enormous," I said. "Tell me again how many patients you have."

"This facility once handled thousands of patients. Now, there are little more than a hundred."

"Because?"

"Mental health therapy has changed in the past fifty years. Many former patients can lead almost normal lives with the use of newly developed drugs," Celeste said. "Only the worst cases remain."

"You had a dairy and truck farm and raised your own produce. How were the patients able to help?"

"Not all of the patients had debilitating conditions. Many were released after therapy. The facility helped many Louisianians overcome mental health problems. They were able to hold down normal jobs on the farm."

Celeste took me through the old dairy barn and pointed out the fallow fields. Down the hill, I could see the little town of Pinebridge. It was getting late when we started back up the hill to the Pinebridge Mental Hospital, and Celeste had a call on her cell phone.

"I have a minor emergency that needs my attention," she said. "Feel free to wander the grounds as you please."

I watched Celeste hurry up the hill toward the hospital. The sky had turned cloudy, and a slight breeze was moving Spanish moss and Resurrection Ferns in the branches of the old oak trees shading the surroundings. I had the distinct feeling that someone was staring at me. Someone was.

I had stopped on the cobblestone path and stood beside a beautiful rose garden. A young woman was kneeling in the middle of the red roses. When I glanced at her, she clenched her fist in the universal sign language that I knew meant, 'Help me.'

Chapter 6

The young woman's curly, ash-blond hair draped to the small of her back. Her eyes were pale blue, the color of the sky above us. Ringlets of flowers hung from her neck and laced her hair. I knelt beside her.

"You need help?" I asked.

When she showed me her bleeding finger, I wrapped it in a tissue I had in my pocket. She wasn't quite smiling when she stared into my eyes.

"I'm Wyatt," I said. "What's your name?"

"Rica," she said.

Her finger wasn't the only thing needing attention. She had a bruise on her face, and her arms were scratched. Her light blue gown was also torn and seemed far too revealing to be a standard-issue hospital gown.

She didn't answer when I asked, "What happened? Did you fall?" She only stared at me. "Your scratches need to be looked after. Come with me."

I helped the young woman to her feet and led her up the hill to the back of the hospital. Her gown was sheer and all but transparent when backdropped by the sun. It was impossible for me not to recognize what a beautiful woman she was.

We entered Celeste's office without knocking and found her embroiled in an argument with a large man dressed in the same uniform as Marshall, the murder victim. They both grew instantly silent.

"Return to work," Celeste said. "We'll take up this matter again later."

"Sorry to interrupt," I said. "I didn't realize you were busy.

"It's all right. Our business is complete," she said.

"This is Rica," I said. "She must have taken a spill because she has bruises and is all scratched up."

Celeste's expression was sorrowful when she grabbed Rica's shoulders.

Rica didn't answer when she said, "What happened to you, baby?" She punched a button on her intercom. "Gayla, I have an injured patient in my office."

Gayla, a sixty-something nurse with short hair and light blue scrubs, knocked once before entering Celeste's office. After looking at Rica, she took her hand and started for the door.

"I'll clean her up and doctor her wounds," she said.

"You don't look worried," I said when they were gone.

"Lyrica is a klutz," Celeste said. "This isn't the first time she's fallen and hurt herself."

"Lyrica?"

"Her name is Lyrica Winter. She is one of our patients who is beyond help."

"What does she suffer from?" I asked.

"Severe schizophrenia, PTSD, you name it. She's been here five years and has never spoken."

"She spoke to me," I said.

Celeste shook her head as if she didn't believe me.

"What did she say?"

"She told me her name is Rica."

"She's in good hands with Gayla. Right now, I have work to do. Harper and I are eating at the Raven's Roost tonight if you want to join us."

"What time?" I asked.

"Eightish," she said.

"I look forward to it," I said. "I'll let you get on with your work."

I saw the nurse's station down the hall from Celeste's office. The door was cracked, and Gayla was busy tending to Rica's wounds. As I watched, the big man who had been arguing with Celeste entered the nurse's station without knocking.

The man was every inch of six feet six inches and weighed somewhere north of two hundred pounds. Crimson tattoos decorated both of his massive arms. He had dark hair and the lidded eyes of an angry reptile and exited a few minutes later, pulling Rica behind him. If I didn't know better, I would have taken the look on her face as terror.

I waited until they had disappeared down the hall before entering the nurse's station to talk to Gayla. She didn't seem surprised to see me.

"I'm Wyatt Thomas, a P.I. from New Orleans. May I ask you a few questions?"

"Do you work for Ms. Gauthier?" she asked.

"No," I said. "A client hired me to locate a missing person. I only met Ms. Gauthier yesterday. Who was that man who just came for Rica?"

"Bud Johnson is one of the hospital's attendants. They handle the most mentally challenged patients. He's the second-in-command behind Inga," Gayla said.

"How many attendants are there?" I asked.

"Only three now since Oliver Marshall's murder."

"Who are the other two?"

"Inga Talladega," Gayla said.

"You don't sound like you like her very much," I said.

"Inga's two hundred pounds of pure muscle and possibly the meanest person I've ever known."

"Who else?" I asked.

"Hank Bauer, a skinhead with swastikas tattooed on his arms and legs, and mean as a cornered snake."

"Why would the hospital hire a Neo-Nazi? Don't they have employment standards?" I asked.

"He fits the bill for what the hospital wants him to do."

"Which is?"

"Keep the problem patients in line," she said.

"I'd like to question them."

"They rule the roost around the hospital. Except for Dr. Felix, the other doctors and nurses avoid them like the plague."

"They'll talk to me if Celeste tells them to," I said.

"The attendants work for Celeste, and she'll never give you permission to talk to them," Gayla said. "Doesn't matter. If you stay here long enough, you'll meet them," Gayla said.

"Any idea who might have killed Oliver Marshall?"

Gayla smirked, though didn't answer my question.

"It wasn't Billy Williams," she said. "He's the gentlest young man I've ever known."

"What about Bud Johnson?"

"I've worked here twenty years, and I'm retiring next month," Gayla said. "The hubby and I have bought a recreational vehicle. We'll park it at the

54

lake and spend the rest of our lives fishing and relaxing."

"I don't want to rock any boats," I said. "Does this hospital have any doctors?"

"Dr. Felix," she said.

"Is he your only doctor?"

"We have half a dozen and access to the staff at the hospital in Alexandria if we feel we need them."

"Does Dr. Felix have an office in the hospital?"

"Yes," she said.

"Tell me where it's located. I'll talk to him."

"I haven't seen him in a while. I think he's out of town."

"Where is he?" Gayla didn't answer. I didn't know if she was covering something up, though it seemed like it. "Do all your patients wear revealing gowns like Rica?"

"You noticed," she said.

"She's practically naked. That can't be normal."

"Dr. Felix has some strange theories on mental illness," Gayla said.

"Like wearing revealing clothes?"

"He's a doctor and has examined her and the other patients many times."

"I didn't notice the other patients wearing revealing nightgowns."

"Lyrica isn't dangerous and has special permission to leave her ward. The others in the ward are considered a risk."

"You mean the ward with the padded cells?"

"Yes," Gayla said.

"If she isn't dangerous, why is she housed with the dangerous patients?"

"A question you'll have to ask Dr. Felix," she said.

"Is she safe here?"

"Like I told you, I'm retiring next month. I don't want to jeopardize my retirement."

Celeste said Billy Williams lives on the grounds. Can you tell me anything about him?"

"The young man is autistic. He can speak and communicate, though he sees life through a much simpler prism than you or I," Gayla said.

"My missing person was a patient here. Maybe you knew her," I said.

"What's her name?"

"Bella Donna Castellano."

"I knew her," Gayla said. "She'd been here awhile when I started work twenty years ago."

"Was something memorable that caused you to recall her so fast?"

"She was a looker—drop-dead gorgeous. We had two dozen attendants then, and they all took turns with her."

Gayla's statement caught me by surprise. "The attendants were abusing a patient?"

"The use of psychotropic drugs was in its infancy, and some of our patients were capable of violence. The attendants had a wink and a nod of approval to deal with the unruly patients however they pleased."

"Even by physical or sexual abuse?" I asked.

"Like I said, it was a different place and time twenty years ago."

"Can you describe Bella Donna?"

"A light-skinned black woman, about five-nine or ten. She had a mouth, which kept getting her into trouble. I treated her for cuts and bruises more than once."

"What happened to most of the attendants?"

"Some powerful person let the Governor know what was happening here. It put him in a public relations bind, and he took action to clean the hospital. Most of the attendants were fired."

"Most?"

"They kept Inga Talledaga because she was young and had only started work the previous year."

"The same Inga Talledaga that still works here?"

Gayla nodded. "She was promoted to head of security and the chief attendant. Attendants have come and gone, though Inga hired Marshall, Bauer, and Johnson."

"What happened to Bella Donna?"

"Disappeared."

"Did one of the attendants kill her?"

Gayla shook her head. "There was a rumor she practiced hoodoo and hexed Inga."

"And?"

"You know all I know about Bella Donna now," Gayla said.

"What about Dr. Felix? Was he working here twenty years ago?"

"Yes."

"What kept him from getting dismissed in the shakeup? Surely, he knew about the abuse."

"Rumor is he had dirt on the Governor, which saved his job."

She laughed when I said, "Must have been juicy."

"That's a fact," she said.

"What about your medical records? Are they computerized?"

"They are now. When the hospital opened, there were no computers. Health records were written on paper and maintained in folders, including patient information, treatments performed, medications prescribed, etc. Only one copy was available."

Gayla laughed when I asked, "Were these paper records later digitized?"

"Nope," she said.

"Where are these paper records stored?"

"In the basement. Want to see?"

"Not now." She nodded when I said, "Can you direct me to where Billy lives."

It was past noon, and my stomach growled as I followed Gayla's directions to Billy William's little house on the grounds of the Pinebridge Mental Hospital. Though the door was unlocked, Billy wasn't home. There was a bench beside the door, and I decided to remain outside until he arrived.

I sat and waited, soon joined by an unusual, solid black cat. The friendly cat jumped into my lap, and I saw it had no eyes. When Billy Williams arrived, I was asleep on the bench, the blind cat purring as he sat in my lap.

"You must be a good person," Billy said. "Noseye is afraid of everyone else but me."

The black cat named Noseye jumped out of my lap and began weaving between Billy's legs.

"Mind if I ask you a few questions?"

"I have a problem with my air conditioning, and my room is warm," he said.

"No problem," I said.

Billy opened the door and motioned me to enter.

"It's not much, but Noseye and I love it."

He smiled when I gave him a thumbs-up and said, "I love it too."

Billy's tiny house was little more than a large room with a bed. There were no pictures on the wall and only one on the dresser of the drab little room. Billy pointed to a worn recliner.

"Have a seat, and I'll get you a glass of water," he said.

"Thanks," I said.

The recliner must have been Noseye's normal perch because the black cat jumped into my lap when I sat down. I stroked him as Billy handed me water in a plastic cup, then sat on the edge of the bed and kicked off his shoes.

"Do you know Rica?" I asked.

"What about her?"

"She's a gorgeous woman," I said. "You know her, don't you?"

"I see her on the grounds," he said.

He shook his head when I said, "Does she know who you are?"

"I talk to her," he said.

"How do you do that? She doesn't talk."

"She can sign, and so can I because the teachers in my school taught me."

"They teach sign language in school now?" I asked.

When Billy smiled, I noticed his dark eyes for the first time.

"My classmates and I were special students. I was ten before I learned to speak with my voice. Until then, I signed."

"Your mom must be proud of you," I said.

"She is," he said.

"Where did you get your wrist tattoo?"

"Efy put it there."

"Who is Efy?"

"A witch. It's a powerful symbol. She said it will always protect me."

"Is that why you wear the gris-gris around your neck?"

Billy touched the talisman hanging from a leather cord. "It has gotten me in trouble more than once," he said.

"Did Mr. Marshall ever do anything to hurt you?"

"He was afraid to harm me," Billy said.

"Because?"

"My witch marking and gris-gris."

"He practiced voodoo?"

"He was afraid. I don't know why," Billy said.

"Did he ever harm Rica?"

"They wouldn't leave her alone," he said.

"They?"

"The attendants."

"Billy, did you kill Mr. Marshall because he was harming Rica?"

Billy shook his head. "Mama taught me to never use my strength against anybody or anything."

He nodded when I asked, "Did you ever confront him about harming Rica."

"He laughed at me."

"Did you tell anyone about the abuse, Gayla or Ms. Gauthier?"

"Only my mom," he said.

"What did she tell you?"

"That God will punish them for their sins."

"Is that what happened?" I asked.

"I don't know what happened."

I glanced out the lone window and saw the sky had darkened.

"I've enjoyed talking with you, visiting your house, and meeting your wonderful cat. It's getting late, and I have a long walk back to town."

"You are the only person who has ever visited us," he said.

He nodded when I said, "You must get lonely."

"Wyatt," he said as I got out of the recliner. "Will you help Rica?"

"I'll do what I can," I said.

"Promise?"

I shook his hand and said, "You have my word on it."

Chapter 7

When I reached the Raven's Roost, it wasn't time to meet Harper and Celeste, so I grabbed a stool at the bar. The bartender was a bald little man whose name tag identified him as Henry Scott.

"You look like you've had a hard day," he said. "What can I get you?"

"If I were still a drinking man, I'd order a double Black Jack with an Abita chaser. Fortunately, I'm not, and I'll have a glass of lemonade if you have it, iced tea if you don't."

When Henry returned with my lemonade, he said, "What's your name?"

"Wyatt."

"In town on business?"

"Yes," I said.

"How long will you be here?"

"A few days; maybe more."

"You waiting on someone?"

"Harper and Celeste," I said. "Celeste is the Administrator of the mental hospital."

"I know who they are. The two of them are in here a bunch," he said. "They aren't teetotalers like you."

"More power to them," I said. "Seems I'm the only person in Louisiana who can't hold his liquor."

"Trust me, you aren't the only one," he said.

"I'll bet you have stories to tell," I said.

"Amen on that one. Most of the people in town are Baptists." He winked and said, "Baptists don't drink or dance. You're not a Baptist, are you?"

"Raised a Catholic, though I'm a practicing agnostic."

"You don't believe in God?" Henry asked.

"I didn't say that."

"Sorry," he said. "My dad was a Baptist deacon. It hastened his death when he learned I worked in a bar."

"I don't believe it," I said. "Baptists drink and dance even if they don't admit it."

"That's a fact," Henry said. "Some of my best customers are Baptists."

"Do you have any stories about Harper and Celeste?"

"A few doozies," he said.

My dinner dates entered the restaurant before Henry had a chance to explain. Harper and Celeste saw me sitting at the bar and joined me.

Harper touched my shoulder and said, "You told me you don't drink."

"Alcohol," I said. "Henry was kind enough to make me a lemonade."

"Put it on my tab, Henry," Celeste said. "Where's Kayla?"

"Right behind you," Kayla said. "I have your table ready." We followed her to where we had dined the previous night. "I'll bring your drinks."

"I love her," Celeste said. "She takes such wonderful care of us."

When Kayla returned with our drinks, Celeste said, "I'd like to start with a shrimp cocktail."

"Make it two," Harper said.

"You got it," Kayla said.

"Any crawfish?" Harper asked.

"Crawfish is in short supply this season, but if you can afford it, we had a shipment today," Kayla said."

Celeste grinned and said, "I think we can handle it."

"Have any raw oysters?" Harper said.

"Absolutely. Can I get you a dozen?"

"What about you, Wyatt? Do you eat oysters and crawfish?"

"Every chance I get," I said.

"Then bring the oysters, and we'll all have your special," she said.

"You got it," Kayla said. "I'll put your order in."

When Kayla left the table, Celeste said, "How did the rest of your day go?"

"I talked to Gayla, your resident nurse, and learned some things about Bella Donna," I said.

"Such as?"

"Gayla was working at the hospital while Bella Donna was a patient. She gave me a physical description and told me the attendants at the time frequently abused her and many of the other patients."

"They were all fired for their actions, which marked a new era for the hospital," Celeste said.

"All except Inga Talledaga," I said.

"Inga had just started work at the hospital and wasn't involved in the abuse," Celeste said.

"Is she now?"

"There is no abuse at this hospital. Did Gayla tell you that?"

"Gayla's ready to retire. If she is aware of any patient abuse, she kept it to herself," I said.

"Then who told you?" Celeste said.

"Billy Williams."

"Billy is autistic. As I said, his perception of reality differs from yours or mine."

"He seemed cognizant to me," I said.

"Did he provide you with any specific details?" she asked.

"He was vague. Nothing he said would stand up in a court of law," I said.

"Are you a lawyer now, Wyatt?" she asked.

"In another lifetime," I said. "I was disbarred."

"You seem to have resolved your past," she said.

"I'm a survivor. I became a private investigator and found I'm good at it."

"What else did Billy tell you?" she asked.

"He seemed to think Rica got her scratches and bruises from Oliver Marshall."

"If he wasn't the murderer himself, how would he know?" Celeste asked.

"The thought crossed my mind," I said.

"What do you think?" Harper asked.

"I have a hard time believing Billy Williams would ever harm another person."

"Then what is your conclusion?" Celeste asked.

I smiled and said, "I'm still at square one. I may have to tell Mr. Castellano I've encountered a dead end. If so, he'll probably want me to wrap up the case and return to New Orleans."

Celeste smiled and tapped my lemonade glass with her martini glass. "Then let's have some fun until you tell him," she said.

Kayla interrupted us with the oysters and more drinks. Celeste seemed to have forgotten about my less-than-veiled allegations of patient abuse. Unlike the previous night, she kept up with Harper, drink for drink.

Harper seemed introspective, possibly afraid I would tell Celeste about spending the night with me. She barely spoke and avoided making eye contact. Celeste didn't seem to notice.

When we'd finished eating and Celeste cleared the tab, I asked, "Do I need to drive you home?"

Celeste patted my cheek and said, "Only if you want to spend the night."

"Nothing I'd love better, though I have notes to prepare if I'm going to conclude this case."

Celeste was slightly sloshed when she said, "Then we'll take a rain check, and tomorrow is scheduled for rain."

Kayla was looking at her watch when Celeste and Harper walked out of the door.

"I'm not off for another hour. Will you wait on me?"

"I have nowhere to go except back to my hotel room. Nothing exciting about that," I said.

"I'll bring you more lemonade," she said.

"Take your time," I said. "I'm not going anywhere."

The age difference between Kayla and me was a warning that I should nip the relationship in the bud. I didn't because something, perhaps Kayla's mom's description of her abuse signaled that her interest in me was more than sexual. Kayla's hour wait was optimistic, and it was late when she finally joined me with a colorful mojito in hand.

"Hope you don't mind if I drink," she said.

"Knock yourself out," I said. "What can you tell me about Celeste and Harper?"

"They are a couple," she said.

I laughed. "It doesn't take a private dick to see that. What else have you got."

Kayla leaned forward and clasped my hand. "I have a confession to make. That's all I have. I broke up with my longtime boyfriend last month and desperately need a little male attention."

"So, this is a date?" I asked.

"I'm sorry," she said.

"Don't be sorry. I'm happy to oblige. How about a dozen oysters?"

Kayla and I were soon feasting on oysters, and she was on her third mojito.

"I already ate, but I'm a sucker for raw oysters," she said.

"Me too." She smiled when I said, "Let's have another dozen."

She hiccupped and said, "Are you in Pinebridge to investigate Harper and Celeste?"

Kayla, I sensed, was playing a game with me. I lied and said, "They aren't on my radar."

"They often have parties."

"What's unusual about that?" I asked.

Kayla didn't answer my question. Instead, she said, "I think I've led you along. You're a beautiful man, and I wouldn't mind spending the night with you. It doesn't matter because I have an exam tomorrow at seven. I have to go now."

"No problem," I said. "I enjoyed it. See you tomorrow?"

Kayla kissed me and said, "I can't wait."

After ten, the Raven's Roost had cleared out, and no one left but Henry and me.

"Looks as if you're ready to close," I said.

"I'm here until midnight," he said. "Customers or not. Lemonade?"

Henry smiled when I said, "Make it a double."

"Sure you don't want a shot of vodka in your lemonade," he asked when he returned.

"Nothing I'd like better, though straight lemonade will have to do."

Henry rested his elbows on the bar and said, "Mind if I smoke?"

"It doesn't bother me," I said.

Henry removed a cigar from his shirt pocket and lit it with a match he had produced from somewhere.

"The boss would fire me if he knew I was smoking in the restaurant."

I didn't remind him it was also illegal. Instead, I said, "If you don't tell him, neither will I."

Henry took a few puffs before producing an ashtray and extinguishing it. After knocking off the ashes, he returned the cigar to his shirt pocket, washed the ashtray, and hid it under the bar.

"Just needed a puff or two," he said.

"Are you from Pinebridge?" I asked.

"Lived here all my life. Graduated from high school and went a couple of semesters at Pinebridge College until I knocked up my girlfriend and had to marry and get a job."

"Still married?"

"Kids are grown and moved away. Wife died a few years back."

"I'm so sorry," I said.

"You never miss the water till the well runs dry," he said.

"Truer words were never spoken," I said. "Let me buy you a drink."

"Appreciate it," he said.

Henry poured himself a tall glass of scotch with no ice or water.

"Thanks," he said. "I helped put together our fortieth high school reunion last year. It kept me busy. You'd be surprised how many people in my class have died already."

"Sounds like fun," I said. "You must have a handle on what's happening around town."

"You can't live in a small town for almost sixty years without knowing all the dirt."

"Bet that's right," I said. "Where do people work?"

"The college and the hospital," he said. "There's a garment factory and a boat factory. Lots of folks work there. Some work across the river in Alexandria and others in Leesville."

"Leesville?"

"The town outside of Fort Polk, the nearby Army base. They changed the name to Fort Johnson, but it will always be Fort Polk for me."

"How far away is Leesville?"

"Fifty miles or so," he said.

Henry finished his tall scotch. "Have another drink," I said.

"You on an expense account?" he asked.

"I am," I said. "Drink as much as you want."

"Thanks," he said. "Guess you want some information for these drinks."

I waved my hand and shook my head. "No pressure," I said. "I'm enjoying your company."

"I wasn't born yesterday. "Everyone in town knows you're a private dick. Doesn't matter because you're not pushy. I like that."

He smiled when I said, "You like oysters, Henry?"

Henry and I had soon consumed a dozen oysters. Since I was full, he did most of the damage. I nodded when he motioned to his empty scotch glass.

"You want to know the straight scoop on Harper and Celeste?"

Kayla was going to tell me, but she crapped out when it came time to spill the beans," I said.

"I'm surprised she told you anything. Kayla's as thick as thieves with Celeste."

"I sensed I was pushing some boundaries," I said.

"Celeste is from New Orleans," Henry said. "People didn't trust her when she moved here."

"They do now?"

"She won their trust," Henry said.

"How did she do that?" I asked.

"Sex parties," he said.

"Excuse me?"

"I didn't stutter. Celeste is a striking woman. Within a month of arriving in Pinebridge, she'd had sex with the mayor, the president of Pinebridge College, and the pastor of the largest church in town."

"Damn!" I said. "To what purpose?"

"Don't know," he said. "When they had sex with one of the patients, their loyalty was sealed."

"The city fathers had sex with a mental patient?" I asked.

"More than once, from what I've heard," he said.

"Let's have more oysters," I said.

"You got it," Henry said.

We finished the oysters, and Henry had another tall scotch. It was nearing midnight.

"I have a blockbuster to tell you about the hospital, but it's almost midnight, and I must start closing."

Henry's eyes focused on something behind me. I turned to see Kayla standing in the shadows.

"Forgot my purse," she said. "Got to go now."

When she was gone, I asked, "How long was she standing there?"

"Long enough," he said.

I handed him a credit card and said, "Better tab me out."

"You got it," he said.

From the look in Henry's eyes, Kayla's appearance spooked him to the core.

"You're not worried about Kayla, are you?" I asked.

Henry's expression grew dark. "A big mouth can get you killed in Pinebridge."

Chapter 8

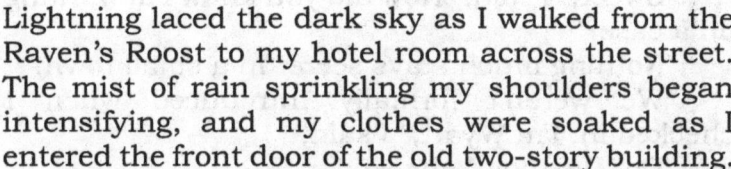

Lightning laced the dark sky as I walked from the Raven's Roost to my hotel room across the street. The mist of rain sprinkling my shoulders began intensifying, and my clothes were soaked as I entered the front door of the old two-story building.

The woman who had checked me into the hotel the previous night was behind the counter, reading a magazine. Dark hair draped her shoulders, and her equally dark eyes flashed when she saw me.

"Looks like you got caught in the rain," she said.

"It was barely sprinkling when I left the Raven's Roost. The bottom fell out before I made it to the hotel," I said.

"Any luck finding what you're looking for?"

She grinned when I said, "One step forward and two steps backward."

Not satisfied with my terse answer, she asked, "What exactly are you looking for?"

"A former patient at the hospital about twenty years ago who disappeared," I said.

I started to walk upstairs when she said, "Lots of strange things happened twenty years ago."

I spotted a coffee urn on the counter and stopped to pour a cup. "Have you lived here all your life?" I asked.

"My husband's family owns this hotel," she said. "We met in college and moved to Pinebridge after he graduated."

"Oh? What does he do?"

"Petroleum engineer. Helps drill wells in the Gulf. Twenty-one days out, seven days in."

"Must get lonely," I said.

"I stay busy. I'm a librarian at Pinebridge College during the day, and I help out Bert's parents here at night," she said. "Bert's mom watches my two kids during the day, and I work at the desk at night."

"Sweet," I said. "How did you know I'm working on a case?"

"Nothing much stays secret in a small town."

"We weren't formally introduced when I checked in. I'm Wyatt," I said.

"Dot Beaufoy," she said.

"It's nice to meet you, Dot. As a librarian at the college, you must know the history of Pinebridge well."

"It's fully documented," she said. "Come to the library, and you can read it yourself."

"Authors tend to put their own stamps on things, if you know what I mean," I said.

"You're talking about the hospital, aren't you?"

"There's a website online that claims patients were treated like prisoners and kept in cages."

"You can't believe everything you read online," Dot said.

"Where there's smoke, there's usually fire," I said. "What difference does it make to the town fathers?"

"What happened or didn't happen at the hospital isn't discussed much."

"Why is that?"

"Call it a culture of silence," Dot said.

"Because?"

72

"Maybe fear of the stigma associated with mental health, outsiders, or things that happened in the past."

"You mean like a scandal?" When she nodded, I said. "What scandal?"

Dot laughed and put her magazine under the counter.

"I read too much. Talk of scandal was hyperbole created by a lonely librarian with little to do all day except conjure up fictional scenarios."

When a traveling salesman looking for a room for the night hurried through the door, I waved and started up the stairs.

"I'll let you get back to business," I said. "Catch you later."

Dot knew something about my case. So did Henry and Kayla. Everyone seemed to know more about the Pinebridge Mental Hospital than I did.

My little room was stuffy, so I cracked the window and turned off the lights. My clothes, down to my underwear, were damp from the rain. I pulled everything off and crawled under the covers. The sound of rain outside my open window soon lulled me into a deep sleep. The haunting melody of frogs awaiting an approaching storm awoke me sometime later. Or did it? If I were awake, I wasn't in my room at the Beaufoy Hotel.

The only thing separating a nightmare from a dream is the gut-wrenching fear you feel when you wake up screaming. I wanted to scream, though I couldn't open my eyes.

Something that didn't seem quite human was screaming in the distance. Some animal, likely a big cat, was stalking me through a pine forest. I was barefoot and naked as the day of my birth. I had no weapon, not even a rock or big stick. The cat was tracking me, and I inherently knew there was no place to hide.

Fear is the most basic human emotion. Human nervous systems are programmed to respond to danger, and my primordial heart was racing as the killer drew closer. It didn't matter because I was in a dream or a nightmare. It wasn't real, or was it? My heart-racing anxiety morphed into a Technicolor hard-on when a beautiful woman dressed in a blue nightgown blocked my path.

"Help me," she said.

❦

When a persistent knock on my door awoke me, I was still half-asleep. Officer Maya Henstooth was grinning when I opened the door.

"Do you always greet people in the nude?" she asked.

"Oops!" I said, turning and rushing to the bathroom. I returned covered in a robe. "Come in," I said. "So sorry. I'm not a flasher; I promise."

Maya followed me into the room. "Did I wake you?" she asked.

"Guilty as charged," I said.

"You're shaking," she said.

"You awoke me from a nightmare."

"Sorry."

"I should be sorry. It wasn't my intention to answer the door naked."

"I'm a cop," she said. "Nothing much I haven't seen."

She laughed when I said, "I wasn't trying to traumatize you."

"I have four brothers," she said. "Trust me when I tell you male nudity doesn't bother me."

"This is early even for you. It isn't light outside," I said.

"Another long day," she said.

"Any new leads?"

"Nothing much. I was hoping you had something," she said.

"How about a cup of plastic coffee?"

"Plastic coffee is better than no coffee."

Maya laughed when I said, "Not much."

"What was your nightmare about?" she asked.

"Some wild creature, probably a panther, was chasing me through a forest. It was dark; I had no weapon and was afraid."

"Your subconscious was focusing on the ghost cat who left the lacerations on our murder victim," she said.

"Probably," I said. "It didn't make it any less unnerving."

"Are you getting anywhere on your case?"

"Every time I open a door, there are two more closed ones behind it," I said.

"I'm having the same problem," Maya said. "My people combed the murder scene for clues. We found nothing. No footprints, fingerprints, or DNA, and no murder weapon. It's almost as if he were killed by a ghost."

"Or a ghost cat. Why not? We found the victim in a cemetery," I said.

"I don't believe in ghosts, and I'd bet neither do you."

"Did your death investigator have any idea what the murder weapon was?"

"Probably a knife with a serrated edge," she said.

"A hunting knife?'

"Could have been a kitchen knife," she said. "Whatever killed him, we didn't find it."

"It didn't look like he put up a struggle," I said.

"Maybe he knew the killer," Maya said.

"Maybe," I said. "Let's hit that café again. I'll buy your breakfast and tell you what I learned yesterday that could impact your case."

We were soon drinking coffee in a booth at Abner's on Main Street. A dozen farmers occupied several large tables, discussing everything from politics to the weather. They recognized me as a stranger to town and were undoubtedly eavesdropping on our conversation. We kept our voices low and hoped no one read our lips.

It seemed as if Maya hadn't eaten in a while. She poured extra syrup on her short stack of pancakes and ate with gusto.

Between bites, she said, "You have something pertinent to the murder case?"

"Celeste Gauthier gave me a tour of the hospital grounds yesterday. We were in the garden when she got a call. She hurried to her office and left me outside."

"And?"

"A young woman was sitting among the roses, and she signed to me as I walked past her."

"Signed?"

"I don't know much sign language, but I do know the universal sign for help." I closed my fingers over my folded thumb to show her. "I asked her if she needed help. She didn't answer, though I could see she did."

"What help did she need?" Maya asked.

"The first thing that caught my attention was her blue nightgown."

"You mean her hospital gown?"

"She wore a torn baby doll nightie that did nothing to hide the fact she had nothing on underneath. That's not all."

"Tell me," Maya said.

"She had a black eye, swollen lips, and scrapes on her arms and chest as if someone had raked her through the gravel."

"And?"

"I took her to Celeste's office. Celeste called Gayla, a nurse. Gayla took her to get cleaned up and to check out her cuts and bruises."

"What did Celeste say?" Maya asked.

"The woman's name is Lyrica Winter. Celeste said she has PTSD and severe schizophrenia and is usually confined to a padded cell. When I asked about her cuts and bruises, Celeste told me she was a klutz and often injured herself."

"What was she doing in the garden?" Maya asked.

"Celeste informed me she was neither violent nor dangerous and often spent time in the garden."

"What was her explanation about the baby doll?"

"I didn't bother asking her because her answer would have been bogus. I stopped by the nurse's station when I left Celeste's office. I arrived there as attendant Bud Johnson was returning Rica to her room."

"Rica?"

"Seems she could speak enough to tell me her name," I said. "I went into the nurse's station and quizzed Gayla."

"What's Gayla's last name?" Maya asked.

"I didn't ask her. Turns out, she'd met my missing person shortly after starting work at the hospital some twenty years ago."

I nodded when she said, "Gayla knew Bella Donna Castellano? Did she know what happened to her?"

"She's about to retire and didn't want to tell me anything that would affect her retirement. She said that twenty years ago, there were many allegations of the attendants abusing patients. There was a whistleblower, and the governor stepped in and fired them all except one."

"What's his name?" Maya asked.

"Her name is Inga Talledaga. She still works at the hospital."

Maya was writing everything I told her on a notepad. "What else?"

"Gayla gave me directions to Billy Williams's little one-room house. He told me the attendants regularly sexually abused Rica."

"If she doesn't speak, how did she tell him?"

"Billy is supposedly autistic and went to special classes where he learned to sign."

"Supposedly?"

"I'm no mental health expert, though Billy seems normal to me," I said. "I asked him where he got the witch mark, and he said someone named Efy tattooed it on his wrist."

"Efy?"

"He said she was a witch. He was hesitant, and I didn't press him on it."

"What else?"

"He said the three attendants feared him because of the witch mark and the gris-gris he wears around his neck."

"Gris-gris?"

"A talisman, amulet, or voodoo charm believed to ward off evil and bring good luck to oneself or misfortune to another," I said.

"Now, I am confused," Maya said. "How are voodoo and witchcraft connected?"

"Billy's mother gave him the gris-gris."

"Billy's mother practices voodoo?"

"Lots of people in New Orleans wear gris-gris," I said. "It doesn't necessarily mean they practice voodoo."

"I'll run these names," Maya said. "You've opened a can of worms. What do you intend to do about it?"

"Nothing, at least until we have more evidence," I said.

"I don't know if I can keep the abuse part secret for long," she said.

"Whatever's going on here likely has deep political roots. Harper Devereaux is the daughter of one of the most powerful families in New Orleans. She was the Queen of the Krewe of Illusion. If we play our hands too soon, I predict it'll be covered up in a heartbeat with you and me left holding aces and eights."

"What do you suggest?"

"Inga, Bud, and Hank are pawns in a complex chess game. We set a trap, bide our time, and see who takes the bait. If the people we're dealing with are too powerful, we'll likely get hung up by our thumbs."

"How do you know so much about the rich and powerful?" Maya asked.

"My grandfather was a former Louisiana governor, my dad, a politician, and my mom a New Orleans socialite. I was a lawyer and ran in all the right Garden District circles until I got disbarred."

"Not good," she said.

"What's good is I'm still alive. We're likely dealing with people who control the power of life and death."

"You're scaring me," she said.

She smiled when I said, "I'm betting you've never been scared of anything."

"The panther wasn't the only thing in your dreams, was it?" she asked.

"I remember being confronted by Rica Winter before you woke me. She was all but naked."

My face turned red when Maya said, "I could tell something had excited you."

Chapter 9

My face was still red, and Maya grinning when a waitress topped up our coffee cups.

She stopped grinning when I asked, "What else do you know about Billy Williams?"

"A dead end," she said. "There's no record that he even exists. No birth certificate. No fingerprints or DNA matches. No records at all."

"Maybe Billy Williams isn't his real name."

"The thought crossed my mind," Maya said. "We've entered his mug shot into our facial recognition program. No luck so far."

She shook her head when I said, "No social media accounts?"

"Nothing."

"How old is he?"

"He told us that he's twenty-one."

"Have someone check the high school yearbooks for all schools within a hundred-mile radius."

"I have someone working on it. It's time-consuming, and human eyes tend to overlook things right in front of them."

"Amen to that. What about his parents?"

"His mother is a woman named Wanda Spivey. He has no father," Maya said.

"Let me guess. There are no records for Wanda Spivey."

Maya sipped her coffee before answering. "Zero."

"What now?" I asked.

"Billy Williams led us to the body. My guess is he knows more about the murder than he's letting on, and we know little about him."

"We need to locate his mother," I said. "If she truly practices voodoo, it might be her that conjured up the ghost panther."

"You don't believe in voodoo, do you?"

"My business partner in New Orleans is a voodoo mambo. I've seen her do things I wouldn't believe possible," I said.

"Like what?" Maya asked.

"Summon spirits of the dead," I said.

"I'm a cop, not one of your clients. If I haven't seen it, I don't believe it," she said.

"Suit yourself."

"Doesn't matter because we have no idea how to find Billy's mother," she said. "If we had a picture of her, we'd have a chance of locating her with facial recognition."

"Billy has her picture in his house," I said.

"You didn't tell me that," she said.

"I'm telling you now," I said.

Maya finished her coffee and said, "I'm going to visit him. Can you show me where he lives?"

"If you'll let me go with you," I said.

"This is a police matter. It wouldn't be proper."

"Billy trusts me. You're likelier to get the answers you want if I tag along."

"Then let's tab out and go," she said.

It was only a mile to the hospital. I took the opportunity to quiz Maya on the way to the abandoned hospital parking lot.

"You have four brothers?" I asked.

"And two sisters. I'm the youngest of seven kids."

"How did that work out?"

Maya smiled and said, "I never wore new clothes, not even new shoes, until I went away to college and got a part-time job. What about you?"

"Born with a silver spoon in my mouth. I was four before I realized my black nanny wasn't my mother."

"Must be nice," she said.

"Neglect is a form of abuse," I said. "I was in college before I finally resolved my parent-son relationship. Or at least the lack thereof."

"We all have our crosses to bear," she said.

"The red Corvette my parents gave me when I graduated from Ben Franklin High School helped salve many wounds."

I laughed when she said, "So sorry for your broken childhood."

Maya parked the car, and we headed across a vacant field to Billy Williams's little house in a loose pod of abandoned hospital buildings. The door was unlocked. When no one came to the door after I had knocked, I pushed it open and entered.

"We don't have a search warrant," Maya said.

"You may need one. I don't. If anyone asks, tell them you thought I was a burglar."

Maya frowned and followed me into the stuffy little room. Billy's blind cat, Noseye, jumped off the bed and began weaving a path through my legs. Seeing the picture of Billy's mother on the dresser, Maya took a picture with the camera on her cell phone. I picked up Noseye and was rubbing his head when Billy Williams entered.

"What are you doing here?" he asked.

"Looking for you," I said. "Detective Henstooth has questions."

"I already told her everything I know," Billy said.

"Not everything," she said. "Where did you go to high school?"

"Leesville," he said. "My mom worked at the army base."

"Fort Johnson?" she asked.

"It was Fort Polk back then," he said.

Billy shook his head when Maya asked, "Does your mom still live in Leesville?"

"Not anymore."

"Where does she live?" I asked.

"A cottage in the Kisatchie National Forest," he said.

Billy nodded when Maya said, "She lives in a national forest? How does she do that?"

"She just does," Billy said.

"Does your mom still work?" Maya asked.

"She gathers herbs and medicinal plants and makes potions for people."

"Your mom is an herbalist?" Maya said.

"I guess you could say that," Billy said.

"What's her real name?"

"Wanda Spivey. Like I told you."

"You know what a lie detector is, Billy?" Maya asked.

"I'm telling the truth."

Billy didn't answer when Maya asked, "Then why don't I believe you?"

"Can you give us directions to your mom's house?" I asked.

"You'll never find it," he said.

"Then maybe you can take us there."

"She doesn't like unexpected visitors," Billy said.

"Call and tell her we're coming," Maya said.

"Can't do that," Billy said. "She has no phone."

"What are you hiding?" Maya asked.

"Nothing," he said.

Billy smiled when Maya said, "Your nose is growing again."

"Your mom isn't a suspect," I said. "Detective Henstooth and I have a few questions. Won't you take us to her?"

"What can she tell you I haven't already told you?" Billy asked.

"The truth," Maya said.

"I'll think about it," Billy said.

"Wyatt said you told him that the attendants were sexually abusing some of the patients."

Billy glanced at me with a frown and said, "I don't remember saying that."

"Are the attendants sexually abusing the patients?" Maya asked.

"Ms. Gauthier told me not to talk about it," Billy said.

"Did she now? Maybe I need to question her again."

"Don't tell her I said anything," Billy said.

"You don't have to be afraid of Ms. Gauthier," Maya said.

"I don't want to lose my job."

"She can't fire you for telling the truth. Who taught you to sign?"

"My teacher, Ms. Donaldson."

Billy nodded when Maya said, "She teaches at one of the schools in Leesville? Is she still there?"

"I don't know," Billy said. "She taught me to read and write and how to use sign language. It was the only way some of the students could talk."

"And that's the way you converse with Rica Winter?"

"Yes," he said.

"If I have questions for her, will you translate?"

"I can't. Ms. Gauthier would fire me," Billy said.

"Why does she care?" Maya asked.

"She does," Billy said.

When I glanced at Maya, she motioned to the door.

"We're done with you," she said. "You can get back to work now."

I put the cat on the floor and followed Maya out of the stuffy little house. When we reached the front seat of her police cruiser, she rolled down the windows.

"What do you think?" she asked.

"He's covering something up," I said.

"My thoughts exactly."

"You struck gold when you asked him to interpret for Rica," I said. "When are we doing it?"

"Not you," she said. "Me. This is police business."

"Give me a break," I said. "She can help with my case as well as yours. I've scratched your back. It's time for you to scratch mine."

"I'll think about it. As you said, we should probably keep allegations of abuse out of things until we have the murder solved. Right now, I'm more interested in finding Billy's mother."

"We could start by driving to Leesville and speaking with Billy's teacher, Ms. Donaldson."

"Leesville is in Vernon Parish. I have no jurisdiction there," Maya said.

"That sucks! How about we look at aerial photos of Kisatchie National Forest? We can find the house that way," I said.

"Billy's probably lying about where his mom lives. Even if he's not, Kisatchie is the largest forest in Louisiana and covers parts of seven parishes, more than six hundred thousand acres."

"How do you know so much about the forest?" I asked.

"We had an escaped convict a few years ago who took shelter in the forest. We only found him when he went into town for supplies."

"If she sells potions to the locals, they must know where she lives," I said.

"I only have jurisdiction in Rapides Parish," Maya said. "Even if she does have a house in the Kisatchie National Forest, it'll do me no good unless the house is in Rapides."

"Doesn't stop me," I said. "I can interview Billy's mom and Ms. Donaldson no matter where they live."

"If she doesn't live in Rapides Parish, then we forget her," Maya said.

"We could at least speak with some of the people in the Rapides Parish towns abutting the forest," I said.

"You think Billy's a liar. Try getting a truthful answer from one of the locals around here."

"I'm starting to figure that one out," I said. "What now?"

"I'm taking this picture of Billy's mom and running it through our facial recognition program. I'll drop you off at the hospital."

My cell phone rang as Maya started the car. It was Frankie Castellano.

"What do you have for me so far?" he asked.

"A bucket of worms and no fish," I said.

"What's the problem?" he asked.

I could hear him chuckle when I said, "The people around here are more tight-lipped than you are. I did talk with a nurse who knew your sister when she was at the hospital."

"Did she tell you where she is?"

"No," I said.

"What else?"

"Your sister's disappearance isn't the only thing around here being covered up. I've been using a pick hammer on a brick wall. It's time to move to a wrecking ball."

"Keep at it," Frankie said. "I have confidence in you."

Frankie signed off without saying goodbye.

"Who was that?" Maya asked.

"My client."

"Is he ready for you to give up?"

"Frankie Castellano's like a bulldog. He doesn't let go once he sinks his teeth into your neck."

"Frankie Castellano, the mob boss?"

"That's him," I said.

"He has a restaurant slash illegal casino and house of prostitution just off the Interstate."

"You haven't busted him?"

"Castellano has more tentacles than an octopus, and every one of them is connected to people in high places."

"Tell me about it," I said. "Frankie was the King of the Krewe of Illusion and the only person in south Louisiana more powerful than the Devereaux family."

"How do you square it working for a mobster?" Maya asked.

I grinned and said, "I'm a sleazy French Quarter P.I. and not a Baptist deacon. Remember?"

"Castellano's a crook," she said.

"He's not convicted of anything, and he didn't hire me to do anything illegal."

I laughed when she said, "You're getting paid in blood money."

"If you could see where your paycheck comes from, you'd find a few bloodstains along the way," I said. "At least that's my bet."

"That may be so, but right is right, and wrong is wrong," she said.

"Not everything is black or white. Sometimes it's a shade of gray," I said.

"An overused platitude," she said.

"Clichés persist because there's a certain amount of truth to them," I said.

"You're Catholic, aren't you?"

"What's that got to do with anything?" I asked.

"Catholics are loose and easy with their interpretation of the Bible," Maya said.

"We aren't talking about religion. Even if we were, I gave it up long ago, so let's not go there," I said.

Maya stopped the police cruiser in front of the entrance to the Pinebridge Mental Hospital.

"Thanks for your help," she said.

"Does this mean you won't be knocking on my door at six tomorrow morning?"

When Maya smiled and said, "Wouldn't miss it for the world. I like surprises, and you made my day this morning," my face turned red again.

Chapter 10

When I entered the revolving door, it was the first time I had a good look at the hospital. Visitors sat in the large reception area, some reading magazines and others chatting with patients in hospital gowns. At least three doctors in white coats and numerous nurses and orderlies in blue scrubs were hurrying about. One of the people in the reception area fitted the description of Inga Talledaga.

The short-haired woman had the shoulders of a professional wrestler and a snarling expression to match. When she walked past me, I saw her name tag. She turned when I spoke.

"Excuse me. Are you Inga Talledaga?"

"That's me," she said. "Who are you?"

"Wyatt Thomas," I said. "A private investigator from New Orleans."

"What can I do for you, Mr. Thomas?"

"I'm looking for a missing person, a patient here at the hospital twenty years ago."

"There were many patients here twenty years ago," Inga said.

"Her name was Bella Donna Castellano. Gayla informed me she remembered her. She'd just started working at the hospital, and you were also working here at the time."

"I don't know any Bella Donna Castellano," Inga said.

She started to walk away, stopping when I said, "The rumor is you made her disappear because she hexed you."

"That's bullshit! Who told you that?"

"Doesn't matter," I said. "Is it true?"

Inga's normal scowl turned into an ugly frown as she approached my face, so close that I could smell the garlic chicken she'd eaten for lunch.

"You're stepping on the wrong toes." She turned to walk away but stopped and said, "Go back to New Orleans before you step in a pile of shit."

"Is that a threat?" I asked.

"Consider it a piece of good advice."

Inga was walking away when Harper spotted me in the crowded reception room. She smiled, put her arm in the air, and hurried to join me. When she reached me, she took my hand and led me to a corner of the reception area dominated by a large potted plant.

Harper could have easily made a living as a Vogue cover model. She was dazzling and very noticeable in light blue designer shorts, a white frilly blouse, and expensive matching shoes.

"What's up?" I asked.

"Celeste said you were wrapping up your investigation and returning to New Orleans."

"That was my plan," I said. "Frankie called me earlier and told me he wasn't satisfied with not locating his sister. He ordered me to stay on the investigation until he informed me otherwise."

"I know. He also called me," she said. "What are you going to do?"

"I'm not very smart, though I know better than to piss off Frankie Castellano."

Harper grinned and said, "He's a powerful man."

"He reminds me of your dad," I said.

"You know my dad?" Harper asked.

"I helped him on a legal matter before I was disbarred."

"He never told me that."

"I doubt he remembers me."

"Dad never forgets anything," she said. "He remembers. What are we going to tell Celeste?"

"The truth," I said. "I was on my way to see her."

"Then I'll go with you."

Harper held my hand as we pushed through the crowded reception area arm-in-arm, every person we passed eyeing her shapely legs. I sensed she was somewhat of an exhibitionist, and her sly smile as she eyed the crowd did nothing to belie my observation. She didn't bother knocking when she entered Celeste's office.

I wondered how to explain my continuing investigation as Celeste and Harper hugged. I didn't have to, as Harper did it for me.

"Frankie called me earlier," she said. He's having Wyatt continue his investigation. I guess we have a few more days to enjoy him."

Celeste turned her attention to me and asked, "You've talked with everyone. What more can you do?"

I put my hands in the air and shook my head. "Mr. Castellano is very direct in his desires. I'll stay and do what I can until he tires of the search and calls me off the case."

Celeste seemed satisfied by my lie. I wondered how she would feel after learning about my conversation with Inga. I decided to press forward and not worry about it.

"Will you join Harper and me tonight at the Raven's Roost?" Celeste asked. "Same time as usual."

When she smiled and nodded, I said, "I'll be there."

"Good. I have things to do so I'll see you then. Harper can take you wherever you need to go."

Harper and I passed through the reception area to her expensive Range Rover.

"Where to?" she asked.

"Back to the hotel," I said. "You seemed reticent last night."

"I'm embarrassed. I told you things I shouldn't have," she said.

"You reached out to me," I said. "I could tell you need my help."

"I'm good. I've resolved my past. I'm doing things differently now," she said.

"Don't think like that. You're a victim, not the instigator."

"I love my dad," she said.

"Say what you will, but I got the message last night, and I'm here for you. You took a significant step forward. Keep moving forward, and things will resolve."

Something had occurred, Harper smiling and pretending not to know what I was talking about. She gave me a peck on the cheek after stopping at the front door of the Beaufoy Hotel.

"I'll wait for you if you need to go somewhere else," she said.

"It's too far from here. I'll find another way to get there," I said.

"Nonsense. Tell me where you want to go. I'll take you."

"Leesville," I said. "An old college buddy I haven't seen in a decade lives there. I need to grab something upstairs first."

"I'll park in the shade and be here when you return," she said.

Harper was vulnerable and lying to her about my reasons for visiting Leesville was not my intention. The deceit might prove moot because I had yet to check my P.I. database to determine if I could locate Ms. Donaldson, Billy Williams's special education teacher. Dot was behind the check-in counter, reading a magazine. She smiled when I entered the door.

I stopped when she said, "Got a minute?"

"You bet," I said. "What's up?"

"You're Catholic, aren't you?"

"How did you know?" I asked.

"I saw you cross yourself last night when thunder shook the rafters."

"Not a good Catholic, I'm afraid. Crossing myself when startled seems a habit I can't break."

"There aren't many Catholics in Pinebridge. About thirty people, counting the Beaufoy family, Bert, and me. We attend Mass at the Chapel in the Trees."

I didn't know what Dot was getting at, so I said, "Okay."

"Father Piastri is the priest."

Dot waved a placating palm when I said, "I haven't attended Mass in many years."

"Father Piastri lives on the grounds. He was the priest here during the scandal."

"And?"

Dot looked at me as if I were a blithering idiot and said, "I hope your room is comfortable and you're having a great time here in Pinebridge."

"I may have to change my evil ways. Where exactly is the Chapel in the Trees?"

"About a mile due north of town," she said.

"Thanks, Dot," I said before hurrying upstairs.

My room was stuffy again, so I opened the window before retrieving the laptop from my suitcase. It took me about ten minutes to locate a report on Debra Donaldson, a Special Education teacher in Leesville, Louisiana. Citizens would be incensed, and rightfully so, if they knew how much private information was included in these dossiers. Debra's cell phone number was prominently displayed, and she answered it on the first ring.

"If this is a sales call, I'm not interested," she said.

"Nothing like that," I said. "I'm a private investigator from New Orleans and have questions about one of your former students."

"What former student?"

"Billy Williams," I said.

"I remember Billy," she said. "Is he in trouble?"

"Not at all. Where are you? Sounds like an arcade."

"The casino south of town. I'm meeting my daughter in the bar in about an hour."

"I'll buy your drinks if you answer a few questions," I said.

"You sound cute. Toni and I will be waiting in the bar."

"And you sound beautiful," I said. "See you in about an hour."

I repacked the laptop in my suitcase and hurried down the stairs, waving to Dot as I walked out the door. Harper was playing with her cell phone. She put it away and smiled when I climbed into the passenger seat.

"There's a casino south of Leesville. Do you know where it is?"

"Celeste and I have been there. It's not like New Orleans. All the slots are too close together, and the drinks aren't great. Still, it's not bad for the boondocks of central Louisiana."

"Exactly what my friend Ray said."

"Wyatt, what are we going to do about Frankie?"

"Frankie likes to be the driver, not the passenger," I said.

"He's driving me crazy," she said.

"Why is that?"

"During our time as King and Queen of Illusion, we had an affair. Temporary is all it was for me. Frankie won't let it lie."

"You want me to do something?" I asked.

"Can you?"

"Not me, but one of my partners might possibly intervene," I said.

"Will you talk to them about it?"

"He's on a second honeymoon with his wife in Italy. It's the reason I'm here and not him."

"When will he return from Italy?"

"This weekend. I'll talk to him."

"Thanks, Wyatt. I never want to do anything to hurt Frankie."

"Trust me when I say I understand. I'll see what I can do."

We reached the Calcasieu Rise Casino sometime later, and Harper stopped the Range Rover in the establishment's gravel parking lot.

"You sure you don't want me to come in with you?" Harper asked.

"You're so beautiful, you'd only intimidate Ray. Besides, you won't find a few hours of raunchy frat talk interesting."

"I'm okay with raunch," she said.

I leaned across the console and kissed her. "I'll see you and Celeste at the Raven's Roost."

"How will you get there?"

"Call an Uber if I have to," I said.

Harper smiled as she left me in the parking lot of the Calcasieu Rise Casino. I wondered if she realized how often I'd lied to her in the past three hours. My prevarication became easier as I entered the casino's overly air-conditioned lobby. It didn't take me long to locate the bar. Debra Donaldson and her daughter Toni were waiting for me.

After introducing myself and sitting beside them, Debra said, "I told you he'd be cute."

Debra was retired, on a pension and social security. She didn't seem a day older than her attractive daughter, Toni. Both had short, dark hair and eyes.

"I'm Debbie, and this is my daughter Toni."

"Pleased to meet you. I'm Wyatt." A waiter arrived to take my drink order. "Lemonade if you have it, iced tea if you don't, and put these lady's drinks on my tab."

Debbie and Toni were drinking double vodkas, and they ordered another round.

"You wanted to ask some questions about Billy Williams?"

"He works at the mental hospital in Pinebridge," I said. "Their records show he is autistic. I talked to him at length, and he seems normal."

"Billy is on the high end of the autistic scale. We worked through most of his problems in class, and now he is fully functional."

Debbie smiled when I said, "You must be an extraordinary teacher."

"I did my best," she said.

"She did more than that," Toni said. "She worked her ass off."

"Can you tell me anything about Billy's parents?"

"The students at the school where I taught were mostly impoverished, single-parent children. Billy's father was a soldier, killed, I believe, in

Afghanistan, though that wasn't uncommon. I only met his mother once."

"Can you describe her for me?"

"The students at the school where I taught were predominately black. Even though Wanda's hair was blond and her skin light, I could tell she was black."

"How could you tell?"

"She had a tattooed witch mark on her wrist. She tried to hide it with makeup, but I saw it," Debbie said.

"Why would a witch mark make you think she was black?" I asked.

"Around that time, an old black woman sold herbs and potions to the locals and called herself a witch. For a price, she would tattoo a witch mark on your wrist for protection. All the black girls had one."

"Why was Billy's mother hiding her ethnicity?" I asked.

"In Louisiana, there are lots of reasons. In Wanda's case, I think it was because she was trying to hide her identity."

"Because?"

"I'm just guessing, but it's possible she became involved with an abuser after her husband died. Maybe she'd escaped from the relationship and didn't want the monster to locate her."

"You would have made a good private detective," I said.

"You can't survive thirty-five years in the Louisiana Public School System without a buttload of skill. One more thing about Billy."

"What?"

"He spoke fluent Italian, though it sounded strange because of his southern drawl."

"Did you ask him where he learned it?"

"He was vague, only telling me he was good with languages and had picked it up when he was young."

"Was Billy ever violent?" I asked.

"Never," Debbie said. "He was one of the most nonviolent people I ever met."

Chapter 11

An Uber driver dropped me off in front of the Beaufoy Hotel. As I hurried upstairs, no one was at the checkout counter. When I entered my room, I sensed something was amiss. I'd gone no further than three steps before realizing something was radically wrong.

Someone had cased my room, my suitcase open, and my clothes strewn across the floor. After checking it, I saw they had tried to access my laptop. Their attempt was unsuccessful because the computer was password-protected. When I tried to boot it, I was presented with the dreaded blue screen of death. I put it aside, deciding to worry about it later.

Whoever had ransacked my room hadn't done so to steal anything. They had other reasons and intimidation came to mind. I realized it when I saw the bedcovers pulled down on my bed.

The rifled bed revealed a Satanic symbol on the bedsheets. The red stain had bled through the sheets, and it looked as if the color was blood. My mind was racing, processing what I needed to do. Ignoring the intrusion, I hurried to meet Celeste and Harper at the Raven's Roost. Having run late, I found them waiting at the usual table.

"We thought you'd blown us off," Harper said.

"Someone invaded my hotel room and rifled through my belongings," I said.

"Did you call the police?" Celeste asked.

"Nothing anyone can do tonight," I said. "I'll call them tomorrow."

"Did they steal anything?"

"No," I said. "They desecrated my bed with a bloodstained Satanic symbol."

"How horrible," Celeste said. "You can't return to the room. Come home with us and stay the night."

"Thanks," I said.

Kayla arrived at our table with drinks and a come-hither look as Harper and Celeste excused themselves to visit the ladies' room.

"I don't have a test tomorrow morning. Any chance of hooking up tonight when I get off work?"

"Someone ransacked my hotel room," I said. "I'm spending the night at Harper and Celeste's."

"Have fun," Kayla said with a wink.

When Harper and Celeste returned, Harper asked, "How was your visit with Ray?"

It took a moment to remember that I'd told her a lie to prevent explaining my real reason for visiting Leesville.

Not wishing to add to my deceit, I said, "Good."

Though the pepperoni pizza we shared was tasty, I realized that Raven's Roost cuisine had no theme and was anything other than inspired. I'd be back in New Orleans soon enough, so I decided not to worry about the food. Kayla winked again when we walked out the door, adding to my certainty that she had an agenda.

I sat in the backseat of the Land Rover on the way to Harper and Celeste's house. Celeste opened the front door, and I followed them into the darkened foyer. I felt a sharp pain when something struck me in the back of the head. It was the last thing I remembered for a while.

෧෨෯෩

I was naked when I came to on the floor of a dimly lit bedroom. My hands were cuffed behind my back, and I had no way to rub the throbbing pain on my scalp. A trickle of blood dripped down my neck. I wanted to call out, but a red rubber ball was stuffed in my mouth. My ankles were also cuffed, locking me in place on the light-colored shag carpeting.

The bedroom was like something out of 1001 Arabian Nights, with candles and fruity incense burning and the melodious strains of one of Mozart's symphonies pouring from hidden speakers. I wasn't alone.

Three women were in the room. Harper and Celeste were both as naked as I was, except for the silver collars around their necks. They were on their hands and knees.

The third woman was also naked, though her identity was cloaked by a mask covering her head. The masked woman led Harper and Celeste around the room with silver leashes. It seemed apparent from the torpid movements of Harper and Celeste that they were drugged. They weren't the only ones.

My own senses were compromised by some psychedelic drug that engulfed me in dissolving colors and broken sounds. The scenario seemed like a scene from a Fellini movie. It continued until the pain from the wound on my head overcame the power of the psychedelic drug, and my world went dark.

෧෨෯෩

Harper, Celeste, and I opened our eyes around the same time the following morning. We were lying naked on the shag carpeting. My hand and ankle cuffs were gone, and the first thing I did was feel the open wound on the back of my head. Harper rubbed her forehead. Becoming nauseous, she rushed to the bathroom to throw up.

The red whelps covering Harper and Celeste's arms, legs, back, and chest revealed that they had been flogged. Celeste struggled to reach the house phone on the nightstand beside the bed. She used it to call the hospital.

"Gayla, this is Celeste. Can you come to my house? And please bring your medical kit. Don't bother knocking. Just let yourself in and find your way to the kitchen."

When Celeste hung up the phone, I used it to call Detective Maya Henstooth. We were dressed in bathrobes, sitting at the kitchen table, drinking coffee when Gayla arrived. Silkie was in my lap and jumped to the floor, sniffing the food bowl in the corner.

"What happened?" Gayla asked.

"The police are on their way, and you'll hear when they arrive," Celeste said. "I don't want to tell the story more than once."

Gayla checked everyone's bumps and bruises, cleaned my headwound, and bandaged it. When Maya arrived, we made momentary eye contact.

"Someone attacked and drugged us when we returned home last night," Celeste said.

"Who?" Maya asked.

"Don't know," Celeste said. "They wore full-face masks. They knocked Wyatt unconscious and then forced Harper and me to perform a sexual show for them in my bedroom."

"Show us the bedroom." When we entered the room, she said, "This is a crime scene. Treat it as such."

Maya's forensic technicians began searching the bedroom for clues, and we returned to the kitchen.

Tears streamed from Harper's eyes. "They beat us," she said.

"How many intruders were there?" Maya asked.

"I counted three of them," Celeste said. "They were cloaked from head to toe, and the house was dark. I think the two people who held my arms while I was being injected were males, though I can't be sure."

"Can you describe what happened after that?" Maya said.

"Harper and I were stripped and forced to perform unspeakable sex acts. When we resisted, we were beaten."

"What were you beaten with?" Maya asked.

Harper shook her head. "It was wet and stung like hell. It could have been a wet leather whip."

"Can you add anything, Mr. Thomas?" Maya asked.

"Not much," I said. "I was only conscious briefly before blacking out."

"Who was the last person you spoke with before the attack?" Maya asked.

"Kayla, the waitress at the Raven's Roost," Harper said.

Hours passed before Maya's team finished their investigation. They'd found my clothes and cell phone and allowed me to dress.

"We've done all we can here," Maya said.

"Wyatt," Celeste said. "You haven't told Detective Henstooth about your hotel room."

"What about it?" Maya asked.

"When I returned to my room last night, I found someone had rifled through it," I said.

"What else?" Maya asked.

"My bedspread had been pulled back, and someone had drawn a Satanic symbol on the sheets. It appeared whoever did it used blood."

"Why didn't you call the police?" Maya asked.

"Harper and Celeste offered me a spare room for the night. I intended to call you this morning."

"Room service at the Beaufoy Hotel found the mess in your room this morning. They called the police. Will you accompany me to the scene and tell me what you know?"

"Of course," I said.

Maya glanced at Celeste and said, "You and Ms. Devereaux are free to go. Get some rest. I'll post police security outside your house if the perps decide to return."

I felt like hell as Maya and I traveled the short distance back to the hotel. Dot Beaufoy averted her eyes as Maya and I started upstairs to my room. A crime tech met us at the door.

"Find anything, Ike?" Maya asked.

Like Maya, the officer wore a brown and blue Rapides Parish police uniform.

"Just finishing up," he said. "We'll know more later."

Maya walked over to my bed and stared at the bloody symbol.

"Do we have any Satanists in the parish?"

Ike chuckled. "Doesn't take a Satanist to draw a Satanic symbol," he said.

"Thanks, Ike," Maya said. "I'll get with you back at the office." She looked at me and said, "Let's take a ride."

"Right behind you," I said.

We were soon back in Maya's cruiser. She drove to the unused hospital parking lot and stopped.

"Explain to me what's going on," she said.

"It's complicated."

"Give me the short version," she said.

"When you let me off in front of the hospital yesterday, I spotted Inga Talledaga in the lobby. I told her I was looking for a missing person and heard she was working at the hospital then."

"And"

"When I suggested Bella Donna had disappeared after hexing her, Inga took offense. She threatened me, at least in so many words."

"What did she say?" Maya asked.

"'Go back to New Orleans before you step in a pile of shit.' When I asked if that was a threat, she told me to consider it good advice."

"You pissed her off, and it sounds like you did it on purpose."

"I wanted to see her reaction," I said.

"That doesn't make her a suspect," Maya said.

"Inga is tall and built like a football linebacker."

"Go on."

"I didn't see much last night. I did see a muscular woman holding a leash as she put Harper and Celeste through their paces. Except for the mask covering her head, the woman was as naked as they were."

"Let me guess," Maya said. "You suspect it was Inga Talledaga."

"You got it. I'm guessing she and her cohorts rifled through my room at the hotel to ensure I wouldn't spend the night there. She was right. When I met Celeste and Harper for dinner at the Raven's Roost, they invited me to stay in their spare bedroom."

"Are you sure you didn't participate in the bondage scene?"

"And hit myself in the head, giving myself a concussion as an alibi?"

"How did she know you were having dinner with the two women?"

"It's Celeste's and Harper's go-to restaurant. Probably everyone at the hospital knows it," I said.

"Maybe," Maya said. "I'd better round her up for questioning. What else?"

"I went to Leesville and spoke with Debra Donaldson, Billy Williams's Special Ed. teacher. She told me a couple of interesting things."

"Like what?" Maya said.

"She'd met Billy's mother and described her as a light-skinned black woman attempting to pass as white."

"For what reason?"

"To hide from a male abuser. She didn't know that for a fact, and it was only her conjecture."

"What else?" she asked.

"She confirmed what I think we both believe: Billy Williams isn't capable of violence."

"You've been busy since the last time I saw you," Maya said.

"That isn't all. The night before last, I spoke with Henry Scott, the bartender at the Raven's Roost. He told me something that Kayla, the waitress, had alluded to."

"Tell me," Maya said.

"He said that Harper and Celeste have sex parties and had compromised many of the citizens of Pinebridge, including the president of Pinebridge College and the local Baptist minister."

"You believed him?"

"I don't believe anything I can't corroborate," I said. "Dot, the night receptionist at the Beaufoy, told me something that gave the theory some credence. She came close to telling me about a scandal at the hospital."

"You believe her?"

"When I pressed her for more information, she clammed up," I said. "Yesterday, she told me something I have yet to check out."

"Like what?"

"She hinted I should talk with Father Piastri, the local Catholic priest.

"For what reason?"

"Dot and her family are Catholics and don't trust Baptists. She strongly implied that many of the locals, all Baptists, are involved in some conspiracy that dates back to Bella Donna's disappearance."

Maya cranked the cruiser's engine. "Let's go see Father Piastri."

Chapter 12

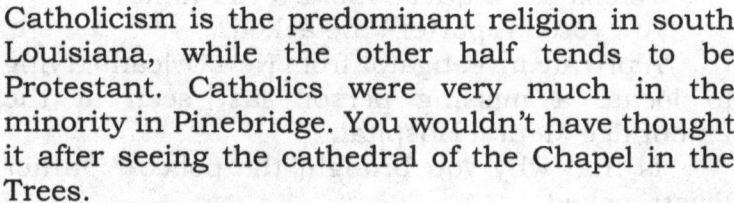

Catholicism is the predominant religion in south Louisiana, while the other half tends to be Protestant. Catholics were very much in the minority in Pinebridge. You wouldn't have thought it after seeing the cathedral of the Chapel in the Trees.

Parishioners had tithed a lot of money to build the lovely cathedral, complete with stained glass windows imported from Italy. The parking lot was small, with room for only about thirty vehicles. Maya parked close to the cathedral's entrance.

"You make the introductions and begin the questioning," Maya said. "I'll chime in when I feel the need."

Maya smiled when I said, "Yes, ma'am."

When we entered the chapel's front door, I realized it was a small version of the St. Louis Cathedral in the French Quarter. Maya, an avowed Baptist, seemed awed.

"First time inside a Catholic Church?" I asked. She nodded. "Don't worry. Satan won't come out of the woodwork and drag you to hell."

She grinned when she said, "Sure about that?"

"You have my word on it," I said.

"Impressive," she said. "Slightly more ornate than the church I attend."

"I don't know why I'm picking on you," I said. "I can't recall ever being inside a Baptist Church."

Our discussion ended as a priest appeared from a door beside the altar. He was short and slender, his spiked hair had turned gray, and his large glasses had black frames.

"Are you here for confession?"

"To see Father Piastri," I said.

From his pronounced accent, the soft-spoken priest was clearly from Italy.

"I'm Father Piastri. What is it you need, my son?"

"To ask a few questions. Do you mind?"

"Are you a reporter?" he asked.

"A private investigator from New Orleans trying to locate a missing person last seen at the Pinebridge Mental Hospital."

"Is that why you brought the police?" Father Piastri asked.

"This is Detective Maya Henstooth. She's a friend, and we're working on separate cases with common sets of facts."

Maya averted her eyes as if she might be struck by lightning when Father Piastri nodded and smiled at her. Ignoring her reaction, the priest motioned us to follow him.

"I have a teakettle aboil in the kitchen. Can I offer you a cup?"

We followed him into his tiny kitchen, where he asked us to sit at the equally small table, its surface ruined by white flaking paint and too many coffee stains. Father Piastri was unapologetic as he poured our tea.

"Sugar or cream?" he asked.

"Two lumps, please," Maya said.

"I'm good," I said.

Father Piastri pulled a vinyl album from its cover, placed it on an old record player, and adjusted the volume before returning to the table. I recognized neither the song nor the artist singing it, though Maya seemed profoundly moved.

"I arrived in Louisiana when I was only twenty-three, a young Italian priest who had visions and dreams of spreading the word of God at the altar of St. Louis Cathedral in New Orleans. I'm now eighty-nine, and I've never gotten further south than Pinebridge."

I glanced at Maya and saw tears dripping down her cheeks.

She shook her head when I asked, "Something wrong?"

Father Piastri showed me the album cover, a picture of a much younger Maya Henstooth dressed in a choir robe, and then answered my question for her.

"Maya is the singer of my favorite album." Father Piastri reached across the table and touched the back of her hand. "Why did you quit singing?"

"I had to make a decision," she said.

"You didn't have to give up one dream to pursue another," he said.

"With me, it was all or nothing," Maya said.

Father Piastri squeezed her hand and said, "It's never all or nothing."

"You're a Catholic," she said.

"Labels are for vegetables in a can. I'm human, just like you."

"I have bills to pay and a large family that needs my help," Maya said.

"I sing, and I'm still a priest," Father Piastri said.

"Singing for yourself and singing for a living are two different things," Maya said.

"It's okay to keep your day job while searching for a dream," he said.

"What could I do?" she asked. "My family still needs me."

"Sing your heart out and never stop." After he and Maya had sipped their tea, he said, "You're here for another reason."

"Dot Beaufoy said you have information about the Pinebridge Mental Hospital," I said.

Father Piastri lowered his head. "I thought someone would knock on my door someday and say the words you just spoke. I was beginning to believe I was wrong."

"Maya and I are here now. Please tell us what you know," I said.

Father Piastri sighed and went to the stove to put on another pot. After pouring our tea, he said, "Where to begin?"

"At the beginning," I said. "We have all day."

"It won't take long because there's nothing I can tell you," Father Piastri said.

"Why not?" I asked.

"Everything I know about the hospital I learned from the confessional. I can never divulge anything I heard there."

"That's crazy," Maya said. "What if someone confessed to murder?"

"Then I would have to live and die with the knowledge," Father Piastri said.

"How can that be?" she asked.

"Priests can never reveal what they have learned during confession to anyone, even under the threat of their own death or that of others," he said. "It's Canon Law that I vowed to live by when I became a priest."

"What if the murderer died?" Maya asked. "Could you reveal the confession?"

Father Piastri shook his head. "Never."

"What difference does it make if the murderer is dead?" Maya said.

"A priest simply cannot reveal what he hears in the confessional. There's no gray area."

"You must be getting close to retirement," Maya said. "Does your vow remain in effect even after you've retired?"

"Canon Law is clear; a priest can never reveal what he hears in a confession."

"I know something about the law," I said. "I was a practicing attorney for years until I was disbarred."

Maya and Father Piastri gave me appraising stares.

"My vows are sacred," Father Piastri said. "I can never break them."

"There are lots of laws out there," I said. "Take Publishing Law, for instance."

"What does that have to do with anything?" Maya asked.

"Hear me out," I said.

"Go for it," she said.

"There are two types of literary works: fiction and nonfiction. Nonfiction deals with the truth. Fiction is literature in prose that describes something imaginary, people who aren't real but created in the author's mind."

"What are you getting at?" Father Piastri said.

"Tell us a story," I said.

Father Piastri glanced at Maya, and she said, "Why not? I like fairy tales. Tell us one."

Father Piastri was smiling as he refilled our teacups.

"Once upon a time, a young priest left his home in Italy to preach in America. He was assigned to a small town in rural Louisiana, thinking a grand cathedral and thousands of parishioners would await him. When he arrived, he found less than a dozen Catholics and a one-room wooden structure that was neither heated in the winter nor cooled in the summer.

"There was a hospital in town where Louisiana patients came for mental treatment. It was called the Hospital of the Insane. Back then, the hospital was large. It grew its own vegetables, had its own dairy, and more than a thousand patients. Many citizens from the little Louisiana town worked there.

"While there were few Catholics in town, the young priest soon learned that the hospital patients were from all over Louisiana, and many of them Catholic. He began conducting Mass there for the believers. It was then that he learned that something was amiss. It started with a person he only knew as Patience.

"Patience was a young woman from New Orleans who showed the priest her bruises from a sexual escapade she had participated in with her guards. Other patients began coming forward to confess. One woman was contrite because she'd helped persuade patients she knew to act as guinea pigs in experimental surgeries that were often unsuccessful.

"The young priest saw examples of unauthorized brain surgeries and limb amputations, many performed for no apparent medical reason. To say he was horrified was an understatement.

"The victims of the unsuccessful experimental surgeries simply disappeared. The priest heard the confessions of those who had helped transport the bodies to a mass, unmarked grave."

When Father Piastri drew silent, I started another pot of water on the stove. The teakettle's whistle echoed off the little kitchen's walls like so many lost souls trapped in a padded cell awaiting a mad surgeon's scalpel. There was no smile on

Maya's face as she stared at the little table's peeling paint.

After sipping his tea, Father Piastri smiled and nodded.

"There is more to the story. Much more."

"Doesn't matter," I said. "We get the gist."

Father Piastri's demeanor changed after finishing his last cup of tea. His smile had returned, and he rummaged through a drawer until he'd found a black marking pen. He handed Maya the pen and the record's album cover.

She nodded when he said, "Will you autograph it for me?"

I glimpsed the cover again as Maya signed her name at the bottom of a smiling picture of herself at a much younger age.

"Thank you, Father," I said. "The tea was delightful, and the fictional story you told us horrifying."

"You have relieved a burden from my shoulders that was growing heavier with every passing day," he said. He glanced at Maya and asked, "Will you ever sing again?"

"I don't know," she said.

"One last thing, Father Piastri," I said. "Did you ever know a young woman named Bella Donna Castellano who was a patient at the hospital?"

"What did she look like?" he asked.

"She would have been in her twenties when she disappeared. She was a striking black woman whose skin was light enough to pass as white. Her father was Catholic and from Sicily."

"I knew them," he said. "Bella Donna was as white as her father."

"How do you know it's the same person?" I asked.

"There aren't many Sicilians in central Louisiana," he said. "I met him. His name was Paco Castellano."

"Tell me about them," I said.

"Paco often visited on the weekends. When he did, he would bring Bella Donna to Mass. Though he was a member of the Black Hand and an evil man, it was apparent that he loved his daughter, and she loved him."

"How do you know that?" I asked.

"You can't be a priest as long as I have without gaining the ability to recognize both good and evil."

"Did you ever see him interact with Bella Donna?" When Father Piastri nodded, I asked, "What was her reaction to him?"

"There was no animosity between the two," he said.

"Is it possible Bella Donna was a victim of her father's abuse?"

"Impossible. There was only love between the two," Father Piastri said.

"Thanks again. It's late," I said. "We'd better go."

We were halfway to the door when Maya wheeled around and embraced the little priest.

"Thank you," she said.

"It's my lot in life to help people. If you need my help in the future, you only have to ask," Father Piastri said.

It was well after dark, and the spring air was humid as we walked the short distance to the little lot where Maya's police cruiser was parked. She put the key into the ignition, staring at me without starting the vehicle.

"Do you believe his story?" she asked.

"He has no reason to lie," I said.

"Doesn't matter because nothing he told us is admissible in a court of law."

"Bones of the dead don't lie either. My guess is there are hundreds of families out there who will be incensed when someone digs up those bones. They'll demand answers. Nothing anyone can do when that happens will prevent the dam from bursting."

"What about Bella Donna Castellano? Why did you think Father Piastri might know her?"

"She's catholic, and so was her father. It was logical to think he would have taken her to Mass and introduced himself to Father Piastri."

"What did he mean when he said Paco was a member of the Black Hand?"

"The Mafia," I said. "Common in Italy and brought to America by Italian immigrants."

Maya turned the key and backed out of the parking lot. She was a half-mile down the darkened road before speaking.

"You hungry?"

"Starved," I said. "I haven't eaten anything since last night, and the Padre's tea is starting to make my hands tremble."

"That's a fact," she said. "Do you like barbecue?"

"Nothing much I like better, as long as it's not the fake variety you get at an upscale restaurant."

"Leo's is neither expensive nor upscale, but he cooks the best ribs you'll ever sink your teeth into," she said. "If you're into desserts, he also makes the best strawberry-banana cake you've ever tasted."

I gave her a thumbs-up and said, "You had me at hello."

Chapter 13

Rain peppered the windshield of Maya's police cruiser as we drove across the Red River Bridge into Alexandria.

"It's been years since I visited this town," I said.

"Nothing much has changed," Maya said. "It's pretty, though the crime rate is among the highest in the country."

She grinned when I said, "Good for your job security. I have a question and am almost embarrassed to ask it."

"Hit me with it," she said.

"You're a black woman with an important job."

"So, you want to know who I'm sleeping with?"

"Something like that," I said.

"The racial breakdown in Alexandria is more than fifty-five percent black or African American and less than forty percent white."

She laughed when I said, "Sounds like racial discrimination to me."

"This is the deep south. Get used to it," she said.

"You're good at what you do. You'd have had my vote even if you were white."

"I don't believe you have a racial bone in your body, Wyatt Thomas."

"I have other faults," I said. "How far is Leo's from here?"

"Not far as the crow flies. Some of the roads to get there are unpaved. Doesn't stop the locals from flocking to it."

The rain continued as we pulled into Leo's broken-shell parking lot. It was little more than a hole-in-the-wall but much more than I'd expected. The bass rhythms of live music and the wonderful aroma of roasting meat met us as we walked up the wooden stairs and entered the establishment. It didn't take me long to realize I was the only white person there.

"Relax," Maya said. "Everyone is civilized."

"Sorry," I said. "I'm not used to being a minority."

"I hear that," she said. "It's something you never get used to."

A wooden stage occupied a portion of the club that proved larger than it had looked from the outside. A band playing Cajun music was halfway through a song, and the dancers on the floor twirling, sweating, and producing their best licks. An attractive woman in a low-cut dress embraced Maya.

"Well, look at you, Miss Maya. You here for some of Leo's ribs?"

"You know it," Maya said. "Wyatt, this pretty woman is Pepper Thompson, Leo's wife and the real proprietor of this place."

"I do the books, though I can't cook like Leo can," Pepper said.

"And you can bounce drunks faster," Maya said.

"I may be an ex-cop, but I haven't lost the old techniques," Pepper said.

I shook the attractive woman's hand and said, "I'm honored. From the aroma wafting from the kitchen, I think I've died and gone to heaven."

"Wait until you sink your teeth into an order of Leo's ribs," she said. "You'll have no doubt."

"Can't wait," I said.

"Can I get you a beer?"

"Glass of lemonade if you have it, iced tea, unsweetened if you don't."

"Maya doesn't drink either," Pepper said. "I should have known."

Pepper seated us in a corner with a good view of the bar's patrons. By now, the spring rain had intensified and was drumming the tin roof, the fan behind us laboring to provide a warm breeze to fight the bar's humidity.

"Are you ready to order, or can I bring you an appetizer first?" Pepper said.

Maya looked at me and asked, "You like spicy food?"

"The hotter the better," I said.

"Then bring us an order of cream cheese poppers," Maya said.

"You got it, baby. I'll tell Leo you're here."

The band finished with a country anthem and launched into a rock and roll classic, and Pepper left us to get our drinks and poppers.

"Do you think Harper and Celeste were in on their home invasion last night?" Maya asked.

"I've had questions about those two since I arrived in town," I said.

"What's your conclusion?"

"From the marks on their bodies, they took lots of punishment. It's hard to imagine they agreed to it—at least not Harper."

"You have reason to believe Celeste is into domination and bondage?" Maya asked.

"At least reason to suspect it," I said. "Something else bothers me," I said.

"What?" Maya asked.

"The age difference between Harper and Celeste. My guess is Celeste is old enough to be Harper's mother," I said.

"Maybe Celeste is attracted to younger women."

"Maybe," I said. "There's another possibility."

"What?" Maya asked.

"Celeste may have targeted Harper."

"Where did she get the chance to do that? Harper is from New Orleans."

"So is Celeste," I said.

"Maybe they met in a lesbian bar."

"Maybe. That bothers me," I said.

"Because?"

"I heard Celeste swings both ways, is more than a bit kinky, and good at manipulation."

"Who told you that?"

A tall man with a winning smile arrived at our table with our drinks and poppers before I could answer Maya's question.

"Here's your poppers and drinks, baby," he said.

Maya got out of her chair. After helping the handsome man put the poppers and drinks on the table, she hugged him.

"Wyatt, this is my brother, Leo," she said.

"I'm honored," I said. "If your ribs taste half as good as they smell, they'll be the best I ever tasted."

Not satisfied with only pumping my hand, Leo slapped me on the shoulder.

"Talk like that will get you a free slice of my famous strawberry and banana cake."

"Can't wait," I said.

When Leo left the table, Maya said, "Maybe Celeste is covering something up."

"I got that feeling the first time I spoke with her. There's something more to Harper's relationship with Celeste," I said.

"Such as?"

"The hospital Administrator is an appointed position. Is Celeste qualified, and if not, how did she get it?"

Maya made a note on her pad. "I'll find out," she said. "Right now, I'm more interested in what Father Piastri told us. Do you believe there's a mass grave on the grounds of the hospital?"

"Don't know," I said.

"If there is a mass grave, how would you locate it without digging up the place?" Maya asked.

Pepper had returned and overheard her question.

"Ground Penetrating Radar," she said.

"Did you just make that one up?" Maya asked.

"No, I didn't, little sister. GPR is real. Are you ready to order?"

"Rib dinner for me," Maya said. "With fried okra and baked beans."

"Make it two," I said.

"Pork or beef?"

"Bring one of each. We'll share," Maya said.

"Got it, baby."

Pepper was in a hurry and didn't elaborate. After she'd left the table, I said, "Is she your actual sister?"

"Sister-in-law. Leo's my oldest brother. Pepper got me the job with the Sheriff's Department. She retired from the force when she and Leo married. She's pretty, isn't she?"

"So are you," I said.

"I wish," she said.

"Does Pepper know you sing?"

122

"Everyone in my family knows I sing. I sing in the choir every Sunday, at least if I'm not on a case."

"Are hymns the limit of your repertoire?"

Maya laughed. "It's the only thing anyone has heard me sing. I do my best impression of Rihanna in the shower. You like Rihanna?"

"Who doesn't? She reminds me of Billie Holliday."

"How so?"

"No one can sell a song like Billie could. Rihanna comes close."

"Forget about my singing for a while. Something else is bothering me."

"Such as?"

"Father Piastri threw us a curve ball. I haven't heard allegations of medical malpractice at the hospital," Maya said. "What do you think?"

"Are the stuffed peppers spicy?"

"Too hot for you?" she said.

I bit into one of the peppers stuffed with cream cheese and said, "Love them. Gayla told me the head doctor at the hospital is a man named Dr. Felix. According to Gayla, he's been with the hospital forever."

"Then he's responsible for the experimental surgeries," Maya said.

"If what Father Piastri told us is true," I said.

"You have doubts?"

"Not me. He's waited a long time to tell his story."

Maya made another entry into her notebook. "I'll run him tomorrow," she said.

We finished the red-hot poppers about the time our ribs arrived. Leo threw in some hot-buttered corn on the cob, and we soon started working on the ribs.

Like Pepper had said, it was the best barbecue I had ever eaten. The rain continued outside Leo's, and a cool breeze blew through the open front door. When Maya excused herself to go to the bathroom, I motioned for Pepper to join me.

"More lemonade?" she asked.

"Can the band play Rihanna?"

"They're professional musicians," Pepper said. "They can play anything. Why?"

"Maya wants to sing," I said.

"We don't do hymns at Leo's," she said.

"Good," I said. "Maya will do a Rihanna song if you let her."

"Get out of here," she said.

"She had an epiphany earlier," I said. "Give her a chance."

"You sure?"

"She's your little sister and not mine. I've only heard her voice on a scratchy old record. You already know what a set of vocal cords she has."

"Sister-in-law," she said. "Emil's the leader of the band. I'll ask him."

The band was coming off a break when Pepper got into Emil's ear. When he glanced at me, I smiled and gave him a thumbs-up. When Maya exited the bathroom, he tapped the microphone to silence the audience.

"Folks, everyone knows there's no better barbecue in the south than Leo's. His little sister Maya is a singer. She needs a bit of encouragement. Can you give her a huge round of applause and welcome her to the stage?"

The crowd went wild and began applauding and chanting Maya's name. She gave me the evil eye as she attempted to beg off the performance. The crowd was having none of it. When the band began playing the intro to Rihanna's *Love on the Brain,* she knew I was responsible.

The crowd grew silent when Maya began to sing. Her voice was evocative, filling the crowded room with pulsating sounds. After the first stanza, everyone went wild, and Maya belted out the song as if she'd done it a thousand times. The audience begged for more. When Emil and his band began playing the opening strains of another Rihanna song, Maya acquiesced and started singing. The result was even more animated than the first song she sang.

"Give it up for Maya Henstooth," Emil said as Maya hopped off the stage.

When Maya returned to the table, she said, "You asshole!"

"Stop it! I could tell by your smile you were enjoying every minute of it."

"Two songs didn't kill me," she said.

"Is Rihanna the only artist you cover?" I asked.

"I know the words to more songs than I can say Grace over," she said. "It's either a blessing or a curse with me."

"From the way Emil is staring at our table, I doubt you'll get away with only singing two songs before the night ends."

"I brought you here to sample Leo's cooking and discuss the case, not to sing."

When the crowd began chanting Maya's name, she shook her head. The band leader motioned her onstage, and she smiled as she pushed through the adoring crowd.

"Irma Thomas," someone in the audience yelled.

"Beyoncé," someone called.

My prediction proved correct. Between bites of Leo's strawberry-banana cake, Maya sang three more songs, each by a different artist. It was midnight before the crowd and the band would allow us to tab out and leave.

"Thank you," Maya said on the way out the door. "I needed that."

"You're a hit," I said. "Emil and his band didn't want to let you go."

"They asked me to perform with them during the French Quarter Fest," Maya said.

"That's wonderful," I said. "Are you going to do it?"

"I loved being onstage tonight. I also love being a detective."

"Maybe you can do both," I said.

"I've never been to New Orleans," she said.

"You have to be kidding," I said.

"My mother believes it's a latter-day Gomorrah."

"Nonsense," I said. "We'll be done here by then. I'll show you the town."

Maya's cell phone rang before she could reply. I could see the exhaustion on her face, even in the dimness of the dashboard lights.

"Something bad?" I asked.

"Another murder," she said.

"Where?"

I drew a worried breath when she said, "Behind the Raven's Roost."

Chapter 14

The rural roads back to Alexandria were slick with rainwater, some of which had yet to have drained into the ditches on either side. Maya's siren blared, rupturing the silence of the night.

When we reached the city limits of Pinebridge, she said, "I'll drop you off."

"No way. I wouldn't miss this for the world."

"Suit yourself," she said.

The rain had stopped, and Pinebridge's sparse streetlights did little to illuminate its sleepy streets. That changed when we turned the corner to Main Street, and the flashing lights of police cruisers signaled the chaos at the Raven's Roost. Maya parked the cruiser, and I followed her to the back of the restaurant.

The alleyway behind the restaurant was on fire with revolving spotlights. Yellow tape surrounded the grease trap and the trash dumpster. We stepped under the crime tape to where several policemen were staring at a body. The victim was on his knees and had been shot through the back of the head.

Maya looked at me when I said, "I know him."

"Who is he?" Maya asked.

"Henry Scott, the nighttime bartender. Someone must have come in after hours, led him to this spot behind the dumpster, and assassinated him."

"What makes you think he was assassinated?"

"His pose—on his knees with hands behind his back—was meant to send a message."

"To who?" she asked.

"Me, probably," I said.

"For what reason?"

"I've been asking too many uncomfortable questions, and someone doesn't like it," I said.

"What did Henry tell you?"

"Tales about the Pinebridge Mental Hospital."

"Like what?"

"The sex parties Celeste hosted when she first moved to Pinebridge."

Maya glared at me and said, "You didn't tell me that."

"I'm telling you now."

"What else haven't you told me?"

"Celeste can't be a lesbian because, according to Henry, she had sex with half the influential men in town after moving here. He said when they had sex with a patient, it sealed their loyalty."

"Why didn't you tell me this?"

"I was going to, but Leo interrupted us. After that, you started singing. I never had the chance."

Maya stared at the victim and shook her head. "How did anyone know Henry shared secrets about the hospital with you?"

"Kayla," I said.

"Who is Kayla?"

"A waitress at the Raven's Roost. I had a date with her after Harper and Celeste had gone home. She was going to tell me what she knew about them but begged off because she needed to get home for an early exam."

"You had a date with a college student?"

"I wouldn't call it a date," I said.

"You just did. What was it?"

"I was looking for information. Kayla seemed to have it. When she left, there was no one in the restaurant except Henry. I bought him drinks, and it loosened his lips."

"So, he was drunk when he told you about Celeste and Harper?"

"It's not like it sounds," I said.

"How did Kayla know you'd talked to Henry?"

"She forgot her purse and returned for it. When she heard us talking, she hid in the shadows and listened to our conversation."

"How much did she hear?" Maya asked.

"Henry was the first to notice her. When I asked him how long she'd been there, he said, "Too long.'"

"So, we've got a suspect. What's her motive?"

"Kayla's not a hitman," I said. "She didn't assassinate Henry."

"Then who did?"

"Kayla had an unusual interest in me," I said.

"Sexual interest?"

"Anything but. I'm a big boy and know when a woman is coming on to me. She was looking for information."

"Such as?"

"What I'm really doing in town, which means she is likely involved in whatever the hell is going on in Pinebridge," I said.

"Who put her up to it?" Maya asked.

"My guess is Celeste. She likes younger women and is probably lonely when Harper isn't in town. Harper already knows why I'm here."

"You think Celeste is involved in the murder?"

"I don't think so. Kayla may have instigated the murder. She didn't pull the trigger. Celeste may not even know about it."

"What does that say about Kayla?" Maya asked.

"Whoever is involved in Henry's murder, Kayla knew about it. If Celeste is in the dark about the murder, it probably means Kayla isn't sharing everything she knows with her."

"I'll bring her in for questioning," Maya said.

"Handle it with kid gloves," I said. "Kayla may know what's happening, but she's only a pawn. The town is tight-lipped enough already. We don't want to make matters worse."

"How do you know so much about crime?" Maya asked.

"I was a defense attorney for much of my legal career. The good defense attorneys learn to think like criminals if they intend to succeed."

Maya smiled and said, "I'll remember that about you."

We left the forensic team to complete their search of the crime scene, and Maya and I returned to her squad car.

When I climbed into the passenger seat, she said, "Your hotel is across the street. You can walk that far."

"You were exhausted earlier today. You need some sleep."

"I wish," she said.

"Come to my room. You can sleep on the bed. I'll take the recliner."

Maya was extremely tired because she didn't put up a fight. No one was in the lobby as we went upstairs. Maya lay on the bed, closed her eyes, and fell immediately asleep. I pulled a light blanket over her, turned out the lights, and slipped into the recliner.

When I awoke the following morning, Maya was gone. She'd used the tiny coffee brewer in the room to make coffee. She had torn a page from her notepad and drawn a smiley face. It was barely dawn, so I took the opportunity to take a much-needed shower. Dot Beaufoy was behind the counter when I walked downstairs.

"I didn't see you come in last night," she said.

"You didn't hear the commotion across the street?" I asked.

"I was reading. What happened?"

"Another murder," I said.

Dot's hand went to her mouth. "Oh my God! Who was murdered?"

"Henry, the nighttime bartender at the Raven's Roost."

"Horrible!" Dot said. "I went to school with his daughter. Why would anyone want to kill him?"

"That's the sixty-four-dollar question," I said.

"Things were quiet until you came to town. Seems as if you've unleashed a shitstorm."

"A common occurrence when snoops start lurking around," I said.

Did you talk with Father Piastri?"

"I did. He couldn't tell me anything important because of his Papal vows, though he's been in town since the late fifties and filled me in on the local color. Thank you."

"Happy to help," she said.

"Maybe you can help me with something else," I said.

"You bet," she said.

"My laptop is on the fritz. Is there a computer repair shop in town?"

"What happened to it?" she asked.

"Whoever rifled through my room tried to get into it. It's password-protected, and they got rough with it. Now, I can't get it to boot."

"Let me have a look. I have a minor in computer technology, and I'm good with computers."

"Thanks," I said.

I went upstairs and returned with my laptop. It took Dot about five minutes to have it back up and running.

"Thanks again," I said. "How did you get past the password?"

"Trick of the trade," she said.

"Are you a hacker?"

Dot put her finger to her lips and said, "Don't tell anybody. I don't want to go to jail."

"You have to do something illegal for that to happen," I said. "Have you?"

"Let's just say I've taken a few peeks inside well-protected databases. Please keep that piece of information between us," she said.

"Your secret is safe with me," I said.

After returning the laptop to my room, I left the hotel, waving to Dot as I exited the front door. Badly needing coffee, I walked to the little café down the street from the hotel. The same farmers as before were there, and I wondered if they ever left and if they did any farming. My stomach was full, and my caffeine needs satiated, though my questions about the farmers were unanswered as I paid my tab and headed toward the Pinebridge Mental Hospital.

When I reached the hospital, it was still early; neither Celeste nor Harper was there. Gayla was, and she smiled when I entered her little office.

"Morning," she said.

"Good morning to you."

"Do you know a student at Pinebridge College who waitresses at the Raven's Roost?"

Gayla surprised me when she said, "Kayla Duhon?"

"That's her. How do you know her?"

"Our names are so similar that Celeste often calls me Kayla."

"Why would she do that?" I asked.

"I've spoken out of turn," Gayla said. "Celeste wouldn't want me talking about her behind her back."

"Is Kayla Celeste's girlfriend?" I asked.

Gayla averted eye contact and said, "You're going to get me in trouble."

"Because Harper doesn't know?" I asked.

"I'm sorry. I've said too much."

"I've already forgotten what you told me," I said. "Do you have time to show me your records room?"

"Come with me," she said.

We took the elevator to the basement. When the door opened, I could almost feel the darkness. When Gayla flipped a switch, fluorescent lighting flooded the hallway. She led me down the barren hall to a single door.

She shook her head when I asked, "Where are your keys?"

"It isn't locked," she said. "Who would want to steal old medical records?"

I didn't reply as she flipped another switch, illuminating a large windowless room with thousands of hanging file folders.

She laughed when I said, "Are they in alphabetical order?"

"Good luck on that one," she said.

"Mind if I have a look through the files?"

"Knock yourself out and try not to let the dust kill you. Now, everything is computerized, and you're probably the first person who has been inside here in a decade or more."

The moment Gayla was gone, I felt the solitude of the place. She wasn't wrong about the dust.

After several powerful sneezes, I wondered if I was prepared for the task. I tied a handkerchief around my face in a makeshift mask. It didn't help much.

Gayla was correct. The files weren't in alphabetical order—not even close. I randomly picked a folder and soon learned how futile my search was. The dust wasn't the only hardship I had to deal with. There was no air conditioning, and the conditions were stuffy and humid. The fluorescent lighting was also unreliable and began turning on and off.

All the information was in pencil, some in ink. It didn't matter because everything was handwritten and often all but illegible. I attempted to remain positive. My good intentions were thwarted by the often incomplete information in the files. I'd studied files for hours before finding the medical documents of a woman named Patience.

Father Piastri used the name Patience when telling his fictional story of the patient who had confessed to his imaginary priest. Had he made up the name, or did he slip in a bit of real detail in his story?

The date comported with the timeline of the good father's tale. I opened the file, hoping not to be disappointed and the likelihood I'd never find anything of interest, much less incriminating.

What I had stumbled upon was the proverbial jewel in a pig's ass. I knew it from the first paragraph I read.

Patience Bianchi was from Italy and had no relatives in the States. Driving without a license had resulted in time in jail, where it was determined she had untreatable mental illness. During her time at the hospital, she'd had several abortions and was finally sterilized.

Dr. Felix had signed the order to operate. A handwritten letter from Axel Devereaux, Harper's father, to Dr. Felix was also present. Deciding to read it later, I put the file folder under my arm and prepared to return upstairs when the fluorescent lights went off, and I was suddenly in total darkness.

Chapter 15

Total darkness isn't a usual occurrence. There's almost always a light to which the eyes can gravitate and orient. It's different when it's completely dark. There's no light to orient yourself. When the basement lights went out, I stopped in my tracks, waiting for them to come back on. When they didn't, I proceeded slowly to where I thought the door was, quickly grew disoriented, and bumped into a row of folders.

Rows of suspended file folders filled the large room, and I had counted three aisles between them. A path perpendicular to the files led back to the door. At least that's what I thought. After an indeterminable time, I still hadn't found my way to the door, and the air was becoming stuffy. I called out in case someone was listening.

"Can anybody hear me?"

The hundreds of paper files muted my voice, and there was no echo. It was as if I were in a corn maze, except there was no light, and the rows of files were the corn. After more time passed and I couldn't find a path back to the door, I decided on another plan.

If I could push through the files, I would eventually reach a wall. When I did, I could follow the wall until I found the door. My plan proved difficult to implement because of the density of the files. I began removing enough files until I could penetrate to the next row. I almost panicked when I finally touched a wall.

The hanging folders filled the space all the way to the wall, and I found it impossible to push through them. Sweat saturated my shirt as I sat on the floor, wondering why I had forgotten to use my cell phone. I felt a momentary twinge of relief, at least until I tried to dial the hospital. My heart sank when I realized there was no signal.

The files didn't hang all the way to the floor, and I began crawling along the wall and the open space beneath them. By now, I was totally disoriented and had chosen the wrong direction for the door. I must have been close to it when I started because much time had passed, and I took four turns before I located it. When I grasped the doorknob, I had another disappointment. It was locked.

"Help me!" I called.

I had one reason for hope: Gayla might realize I'd been in the basement for hours and come looking for me, assuming it hadn't been her who had locked the door.

I was hoarse from shouting at the top of my lungs, and my muscles were sore from trying to open the door forcefully. There must have been a vent because there was air, albeit stuffy, to breathe. It was a small favor, as I knew I'd die of thirst if someone didn't unlock the door. I sat on the concrete floor, trying to devise a plan for escaping the basement that might soon become my tomb, when someone turned the door handle.

Jumping to my feet, I grabbed the handle and flung open the door, thinking I would see Gayla. It wasn't her. The hallway was dark, with dim bioluminescence lighting the form of someone standing before me. It was Lyrica Winter. When I clutched her hand, she didn't pull away.

"Rica," I said. "How did you know I was here?"

She didn't answer, only shaking her head. Remembering she wasn't verbal, I pulled her up the hall to the elevator, relieved that I saw a light behind the up button. When the door to the elevator opened, my dilated eyes rebelled because of the sudden glare. When they stopped watering, I had a good look at Rica.

She was clad in the same transparent nightgown as the first time I had seen her. There were more than marks on her this time. Blood oozed from her nose and split lip. I pushed the up button.

The lobby was empty when the elevator reached the ground floor. In the full fluorescent lighting, I could see close up the abuse Rica's body had taken.

"You're not going back there," I said.

I quickly pulled her through the lobby and out the front door. I couldn't take her to my hotel room because if she were reported missing, my ass would be in a jail cell within hours. It was dark, and I headed toward Billy Williams's little house. Billy met me at the door.

"What did you do to her?" he asked.

"Not me," I said. "I was locked in the basement. She looked like this when she rescued me. We can't let her go back to the hospital. Can you help?"

Grabbing Rica's arm, he pulled her into his house. From his muted lights, I quickly realized he had electricity. He sat Rica on the couch, and she smiled when Noseye bounded into her lap. Billy began conversing with her using sign language.

"She verified your story," he said.

"How did she know I was in the basement?" I asked.

"The patients communicate through the heat and air vents. She heard you."

"How did she get out of her cell?"

"She's an escape artist," Billy said. "I don't know how she does it."

Billy had a first aid kit. He retrieved it and began cleaning Rica's wounds.

"You look as if you know what you're doing," I said.

"Gayla taught me," Billy said.

"Can Rica stay with you for a while?" I asked.

"You bet she can. Noseye and I will take good care of her."

"She'll need food and something to wear."

"Rica is in good hands," he said.

Billy smiled when I asked, "Where did you get the electricity?"

"Wasn't hard," he said. "I wired into the main transformer."

"Who taught you how to do that?" I asked.

"I may be autistic," he said. "I'm not stupid."

"One more thing. Someone told me you speak Italian."

"A little," he said.

"Who taught you?"

"No one taught me," he said. "I picked it up when I was a boy."

"From who?" I asked.

"My grandmother," he said.

"Your grandmother is Italian?"

"No, though she speaks Italian when flustered," he said.

"I have to go. I'll check back," I said.

"Thank you," he said. "I've tried to get my courage up to rescue Rica for months. She is safe now that you did it for me.

It was well after dark as I hiked to Pinebridge. The Raven's Roost was alive and open for business, and I wondered if the patrons knew about the murder there the previous night. The lobby of the hotel was empty. When I walked upstairs to my room, Dot wasn't at the check-in counter. I found Maya waiting at my door.

"You look like hell," she said. "Where have you been?"

"Hello to you, too," I said. "Come inside and wait until I shower and change clothes, and I'll tell you."

"What are you carrying?"

I handed the folder to Maya and said, "Evidence, maybe. I won't be long. Have a look and tell me what you think when I return."

I exited the shower clad in a towel around my waist, feeling better than I had in hours. Maya was engrossed in reading the file and didn't bother looking up when I went to the closet for fresh clothes. When I emerged from the bathroom dressed in khakis and a clean shirt, she had a grave expression.

"Where'd you get this?"

"The manual patient file storage room at the hospital. Anything that interests you?"

"You haven't read it?"

"I glanced through it. The hospital file system is in the basement. Someone locked the door and left me to die of thirst. I managed to escape."

"Do you know someone named Axel Devereaux?"

"Harper's father," I said.

"There's a letter from him to Dr. Felix."

"What does it say?" I asked.

"He's giving him the go-ahead to perform the sterilization on Patience Bianchi."

"By who's authority?" I asked.

140

"The letterhead identifies Devereaux as the Louisiana Board of Mental Health Director. He had all the authority in the world."

"So, Harper's father was calling the shots at the hospital when the Governor had most of the attendants fired."

"He survived the house cleaning and has somehow secured the same position with the Louisiana Board of Mental Health for his daughter," Maya said.

"Which means nothing much has changed at the hospital except the firing of the attendants. Devereaux replaced them with other people he could trust. Can you check this out using your police database?"

"Depends," Maya said.

"On what?"

"How corrupt the Rapides Parish Sheriff's Department is," she said.

"You suspect someone?"

"Louisiana is a third-world country regarding graft and corruption." She laughed and said, "I'm beginning to believe that new public servants are issued a manual teaching them how to steal."

"I've lived here all my life," I said. "You're preaching to the choir. You hungry?"

"I could eat something," she said.

"Let's grab a bite. Over dinner, I'll tell you what I know. My client is buying."

"Leo's again?" she said.

"Love it," I said. "My cholesterol level can handle it if yours can."

On the way to Leo's, Maya said, "Thanks for use of your bed. Last night was the most sleep I've had in a week."

"Glad to help. I could tell you were exhausted. Learn anything interesting today?"

"We grilled Kayla Duhon and didn't get much. Though she's young, she's a tough cookie."

Maya smiled when I said, "Guess that ends my hopes of having hot sex with a college girl."

"You talk big," she said. "I don't believe a word of it."

"Are you singing tonight?"

"It's Thursday. Brother Leo only has bands on Wednesdays and Saturdays."

"Damn! You may have to sing a few refrains for me on the way there," I said.

"You'll live," Maya said. "This is gumbo night,"

"Hallelujah! In New Orleans, I'm used to fresh seafood every day."

"Must be nice," she said. "The only fresh fish we get in Rapides Parish is catfish."

"I like catfish," I said.

"If you're here long enough, I'll take you to a camp on the lake. It has Louisiana's best catfish, French fries, and green tomato dressing."

"Can't wait," I said.

"You'll have to settle for gumbo tonight."

"I'll try to persevere," I said.

There was no crowd at Leo's, only a dozen regulars with a taste for south Louisiana cuisine. Leo didn't disappoint. Pepper had something to say when she brought us a dozen raw oysters.

"You think I better tell your mama you've had dinner twice this week with a white man?"

"Don't you dare!" Maya said. "This isn't a date. Wyatt and I are associates."

"I doubt your mama or your deacon daddy will see it that way," Pepper said.

I glanced at Maya and said, "Your dad is a Baptist deacon?"

"Don't remind me," she said.

"Your parents aren't racists, are they?"

"You kidding me?" Maya said. "This is the deep south. Everyone's a racist."

"I'm not," I said.

"Bet your mama is," Pepper said.

"And my dad," I said. "I confess."

"Doesn't matter," Pepper said. "Tonight, we're all family."

Last night's rain had heralded a cool front, and the breeze blowing through the open door was refreshing. As I ate a bowl of Leo's gumbo and a cup of red beans and rice, I thought I had died and gone to heaven.

Between bites, I said, "Where are you on your murder investigation?"

"Which one?" she said.

"Either one. Are you getting anywhere?"

"Nowhere fast," she said. "The file you brought from the basement is the closest thing I have to a smoking gun."

"A jury is never going to believe our interpretation of the letter," I said. "It does give us a roadmap of how we should proceed."

"I'm all ears," Maya said.

"Something is lurking just beneath the surface. My guess is there's money involved. It would be big money if Axel Devereaux had anything to do with it. That's a problem."

"What problem?"

"The Devereauxs are an elite Garden District family. They have their fingers in every political pie."

"And?" Maya said.

"You don't take out a tank with a peashooter," I said.

"Is that all we have?"

"I was being generous. Axel Devereaux is connected. We aren't. If we pursue it, we could wind up dead like Henry."

"You aren't throwing in the white flag, are you?"

"Not even close. I think our case lies in the hospital files."

"The ones in the basement?"

"That corruption and abuse was already outed and temporarily corrected. I'm interested in what has happened at the hospital since the purge."

"How do you intend to do that?" Maya asked.

"Get a look at the hospital's computer files. The people controlling the hospital are communicating somehow. We need to tap into that stream of information."

Maya's cell phone rang while we worked on tasty bites of Leo's famous strawberry-banana cake. She glared at me after ending the call and returning the cell phone to her pocket.

"The hospital has reported a missing patient. You wouldn't know anything about it, would you?"

"I'll tell you in the car."

Chapter 16

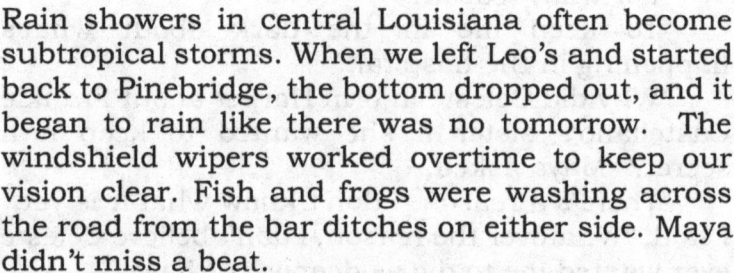

Rain showers in central Louisiana often become subtropical storms. When we left Leo's and started back to Pinebridge, the bottom dropped out, and it began to rain like there was no tomorrow. The windshield wipers worked overtime to keep our vision clear. Fish and frogs were washing across the road from the bar ditches on either side. Maya didn't miss a beat.

"We're in the car. What do you know about the hospital's missing patient?" she asked.

"I didn't tell you everything that happened to me in the basement of the hospital."

"While you were looking through the files?"

"Yes."

"Tell me now," she said.

"The hospital files weren't computerized until the late seventies. Before then, they were kept in handwritten file folders. The hospital stores them in the basement."

"And?"

"The day I met Celeste, she provided me with Bella Donna Castellano's paper file. She let me look at it for about an hour and then took it back without allowing me to make a copy."

"What's your point?" Maya asked.

"The folder contained no handwritten notes. It was neatly typed and said that Bella Donna was a victim of sexual abuse by her father."

"Spare me the details and cut to the good part," Maya said.

"I spent multiple hours looking through the basement files today. None were typed; all were handwritten in pencil or ink."

"What's that supposed to mean?" Maya asked.

"Bella Donna's file that I looked at in Celeste's office wasn't real. Someone had created it for the specific purpose of showing it to me."

"For what reason?"

"To keep me in the dark about what's happening in the hospital."

"Why did Celeste inform Harper about Frankie Castellano's sister if she wanted to keep it a secret?" Maya asked.

"There's a reason. I don't know what it is yet," I said. "Whatever the reason, I don't believe Celeste ever wanted me to dig as deeply as I have."

"You think Celeste is in on this?" Maya asked.

"Up to her neck. I can't prove it. Doesn't mean it isn't so."

"What do you know about her?" Maya asked,

"Nothing, other than what she's told me," I said.

"You think Bella Donna's real files are in the hospital's basement?"

"Bingo!"

"You said the files were in no alphabetical order. Even if it is in the basement, how do you propose to find it?"

"The file I showed you was dated twenty years ago, about the same time Bella Donna went missing."

"Go on," Maya said.

146

"The files aren't in alphabetical order. They are filed by year. We should find Bella Donna's real file near the one I gave you."

"So you don't have it?"

"Let's get it now," I said. "You can watch the door while I return to where I found Patience Bianchi's file. I should be able to locate Bella Donna's real file nearby."

"You're suggesting I assist you in a breaking and entering?"

"Yes. We can't legally look at the files in the basement because of government HIPAA rules. If we want to see Bella Donna's actual file, we must make a midnight acquisition."

"I'm a law officer. There are rules I can't break."

"You don't have to. I'll break them for you. The file will help both of us, and I can't do it without you," I said.

"I'll think about it on the way into town. You still haven't told me about Lyrica Winter," Maya said.

"Someone locked me in the basement, either with the intent of killing me or else scaring me. The lights went off, and I was in total darkness. It was locked when I managed to find my way to the door. Rica heard me calling for help through the heating and air conditioning vents. She came to the basement and unlocked the door."

"She had a key?"

"I have no idea how she opened the door."

"How did she get out of her cell?" Maya asked.

"I wish I had an answer," I said. "Billy Williams told me she's an escape artist."

"What happened when you left the file's room," she said.

"When I got Rica into the light, I saw she was beaten to hell, her nose and lip recently busted. I couldn't return her to the abuse she was enduring, so I took her to Billy's house. He cleaned and doctored her wounds and conversed with her in sign language."

"What's going to stop him from abusing her?"

"Gayla told me he is the gentlest person she knows. I trust him."

"How will we get into the basement without being seen?" Maya asked.

"The lobby was empty earlier. It's later now, and there's less reason for anyone to be there."

"What about the squad car?"

"There's covered parking near the entrance. If someone sees the car, they'll think it's because you're responding to the missing patient report. If anyone asks, that's what you'll tell them."

No one, not even a person at the reception desk, was in the lobby when Maya and I punched the down button on the elevator. She'd brought a flashlight, so we didn't bother turning on the overheads when exiting the basement hallway. We found the door to the storage room unlocked.

"Wait here and keep the door open," I said. "I won't be long."

Reentering the darkened room where I'd experienced so much mental anguish earlier in the day resulted in a certain uneasiness in the pit of my stomach. It didn't go away.

I'd purposely left a gap in the filing sequence if I needed to return the file I'd taken. Bella Donna had disappeared shortly after Patience Bianchi had confessed to Father Piastri. It was logical I would find Bella Donna's file near the one I had taken. I was prepared to browse through as many files as it might take. It didn't happen that way.

Bella Donna's file was beside the empty spot where I had removed Patience Bianchi's. I had to look twice to make sure I wasn't seeing things. After reassuring myself there were no other adjacent files on Bella Donna, I secured the folder beneath my arm and returned through the darkness to the door where Maya awaited.

"Got it," I said.

"That was quick," she said.

"Let's get the hell out of here before our good luck turns bad."

I handed Maya the flashlight and followed her to the elevator. We soon exited the hospital's front door and gazed at Bella Donna's folder in the dim illumination of dashboard lights.

"It's late," I said. "Let's look at it in my room. After that, you can get some sleep in the bed. I'll take the recliner again."

"My daddy will be on his knees praying for my soul this Sunday if he knew I was spending the night with a white man."

"There's a difference between spending the night in the same room and sleeping together," I said. "If you're half as tired as I am, you're a danger to yourself driving home. I'm sure he would understand."

Maya didn't put up a fuss.

Once again, the Beaufoy Hotel lobby was empty as we climbed the stairs to my second-floor rental. When I opened a window, damp air flooded the room.

"Mind if I take off my shoes?" Maya said. "My feet are killing me."

"Make yourself at home. Looks like there's even plastic coffee."

We were both shoeless, sitting on the bed, drinking coffee from plastic cups and enjoying the breeze blowing through the open window as I opened Bella Donna's file.

After a few minutes, Maya said, "Well?"

"This isn't the same file Celeste showed me. All the entries are handwritten."

"What else?"

"Celeste's report said Bella Donna was a victim of her father's sexual abuse. I had wondered about that because Gayla told me she remembered Bella Donna's father visiting often and that she seemed happy when he was in town."

"And Father Piastri corroborated it," Maya said. "What reason would Celeste have for wanting you to believe Bella Donna was abused by her father?"

"Don't know," I said. "Paco Castellano was a powerful man. Maybe he was the person who put the Governor on the spot such that heads had to roll here at the hospital."

"Is he still alive?" Maya asked.

"Died eight or nine years ago," I said. "There are pictures of Bella Donna. Want to see?"

Maya's expression changed when she took the folder in her hands.

"This is the woman in the picture Billy Williams keeps on his dresser. Bella Donna is Billy's mother," she said.

"I thought she looked familiar," I said. "She fits the description of Billy's mother that Debbie Donaldson gave me.

"Doesn't matter because she's too old to be Billy's mother," Maya said.

"But not his grandmother. That explains why he can speak fluent Italian."

"Excuse me?" Maya said.

"Billy's special education teacher told me he speaks fluent Italian. When I quizzed him about it, he said he picked it up from his grandmother."

"Bella Donna's not Italian," Maya said.

"No, but Paco, her father, spoke Italian. She could have picked it up from him."

"Whatever! It gives Billy Williams a motive to have killed Oliver Marshall." Maya began putting on her shoes. "I'm going to pick him up."

"Doesn't mean he killed Marshall simply because he had a motive," I said. "Rica is with him, remember?"

"And she could be dead by now," Maya said.

Maya was already starting for the door when I said, "I'm coming with you."

"Then get a move on," she said.

I pulled my shoes on without tying them and followed her out the door. When we reached her car, I had difficulty convincing her not to start blasting the siren.

She turned off the engine when I said, "You're making a mistake."

"How so?"

"There are two connected murders here. I doubt Billy even knew Henry, which makes it unlikely that he killed Oliver Marshall."

"What do you suggest we do?"

"Go back upstairs and get some sleep," I said.

"Let's visit Billy Williams. I appreciate your feelings about him, and you may be correct. Even so, I wouldn't be able to live with myself if you're wrong."

She grinned when I said, "Okay, but no sirens."

Billy was awake when we knocked on his door. He glanced at Maya, still in uniform, and then gave me a dirty look.

"You told the police?"

"Detective Henstooth has some questions," I said.

The lights were on in the room, and a laptop screen was alive on a computer table.

"Where's Lyrica?" Maya asked.

"With my mother," Billy said. "She's taking care of her."

"Is your grandmother Bella Donna Castellano?" Maya asked.

"Yes," he said. "Mother and Grandmother live together."

"And Rica is with them?"

"She can't come back here," he said. "They will kill her."

"Who would do that?" Maya asked.

"The same people abusing Rica?" I asked.

"Rica isn't the only patient being abused," he said.

"You have evidence?" Maya asked.

"Just what I've seen," he said.

"Why haven't you told someone?" Maya asked.

"They would kill me, just like they did the reporter from the Picayune."

"I'm unaware of a Picayune reporter being murdered," I said.

"His name was Enrique Navarro. He was my age and a friend of mine."

"When did this happen?" I asked.

"Enrique was working undercover as a patient when I started work here two years ago. He confided in me and was close to wrapping up his investigation when he disappeared."

Billy shook his head when I said, "Maybe he gave up his investigation and left."

"He was murdered like Mr. Marshall."

"You know more about the murder than you told us?" Maya asked.

"It's useless," he said. "There's nothing we can do anyway. They are shielded by the law."

"What law?" I asked.

"HIPAA," he said.

"Who told you that?" Maya asked.

152

"Enrique said the law prevents anyone from accessing the information it would take to prosecute the people responsible. He intended to expose them with a comprehensive article in the Picayune."

"Enrique sounds intelligent, but he was wrong," Maya said. "If the law shields a criminal conspiracy, the veil can be pierced."

"Maya's right," I said. "There's always a path to the truth."

Maya glanced at the computer screen. "That doesn't look like social media to me. Are you studying something?"

"Business Administration with a minor in management," he said. "I'm close to graduating."

"You aren't working here because you like being a caretaker, right?" I asked.

"Enrique didn't deserve to die, and Rica and Bella Donna didn't deserve the abuse they endured. I'm trying to change things. I haven't found a way yet," he said.

"Seems as if we're all searching for the same solution. We'll help you if you help us."

Maya turned to the picture of Billy's mother on his dresser. She picked it up, staring intently at it.

"So, this is your mother and not your grandmother," she said.

"Mom looks a lot like my grandmother. Like I told you the first time, that's a picture of my mom."

Chapter 17

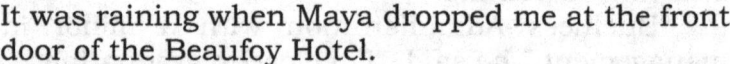

It was raining when Maya dropped me at the front door of the Beaufoy Hotel.

"I haven't slept in my own bed for a week," she said. "I need a shower, and I'm going home."

"Be careful, and remember, you can always spend the night with me," I said.

"Funny," she said.

I watched her squad car disappear into the darkness before walking upstairs, tossing my clothes on the floor, and climbing under the covers. It seemed like I'd just closed my eyes when my cell phone rang. I was wrong; morning light was shining through the window. My cell phone on the stand beside my bed was ringing, and my eyes still closed when I answered.

"Hello," I said.

Frankie Castellano's raspy voice said, "Did I wake you?"

"I've been awake for hours."

"You're a liar, Wyatt Thomas."

Frankie didn't sound angry, and he laughed when I said, "You caught me, boss."

"Give me an update, and I'll let you get back to sleep," he said.

"Your half-sister is alive. She has a daughter and a grandson."

"I want to meet them," Frankie said.

"Her grandson Billy works at the hospital. Billy's mom and grandmom live together in a cottage in the Kisatchie National Forest. I haven't convinced Billy to take me there yet."

"I'll talk to him," Frankie said.

"No," I said.

Frankie sounded miffed when he said, "What do you mean, no?"

"Seems I've opened a bucket of worms. Two murders have occurred since I got to town. I'm up to my neck in the investigation."

"How so?" Frankie asked.

"I need to be blunt," I said. "I know you had an affair with Harper. You may think you still are. You're wrong."

I waited through a long pause. "You don't intend to tell Adele, do you?"

"My lips are sealed. You know that," I said. "What do you know about Celeste and Harper?"

"They're close friends," he said.

"Much more than that," I said. "They are lesbian lovers."

I waited through another long pause. "Harper isn't a lesbian," he said.

"Celeste is knee-deep in the shit going down here at the hospital. I don't think Harper knows about it. Celeste is old enough to be her mother, and I'm convinced she's using her."

"Maybe you'd better fill me in on what's happening in Pinebridge."

"Celeste showed me a file that said your dad Paco was abusing Bella Donna."

"Paco was abusing Bella Donna?"

"There's little doubt Bella Donna was being abused. She isn't the only patient who suffered abuse and worse. It wasn't your poppa doing the abusing."

"What kind of abuse?"

"Rape, beatings, unnecessary sterilizations, experimental surgery. The list goes on," I said.

"Is my family involved in this cover-up?"

"I don't believe so. My thinking is when your father learned of the abuse, he intervened with the Governor," I said.

"I don't doubt it," Frankie said. "The old man was connected. Why do you suspect it was Paco?"

"Your dad was a mean old bastard, but he loved Bella Donna, and she loved him. Bella Donna was abused, and Celeste is trying to pin it on Paco. Since your dad has passed, you could be a target. I'm starting to believe that's why Celeste revealed your sister's stay at the hospital to Harper."

"And you have doubts about Harper's involvement?"

"Don't know yet. You paid me to find your sister. I'll soon have her located. The rest of this bullshit I've walked into is on me. I'm off the clock."

When Frankie raised his voice, I knew for sure he was upset.

"You aren't off the clock until I say so," he said. "I'm working on something and can't cut loose from New Orleans. I'll be in Pinebridge at the end of the week. Keep working on what you've learned."

"Yes, sir," I said.

"You're a smart man," Frankie said. "What's driving this scenario?"

"Power and corruption. I'm unsure which comes first."

"Any idea who the principals are?"

"Best as I can tell, it all starts with Axel Devereaux."

"Oh, shit!" he said. "That man hates my guts, and I have no idea why. You can't imagine the stink he caused when his daughter was named Queen of the Krewe of Illusion."

156

"Though I can't prove it yet, I think it has something to do with your dad and half-sister."

"You've got my attention. Axel Devereaux owns the biggest bank in New Orleans and has his fingers in every economic pie in the State. I'm puzzled."

"About what?" I asked.

"There isn't enough money in the Pinebridge Mental Hospital to pique Devereaux's interest. Something else is at play. I'm counting on you to find out for me," Frankie said. "And Wyatt, watch your back."

"Yes, sir," I said.

Frankie Castellano had already hung up and didn't hear me. It didn't matter because I knew he wouldn't rest until he'd help me reach the bottom of the deceit.

I got out of bed and went directly to the shower, not waiting for the water to grow warm before climbing beneath the cold stream and wetting my hair. I felt better when I exited the shower until I remembered Maya and I had drunk all the plastic coffee the previous night. Pulling on my pants and undershirt, I walked downstairs for a cup from the urn on the counter. Dot Beaufoy smiled when she saw me.

"Morning," she said. "Sleep well?"

"The bed is very comfortable. I drank all my coffee last night and desperately need a shot of caffeine."

"Have you checked the breakroom?" she asked.

"No," I said.

"There's a buffet: eggs, bacon, sausage, pancakes, biscuits. You paid for it. Help yourself."

I returned to my room with a paper plate stacked high with all the goodies I found in the breakroom. I also had a large cup of coffee, and

Dot gave me a couple of extra coffee pods for my little coffee maker.

When I'd finished my last bite of scrambled eggs, I said, "Maya, you have no idea what you missed."

My cell phone rang as I wiped my lips with a paper napkin. It was Harper.

"Where are you?" she asked.

"My room at the Beaufoy," I said.

"The last night you spent with us turned out bad. Let's have dinner tonight at the Raven's Roost. Afterward, you can come home with Celeste and me."

"I don't want to cause a rift between you and Celeste."

"She's the one who asked me to invite you," Harper said.

"I won't get knocked in the head again, will I?"

"The police have watched our house since the attack occurred," Harper said. "I can guarantee our house is safe."

"I spoke with Frankie earlier. He's coming for a visit next week."

"Wonderful," Harper said. "Celeste wants to meet him and has asked me to invite him here since we were King and Queen of Illusion."

"Oh? I can't come tonight. I have something I need to take care of. Maybe tomorrow night," I said.

Thoughts of blackmail began racing through my brain, a scenario of sex and deceit. Celeste would drug me, and I would be unable to resist when presented with three vulnerable women, one of them a patient at the hospital. I had little doubt that Celeste intended to compromise me.

"I'm returning to New Orleans tomorrow," Harper said. "Are you coming with me?"

"Wish I could. Frankie wants more information on his half-sister, so I'm stuck in town for a while."

"Maybe we can have dinner in New Orleans when you finish in Pinebridge. I love Commander's Palace."

"Commander's Palace is wonderful but more expensive than I can afford. How about a Lucky Dog at a stand in the Quarter."

Harper laughed out loud and said, "Whichever, I love them both. Doesn't matter because the treat is on me."

"Can't wait," I said.

When Harper hung up, I dialed Maya's number.

"I have some info that will interest you," she said. "Available for lunch?"

"Sure," I said.

"Pick you up in thirty minutes?"

"Perfect," I said. "I'll be waiting."

When I reached the lobby, Dot was checking in a traveling salesman. The Beaufoy Hotel had no bellboy. When the man headed upstairs with his bag, Dot and I exchanged smiles.

"I have a problem," I said.

"Welcome to the club. I have a test at two, and my youngest kept me up all night with a fever."

"Baby aspirin," I said.

"That's what my mother advised when I called her," Dot said. "My son was bouncing off the wall this morning when I got him off to school."

"Youth is its own remedy," I said.

"Ain't that the truth? What's your problem?"

"I need to hack into the hospital's database."

"What are you looking for?" Dot asked.

"Corruption, abuse, or worse," I said. "Can you help me?"

"I have to live here long after you're gone," she said.

"I don't intend to release anything I learn," I said. "I need to know what's going on at the hospital. I can't do it alone."

"I can hack into the hospital's database," she said. "I've already done it once. I shouldn't even be telling you this."

"We're on the same page. What did you find?" I asked.

"It was so frightening, I wiped it from my mind," she said.

"Help me," I said. "I won't involve you."

"Famous last words," she said.

I heard Maya honking for me and said, "Will you consider it?"

"My kids need their mother," she said.

"I understand," I said.

"Wyatt," she said as I walked toward the door. "I'll think about it."

Maya was waiting outside in her police cruiser. "You said you like catfish."

"Love it."

"Alligator Bayou is on the edge of the Kisatchie National Forest. There's a catfish restaurant called Kool Point Landing that only the locals know about. I think you'll like it."

"My mouth is already watering," I said.

Maya drove out of town and soon left the main highway, exiting onto a nondescript sideroad. Pinebridge wasn't exactly urban, but the area we traversed after turning was like the difference between night and day. The narrow blacktop followed a body of water I can only describe as magically bucolic. Cypress trees with huge trunks protruded from the coffee-colored shallow water. Egrets, cranes, and all manner of other waterfowl occupied the water.

"It's beautiful," I said.

160

"Kool Point is rustic," Maya said. "Nothing like what you are used to in New Orleans. Alligator Bayou is shallow and swampy."

"I'm intrigued," I said. "If the restaurant is half as good as Leo's, I'll love it."

The term bucolic didn't go far enough when describing Kool Point Landing. Giant cypress trees with swollen trunks grew in and out of the water. Small boats lined up on a timeworn pier. A cottonmouth made ripples in the water as it swam into a pile of submerged vegetation.

The old wooden building sat on wood piers over the shallow water. There was no air conditioning, only ceiling fans in the unfinished wooded rafters of the one-roomed building overlooking the bayou.

"Talk about ambiance," I said. "If the catfish tastes half as good as this old cracker box looks and smells, it'll be wonderful."

"There aren't many places like this in the world," Maya said.

"That's a fact," I said.

A waitress dressed in jeans and a Kool Point tee shirt arrived at our table and said, "I'm Sara. What can I get you to eat and drink?"

"Wyatt. This lovely lady with me is Maya."

"Nice meeting you, Wyatt and Maya," Sara said.

"I'll have whatever Maya's having," I said.

"Bring us two catfish dinners, and I'll have a glass of sweet tea," Maya said.

"Tea for me, but make mine unsweetened," I said.

When Sara was gone, Maya said, "Are you Watching your weight? You needn't worry because you don't have an extra pound on you."

"It's because I watch my weight," I said. "Except for the fried food we're about to eat."

"People like you are lucky," Maya said. "I gained five pounds just by walking in the door."

She grinned when I said, "You're in better shape than I am, and you know it."

Neither of us worried about the calories we consumed as we feasted on catfish filets, fried potatoes, and green tomato dressing. A snowy egret, its wings outstretched, landed in the shallow water outside the restaurant.

"Best catfish I ever ate, and the sides were wonderful," I said. "Now, what do you have for me?"

"Celeste Gauthier's bio. It's interesting, to say the least."

"I'm listening," I said.

"Celeste graduated Summa Cum Laude from UNO with a degree in Hospital Management. She worked for a boutique hotel in the French Quarter. That's where she met Axel Devereaux. Devereaux is married, though it didn't stop him from having a wild affair with Celeste."

"Devereaux is old enough to be Celeste's father," I said.

"Even older than you think. Axel Devereaux takes human growth hormones and spends a cool million dollars a year maintaining his youth and physical fitness," Maya said. "Must work because he's well over seventy, and his daughter Harper is in her mid-twenties."

"Damn! I didn't know they had such inside information in the police database," I said.

"I didn't get it all from the database," Maya said. "I called in some chits. There's still stuff out there on him, I'm sure."

"Tell me more," I said.

"Harper's mother is Devereaux's fifth wife," Maya said. "He has thirteen biological offspring, some born out of wedlock."

"Sounds like a busy man," I said.

"Very busy," Maya said. "He graduated from Tulane Medical School in the seventies. His roommate and fellow medical school graduate was Dr. Felix."

Chapter 18

A small boat with a lone fisherman aboard pulled up to the outside dock, unloading his red ice chest and a string of fish. I dropped my fork on the floor, and it bounced under the table.

"Damn! You have been busy," I said. "Dr. Felix seems to be a key player in what's going on at the hospital, and I've yet to see him," I said.

"He lives on an estate on the edge of Pinebridge in a monstrous-sized house that can only be described as a castle. He's reclusive; no one sees him much, not even hospital employees. There are no recent pictures of him. I can't even tell you what he looks like."

"Double damn!"

Sara smiled when she brought me another fork.

"Piece of lemon pie and cup of coffee?" she said.

"I don't have room for more food, though I can't resist lemon pie. Please twist my arm."

Sara looked amused as she glanced at Maya and said, "You, ma'am?"

"Why not?" Maya said.

When Sara left the table to get our lemon pie, I said, "Sounds like you've been working since you left me last night. I feel guilty."

"I actually spent a few hours in my own bed," she said. "My yellow tabby, Bimbo, and blue tick hound, Buster, were happy to see me."

"Buster and Bimbo?"

"My sister Suga checks on them daily so they never go hungry or thirsty. Still, I feel so guilty when working on a case and must be out of the house at all hours."

"You have a sister named Suga?"

Maya nodded. "Her real name is Khinara. She's sweet, and everyone calls her Suga."

"My friend Bertram takes care of my cat Kisses when I'm out of town."

"You have a kitty named Kisses?"

"The love of my life," I said. "Don't know what I'd do without her."

"I know the feeling. There's more I haven't told you."

I licked the last succulent bite of lemon pie off my fork and drank the last of Sara's coffee.

"Sorry I interrupted. Please tell me."

"When Harper isn't in town, Celeste has another main squeeze," Maya said.

"Let me guess," I said. "Kayla Duhon."

"Kayla lives in a little apartment off campus when Harper is in town. When Harper is in New Orleans, she stays with Celeste."

"Does Harper know about Kayla?" I asked.

"No idea."

"Neither Kayla nor Billy killed Marshall or Henry," I said.

"I'm with you on that," Maya said. "Who do you suspect?"

"Marshall's murder occurred on hospital grounds, and Henry's murder seems likely related to the hospital. My guess is the murderer of Marshall is a hospital employee."

"Motive?"

"The Marshall murder was a crime of passion," I said.

"What's your reasoning?"

"Whoever killed Oliver Marshall was close enough to kill him with a single cut. That implies he knew the killer and likely trusted them."

"And Henry Scott?" Maya asked.

"In my opinion, the person who assassinated Henry was a professional hitman. If so, someone paid a lot of money to orchestrate the hit."

"Then maybe the two murders aren't related," Maya said.

"They're connected," I said.

"What makes you think so?"

"No proof. Just a hunch," I said.

"Share your hunch with me."

"The abuse, the cover-up, and the murders are all connected. If we discover who is responsible for these acts, we'll unravel the entire scenario."

"What about the sex act you were forced to watch?" Maya asked.

"Connected," I said. "Meant to intimidate me."

"Is there something about what you saw you haven't told me?"

"I was drugged, though there are things I remember. The woman who performed the dominatrix part was as muscular as a dedicated bodybuilder," I said.

"Inga Talledaga?" Maya said.

"The woman, whoever she was, had a hooded cobra tattoo on her left ankle."

"Sounds as if we need to get a look at Inga's ankle," Maya said.

I smiled and said, "Good luck on that one."

"I'll pick her up and find out," Maya said.

"Let's not play our hand just yet. Even if Inga is involved, she doesn't have the resources to hire a professional hitman. She's an accessory, and implicating her would expose us to the actual person in control."

"Okay," Maya said. "What else do you have?"

"Lyrica Winter," I said. "She was beaten to hell the day I met her. Marshall was murdered the night before."

"You think there's a connection?"

"I'd love to ask her and find out," I said.

"She doesn't speak," Maya said.

"She can communicate using sign language. Billy could talk to her for us."

"Maybe he already has," Maya said.

"We need to get Billy to take us to her," I said.

Sara showed up with a carafe of coffee, smiling as she topped off our cups.

"You're an angel," I said.

"Just doing my job," Sara said.

It was Maya smiling when Sara left the table.

"What?" I asked.

"You're the biggest flirt I ever met."

"I wasn't flirting," I said.

"Whatever," she said. "I need to get to work. Let's get out of here."

Thunder clouds covered the darkened sky when we left Kool Point Landing.

"If I stay in town much longer, I'm going to have to buy new clothes," I said.

"You'll live," Maya said. "I have paperwork to do the rest of the afternoon. Where can I drop you?"

"The hospital, to quiz Celeste and see how much she'll tell me."

"Let me know if you turn up anything interesting."

"You'll be the first person I call."

Maya let me out at the hospital entrance, waving before driving away. Gayla was locking her office door as I entered the reception area.

"Leaving already?" I asked.

"Going fishing with the hubby," she said.

"Have fun."

"You know it," she said, giving me a backward wave.

The reception area was crowded, and I noticed several young doctors chatting as they hurried to a break room. I wondered how much they knew about Dr. Felix. There was no one in the hallway outside Celeste's office.

"Come in," she said when I knocked on her door. "You just missed Harper."

"I thought she was leaving tomorrow."

"She decided to go earlier."

"Sorry I missed her," I said.

"She said you told her that Frankie Castellano was coming next week. Have you had any luck locating his half-sister?"

I lied and said, "My work here has been a total bust. I would have left town with Harper if Mr. Castellano hadn't ordered me to stay."

"Will you still be here when he arrives?" Celeste asked.

"Afraid so," I said. "He's the boss, and I'm at his beck and call."

"Will you introduce us?"

"Of course," I said.

"Maybe we can all have dinner at the Raven's Roost," she said.

"Frankie would love it, and so would I. He wants me to interview Dr. Felix."

"Does he now?" Celeste said.

"Can you arrange it?"

"Dr. Felix is tenured here at the hospital and keeps his own hours," she said.

"Does he still make medical decisions?" I asked.

"Dr. Felix has complete control over what goes on at the hospital. Even I take orders from him. If he wants to talk to you, he will."

"My schedule is flexible," I said.

"He's out of town at the moment," she said.

"When will he return?"

"A couple of days," Celeste said. "He's in New Orleans visiting friends."

"I hear his house is somewhat a parish showplace. Have you been there?"

"Many times," she said.

"How does he take care of such a large place?"

"When he's in town, he has servants, even a cook."

"They get time off when he's out of town?" I asked.

"Dr. Felix is very demanding. When he's in town, no one has a day off. Luckily for his staff, the Dr. travels a lot."

"How does he afford such a wealthy lifestyle on a public servant's salary?"

Celeste seemed taken aback by my question.

"Inheritance," she said. "He works only because he is dedicated and enjoys helping people."

"Good for him. Can you tell him I'd like to speak to him?"

"No problem. Now, excuse me, I have work to do."

"Of course," I said.

Celeste didn't look up from her paperwork as I exited her office. In the hallway outside her door, I ran into Billy Williams.

"I was looking for you," he said.

"How did you know I was in the hospital?" I asked.

"Gayla told me."

"What's up?"

"Grandmother wants to see you."

"Great. I'll call Detective Henstooth."

Billy shook his head. "No police. Just you."

"Okay," I said. "I don't have a vehicle. How will we get there?"

"My truck," he said. "We're taking my cat."

I followed Billy out the hospital's front door and across the grounds to his house. His red Dodge pickup was old but clean and polished. Billy entered his house, exiting with his black cat Noseye in his arms. The truck cranked on the first turn of the key.

Neither Billy nor I spoke as we headed out of town, though I soon saw we were following the same route Maya and I had taken earlier. The clouds had returned, and the sky darkened as we followed the rural road past Alligator Bayou.

"This road gets pretty spooky after dark," he said.

"I can see why," I said. "I've counted two alligators since we turned onto this blacktop road."

"Don't get used to it. There'll be no blacktop when we reach the big pine forest."

Billy was right. We soon exited the blacktop to a dirt path barely wide enough for the truck's passage. The darker the sky became, the narrower the road seemed to get. Billy followed the narrow passageway for half an hour before we emerged into a clearing in the pines, the stone cottage in the clearing seeming like something out of a fairy tale.

"We're here," he said.

"Glad I'm with you. I'd never find my way out of here," I said.

"Planned it that way," he said.

It was raining when we left the truck and ran for the house. When we entered, three smiling women met us. I recognized Rica.

The inside of the house was as rustic as the outside, with pine beams and built-in bookshelves littered with books and knickknacks. There was no electricity, and the room was illuminated only by the fire burning in the stone hearth. With thunder shaking the roof and lightning flashing through the windows, the crackling fire made the large room seem safe and secure. The oldest of the three women took my hand and led me to a comfortable chair.

"I'm Bella Donna Castellano," she said. "I understand you're looking for me."

"At the behest of your brother, Frankie. He has left no stone unturned trying to locate you."

"How did he find out about me?"

"He served as King of the Krewe of Illusion during Mardi Gras. Harper Devereaux was his queen. Celeste Gauthier, the hospital administrator, told her you were a patient there."

"Yes," she said.

She nodded when I said, "You must have an amazing story to tell. I want to hear it."

"We have much to talk about," she said. "Billy is my grandson, Wanda, my daughter, and you know Rica."

The chair I was seated in faced the fireplace, where another black cat lay in a padded bed. Noseye walked to the bed, rubbed noses with the other cat, and joined her.

"Trixie is Noseye's sister. She was born with eyes."

Bella Donna was an attractive sixty-something woman with dark hair and eyes. Her dimpled cheeks gave her the impression of forever happiness. Her long blue dress matched the ones worn by Rica and Wanda. They were all low-cut and coquettish, making them seem party-bound.

Wanda was attractive and looked like a younger version of her mother. For the first time since meeting her, Rica was smiling.

The stone cottage was larger than it had originally seemed. Billy kissed his mother and grandmother before pointing to the stairs.

"Long day," he said. "I'm turning in for the night. Rica is also tired, so I'll walk her to her room."

"Sleep well," Wanda said.

Billy and Rica's disappearance up the stairs was my first clue that I was spending the night. It didn't matter. The chair in which I sat was large and comfortable. Wanda soon brought me a cup of warm broth. It was savory and slightly salty, adding to the warmth and ambiance of the cottage in the pines. Something in the broth warmed my neck and relieved all my doubts as it relaxed me.

"Settle in, Wyatt," Bella Donna said. "The broth will help you relax, and I'll reveal all the secrets of the Louisiana Hospital of the Insane."

Chapter 19

When Wanda brought me another cup of broth, I couldn't turn it away. It warmed my body as I drank it. Outside, the thunderstorm continued to rage. Inside, all was right with the universe, and I sank back into the soft cushioning of the chair.

"I'm sure you're wondering how I ended up in the mental hospital," Bella Donna said.

"The thought crossed my mind," I said.

"I had an issue with one of my teachers. She told my mother I had mental problems and would benefit from a stay at the Pinebridge hospital."

"Your mother and not your father had you committed?" I asked.

"I was conflicted," Bella Donna said. "I was too white for the black community and too black for the white community to accept me. I stumbled into the drug scene and was sexually promiscuous at an early age. To say I was out of control is an understatement. I wasn't mentally ill."

"What did your dad do when he found out you were bound for Pinebridge?" I asked.

"Flipped totally out, though he could do nothing about it."

"Why not?" I asked.

"Though he knew I was his daughter, he admitted it to no one for obvious reasons. He did support Mom and me financially. He used to take me to City Park on Sunday. He was from Sicily and taught me what an honor it was that I had Sicilian blood coursing through my veins. He also taught me how to speak Italian."

"You must have known he had another family."

"I wasn't happy about that and confronted him about it more than once."

"And?"

"He always apologized and promised me things would be different someday."

"So, when your mom had you committed, there was nothing Paco could legally do to unwind the situation."

"Exactly," Bella Donna said. "He tried to compensate by visiting me often. His visits were the only thing normal about my stay at the Pinebridge Mental Hospital."

"I'm aware of the conditions at the hospital. When did the abuse begin for you?" I asked.

"Almost immediately. Hardly a night passed that one of the attendants didn't come to my cell and rape and beat me."

"Your dad found out?"

"It was impossible for him not to see the cuts and bruises I always had," Bella Donna said.

"And that's when he stepped in and spoke with the Governor?"

Bella Donna nodded. "He got most of the attendants fired. It didn't stop the abuse and most assuredly failed to stop the medical procedures the patients were undergoing. Didn't matter because from that point forward, I had a target on my back."

"Is Dr. Felix the head of the snake?"

"One of the snake's heads," she said.

"Pardon me?"

"Dr. Felix controlled what happened at the hospital. Someone else called the shots."

Bella Donna nodded when I said, "Axel Devereaux?"

"Yes," she said.

"The hospital employs a full staff of doctors and nurses other than Dr. Felix. How did he get them to comply with his lack of ethics?"

"He doesn't. They are unaware of the abuse and his medical misconduct."

"How is that possible?" I asked.

"Dr. Felix has a private operating room in his castle," Bella Donna said. "That's where he does the procedures."

"He must have had help," I said.

"He has help," Bella Donna said.

"How do you know?" I asked.

"My friend, Patience, told me."

"Patience Bianchi,"

"Yes," she said.

"Father Piastri, the Catholic priest, suggested he'd heard Patience's confession. He said she underwent extra torment from the staff."

"Because she was from Sicily like my father. The trouble he caused resulted in extra punishment from Dr. Felix and the attendants. Her mental condition continued to grow worse, and she killed herself."

Bella Donna stared at the crackling fire and grew quiet and reflective. Outside, the rain, thunder, and lightning continued.

"I'm sorry," I said.

"When the attendants no longer had Patience to abuse, they focused their attention on me."

"Inga Talledaga was spared from the firings instigated by your father."

"She shouldn't have been. Though she wasn't much older than I was, she was one of the cruelest offenders. She hired three new attendants, indoctrinating them from day one. The abuse never really ceased."

"How did you escape?"

"Inga was obsessed with me and didn't want to share me with the others. She came to my cell one night and took me to her cabin on Alligator Bayou. She kept me there, locked in a dark closet with my hands cuffed behind me when she was at work."

"Damn!" I said.

"I often thought of Patience. If I could have freed my hands, I would have taken my own life. One night, Inga learned something that infuriated her."

"What?" I asked.

"I was pregnant. Inga took me in a small boat out into the bayou to kill me. She was about to cut my throat with her knife. I jumped out of the boat into the water."

"She carried a knife?"

"Always. A switchblade with a serrated edge," Bella Donna said.

"How did you keep from drowning?"

"The water was shallow and only came to my chest. When Inga grabbed for me, she upset the boat and fell into the water. I stuck my head underwater and held my breath. She must have thought that I had drowned because she eventually pushed the boat to shore and righted it. I hid behind a cypress tree, and Inga finally gave up looking for me."

"How did you get the handcuffs off?"

"Efy cut them."

"Who is Efy?" I asked.

"The woman who owns this cottage," Bella Donna said. "The locals knew her as Efy the Swamp Witch and bought potions and native remedies from her. Efy taught me everything she knew, and I was with her until she passed away."

"How did she happen to have a cottage in the middle of a National Forest?" I asked.

"Efy was a real witch. This cottage is enchanted, and nothing can harm those who live here."

Even in the room's dim light, I could see the pain in Bella Donna and Wanda's eyes. Wanda was the daughter of a rapist, and there was no need for me to comment.

"Why didn't you try to connect with your family?" I asked.

"I was afraid. By this time, Wanda was older, and I vowed never to return to the mental hospital."

"What about Billy?" I asked.

"When I was old enough," Wanda said. "I moved to Leesville and got a job at the Army base. I married a young infantry officer stationed there. William was killed in Afghanistan."

"I'm sorry," I said.

"When Billy graduated from high school, we moved in with mom. Billy moved out to take a job at the hospital. I've been here ever since."

"You seemed to have flourished," I said.

"The locals pay good money for Mom's potions and herbs. We also raise bees and sell flowers."

"Your gardens are beautiful. I could see even by Billy's headlights."

Wanda smiled. "Like Mom said, this place is enchanted."

"It's past our bedtimes," Bella Donna said. "I'll bring you a throw to keep you warm."

The brunt of the storm had passed, though the rain continued. I had just dozed off when Billy Williams, wearing pajama bottoms, descended the stairs and stoked the fire. Rica, dressed in a nightgown, was with him. It wasn't hard for me to imagine that they were sleeping together. I opened my eyes and sat straight in the chair.

"Sorry to wake you," Billy said.

"No problem," I said. "I was only half asleep."

Billy and Rica were holding hands and both smiling. It was apparent they were a couple.

"Mom and Grandmother think you are here to help us," he said.

"That's my plan."

"Do you want to hear Rica's story?"

"It isn't my wish to traumatize Rica any more than she already is," I said. "With that said, I'd still like to hear her story."

"She wants to tell it," Billy said.

"I'm listening," I said.

Rica understood me. She nodded and began signing. As she did, Billy interpreted.

"My parents are deceased. I have no family. My foster parents had me taken because they thought I was a threat to their baby. It wasn't true. Amanda's crib was in the room next to mine. She was crying, and I tried to comfort her. They thought I was trying to harm her."

Rica began to cry. Billy kissed her forehead and squeezed her hand.

"She couldn't explain," he said. "It made her feel powerless."

Rica began signing again.

"I was older, and no one wanted responsibility. I moved through the system until it finally ended in Pinebridge. I hated all the drugs I was subjected to and lashed out. I was taken to Dr. Felix's house to undergo a procedure."

Rica quit signing, and Billy stopped talking. Seeing she was overwhelmed with grief, he took her in his arms. They remained silent for what seemed an eternity. I thought they were done. They weren't.

"What procedure?" I asked.

Rica pointed to her forehead.

"They intended to lobotomize her," Billy said.

"But they didn't. Why not?" I asked.

"Oliver Marshall intervened. He threatened the two doctors and took me off of the operating table. I was still groggy from the anesthetic."

"How long after this happened was Marshall murdered?" I asked.

"That very night. He was distraught and knew he couldn't return me to the hospital. Instead, we went to the cemetery. That's where Inga found us."

"Is Inga close to Dr. Felix?" I asked.

"Inga is Dr. Felix's lieutenant and does whatever he tells her."

"She was at his house the night he intended to lobotomize you?"

Rica nodded. "Oliver Marshall was a brute of a man, and Inga was afraid of him. She followed us to the cemetery."

"He trusted her?"

Rica nodded. "They had performed unspeakable acts together. Neither had any friends."

"Marshall thought he loved you?"

Rica nodded again. "Even monsters have feelings," she said, Billy interpreting.

"No, they don't," I said. "You shouldn't feel an ounce of compassion for him."

"I'm not like them. No one deserves to die like he did."

"Let me guess," I said. "Inga killed him with her switchblade."

"She cut his throat, his blood drenching my nightgown. Inga returned me to my cell without bothering to clean me up. I was still covered in

Oliver Marshall's blood the next day when I met you in the rose garden."

"You poor kid," I said. "I'm glad you found Billy."

Rica clutched Billy's hand and nodded. Outside, rain continued drumming on the roof of the enchanted cottage.

"Would you like a cup of tea?" Billy asked.

"Love one," I said.

Rica smiled again when Billy returned from the kitchen with a teapot and three cups. Rica took a dollop of cream and two teaspoons of sugar. Billy didn't touch his, leaving it sitting on the tray.

"What now?" he asked.

"Now I know who killed Oliver Marshall and have a good idea who was responsible for the murder of Henry Scott. Your great uncle will be proud of you," I said.

"My uncle?" Billy said.

"Your grandmother's brother is Frankie Castellano. He hired me to find your grandmother. He's the only person in Louisiana who has the power to right the wrong that has occurred here in Pinebridge."

"Frankie Castellano?" Billy said.

"You'll meet him next week," I said.

Billy smiled. "Thanks for listening to Rica's story. She said to tell you it helped unload the force off of her chest."

I smiled at Rica and said, "You're welcome."

Billy and Rica went back upstairs, and I closed my eyes. They weren't shut for long as the glow of some supernatural being lighted the space before me. It was the flickering image of a black woman wrinkled with age. The purple scarf tied around her head matched the color of the long dress she wore.

"Who are you?" I asked.

"Efy Henstooth," the spirit said.

"The person who owns this cottage?" I asked.

"Yes," she said.

"Are you related to Maya Henstooth?"

"Henstooth is a witch's name, and Maya, like me, is a witch."

"She never told me that," I said.

"Because she doesn't know she's a witch. She knows she has certain powers, though no one has instructed her how to use them properly."

Efy shook her head when I asked, "Does Maya know about you?"

"She's the only person in her family with the power."

"What good is having special powers if you don't know how to use them?" I asked.

"She'll learn in due time," Efy said.

"Why are you here?"

"To advise you what you're up against and to tell you that I'll be here to help."

"What am I up against?"

"An unmovable force," Efy said.

"If it's unmovable, how will I ever prevail?"

"Your brains and my magic," she said before dissolving away in an explosion of colorful spectral embers.

Chapter 20

Billy woke me early the following morning. The storm had passed during the night, and sunlight flooded the cottage through an open curtain.

"It's early, and I must get to work. If we're here when Mom and Grandmother awake, they'll make us wait until after breakfast to leave."

"No problem," I said. "I'm already dressed."

"Sorry," he said. "Next time, we'll come on the weekend."

Billy grabbed his sleeping cat out of the cat bed and headed for the front door. We were soon on the dirt road back to the pavement, Noseye in my lap.

"Thanks," I said. "Your mom and grandmother are wonderful. After you went to bed, I met Efy."

"How did you do that? Efy is dead."

He shook his head when I said, "Must have been her ghost."

"You, my mom and grandmother," he said. "I think you're all crazy."

Billy didn't believe in ghosts, and it wasn't up to me to convince him otherwise.

"Can you drive past Dr. Felix's house before you drop me off?"

"It's impossible to see from the road because it's surrounded by trees and quite a distance from the main blacktop."

"What do you know about Dr. Felix?" I asked.

"He's a creep and molested Rica more than once."

"Rica seemed happy. I'm glad she survived her many ordeals," I said.

"It'll take time, but she's resolving her anger. She wants me to quit my job."

"Why don't you?" I asked. "The cottage seems self-sufficient. You don't have to work at the hospital."

"I'm not there because I like it," he said.

"Revenge can get you killed. Sometimes, it's best to lick your wounds and go on down the road."

"Why aren't you taking your own advice?"

"My motive isn't revenge. Your uncle is paying me to throw a monkey wrench into the skullduggery at the hospital. Your mom and grandmother provided some much-needed ammunition last night."

"I can help," Billy said.

"You already have."

"I'm ready to do more. Why do you want to see Dr. Felix's house?" he asked.

"He's politically connected. I want to pin something on him that smells so rotten that even his friends refuse to protect him."

"Like what?"

"Something too explosive to cover up," I said. "Pictures, maybe."

"How about home movies?"

"Depends on what they show," I said.

"Rica told me he films everything."

"What do you mean by everything?"

"Rapes, beatings, medical procedures. He has a private theatre in his house. He has filmed everything and everybody."

Billy nodded when I said, "Blackmail?"

"He has compromising films of everyone in town, the Parish, and the State. If he can't compromise them, he has them killed."

Billy nodded again when I said, "Like Henry Scott?"

"Where does he keep these home movies?" I asked.

"In a vault in his house, according to Rica."

"Where in the house?" I asked.

"His bedroom," he said.

Billy stopped on the blacktop before getting to town and pointed to a one-lane road leading into a thick grove of trees.

"Dr. Felix's house is at the end of the road. We can't drive there without being seen because he has surveillance cameras everywhere."

"Can you reach the house on foot?" I asked.

"It's a bit of a hike, but you can. I'll show you if you let me go with you," he said. "We'll need to wait until after dark."

"Good idea," I said. "Have you ever broken into a house?"

"No," he said.

"It's dangerous and can get you killed."

"What about you?" he asked.

"I put myself through college helping repossess houses for the FHA," I said. "It's not something I'm particularly proud of. I've probably been in more houses illegally than a cat burglar. Believe me when I tell you it's pretty frightening at times."

"I've been in Dr. Felix's house."

"How so?"

"He hosted a Christmas party for the hospital staff. Oliver Marshall took me on a private tour," he said.

"You were friends with Mr. Marshall?"

"He wasn't a perfect person, and he didn't deserve to die."

"You know the way to Felix's bedroom?"

"Yes, and I can show you where the vault is. How do you intend to open it?"

"Everyone has special talents," I said. "One of mine is opening things."

"Like Rica?"

"There's no magic involved, though I manage."

"Even if you open the vault, how do you intend to get out of the house with the tapes?"

"I only need one," I said.

"Take me. I can help you," he said.

"We'll talk about it later," I said. "Maybe tonight."

"Where can I take you until then?"

"The Beaufoy Hotel," I said.

Though still early, people were out and about, some on the sidewalk, possibly on their way to Abner's Café on Main Street. Two gardeners were working with the flowers in front of the courthouse, and a stray dog was pawing through an overturned trashcan. Dot wasn't behind the reception desk when I entered the hotel and went upstairs. I found Maya waiting for me at my door.

"Out tomcatting?" she asked.

"Hardly," I said. "I have a buttload of information to share with you."

"Wonderful," she said. "You hungry? Maybe we can go to the café down the street."

"The only thing I had to eat last night was a cup of broth. The hotel has a buffet, and the grub is pretty good. Want to try it?"

Maya followed me downstairs to the break area, where several traveling salesmen were smiling as they chowed down on the feast of breakfast items. After filling paper plates and plastic coffee cups, Maya and I returned upstairs.

My room was stuffy, so I opened a window overlooking the town square below. Maya sat on the bed, and I took the only chair as we ate the breakfast feast.

"This is wonderful," she said.

"Thought you'd like it. We may have to make another trip downstairs. Those cinnamon rolls are calling my name."

"I need a cinnamon roll like an extra hole in my head," Maya said. "I could use more coffee."

Despite her protests, Maya and I returned to the breakroom, where we found Dot Beaufoy. She tapped my shoulder and pulled me aside.

"We need to talk," she said.

"You've met Detective Henstooth," I said. "Mind if she sits in on our conversation?"

Dot's anxious expression told me something was wrong when she said, "Just you."

I nodded and said, "I won't be long."

When we returned to my room, Maya and I had cinnamon rolls and a large carafe of coffee, courtesy of Dot. Maya smiled as she sipped her coffee and licked the sugar off her sticky fingers.

"My stomach is going to miss you when you're gone," she said.

"Me too. I'll have to talk to my landlord about a breakfast buffet when I return to New Orleans."

"Good luck," Maya said. "Now, what is it you can't wait to tell me?"

"Billy took me to his grandmother's cottage last night," I said.

"Why didn't you call?"

"Not everyone trusts the police," I said. "Doesn't matter because I'm about to tell you what I learned."

"I'm waiting," she said.

"Inga Talledaga killed Oliver Marshall with her knife. They both had the hots for Rica. Marshall became obsessed with her. When he rescued Rica from Dr. Felix's operating table, Olga followed them to the cemetery."

"Inga killed Marshall? Who told you?" Maya asked.

"Rica Winter," I said. "Inga didn't even bother cleaning her up when she returned her to her cell."

"Rica doesn't talk. How did she tell you?"

"Sign language with Billy Williams interpreting."

"Would her testimony hold up in court?"

"Rica witnessed the murder. Her testimony will hold up, though the cross-examination could get dicey if Inga hires a smart defense lawyer."

"Do you believe Rica?"

"Yes," I said. "Billy's grandmother told me a story about Inga that corroborates Rica's."

"Then I need to arrest Inga Talledaga," Maya said.

"You have two murders to solve, and arresting Inga won't get us there."

"You have a plan?"

"Yes, and it involves what else I learned since I saw you last."

Maya opened the carafe and divided the remaining coffee between us.

"No more interruptions. Tell me what you know."

"Billy's mom and grandmother live in a stone cottage in the Kisatchie National Forest. Billy's grandmother is none other than Bella Donna Castellano. She was a victim of abuse from the time she arrived at the hospital. Her story implicates Inga, the other attendants, and Dr. Felix."

"You said she can corroborate Rica's story," Maya said.

"Inga was particularly attracted to Bella Donna. She took her at knifepoint to a cabin she owns somewhere near Alligator Bayou because she didn't want to share her with the other attendants."

"You think her knife was the weapon used to kill Oliver Marshall?"

"Yes. Bella Donna described it as a switchblade with a serrated edge, the same kind of knife Rica said Inga always carries."

"Damn!" Maya said. "Is she so cocksure she'll never be convicted that she didn't bother disposing of the murder weapon?"

"Seems to be the case. Unless someone tips her off, you'll find it when you arrest her."

"We can add kidnapping, assault, and other charges if we can't make murder one stick. How did Bella Donna escape?"

"Inga kept her cuffed and locked in a closet when she was away from the cabin. She didn't know that Bella Donna was pregnant. When the baby began to show, Inga became infuriated and took her into the swamp in a small boat."

"To kill her?" Maya asked.

"That's what Bella Donna thinks."

"And you don't?"

"Inga wasn't prepared to lose Bella Donna. I think she intended to take the baby by Caesarian and dispose of its body in the swamp."

"Jesus!" Maya said.

"We'll never know because Bella Donna jumped overboard. She didn't drown because the water was shallow, and she somehow managed to escape."

"How did she remove the cuffs?" Maya asked.

"A woman named Efy cut them off. She's the person who owned the cottage in the forest."

"Owned?" Maya said.

"Efy is deceased. Bella Donna lived with her from when her baby was born until now."

"And her baby is Billy Williams's mother?"

"Wanda," I said. "When she was old enough, she moved to Leesville, where she married an Army officer who was killed in Afghanistan. William Williams is Billy's father."

"Where did the name Spivey come from?"

"My guess is she made it up," I said.

"How is It that Efy lived in a cottage in the Kisatchie National Forest?" Maya asked.

"The locals knew her as the Swamp Witch, and she supported herself by selling potions and herbs and casting spells."

"Get out of here!" Maya said.

"That isn't all. Are you prepared for a bombshell?"

"Tell me," Maya said.

"You're aware of the mansion Dr. Felix lives in. According to Rica, it's where he performs all his illicit operations because the rest of the medical staff at the hospital aren't part of the conspiracy."

"How can we prove it?"

"Rica says Felix is a film buff and records all his operations, abuse, and whatever nefarious activity he's involved in. He uses the film for blackmail, and it's how he's gotten away with literal murder for so many years. Rica says he keeps the film in a vault in his bedroom."

"I'll get a search warrant," Maya said.

"Someone would tip off Dr. Felix. When you arrived with your warrant, the evidence would be gone," I said.

"Then how will we get it?"

"Billy's been inside the house. With his help, I'll break in, crack the safe, and retrieve enough evidence to put Dr. Felix and his gang behind bars."

"We can't do that," Maya said.

"You can't. I can."

"What makes you think you can pull it off?"

"It isn't rocket science," I said. "If I weren't a private detective, I'd make a good cat burglar."

I laughed when she said, "Sounds like it's you I need to arrest."

"One more thing," I said.

"I can't handle much more. What you got?"

"The last name of Efy the 'Swamp Witch' is Henstooth."

"Get out of here!" Maya said. "I'm Baptist. There are no witches in my family."

"Do you believe in ghosts?" I asked.

"No," Maya said.

"Efy visited me last night. It may have been a dream, though I don't think so. She verified Bella Donna's story. She also knew who you are."

"You're making this up," Maya said.

"Efy said that Henstooth is a witch's name and that there is only one witch in your family."

"Who?" Maya asked.

"You," I said.

Chapter 21

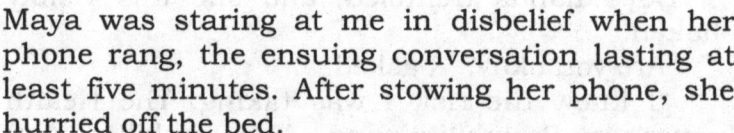

Maya was staring at me in disbelief when her phone rang, the ensuing conversation lasting at least five minutes. After stowing her phone, she hurried off the bed.

"I need to go. We'll have to continue this conversation later."

She nodded when I said, "Another murder?"

"Don't know yet. A motorist spotted a body in the ditch on Highway 116. Probably a hit-and-run and unconnected to the hospital. I'll let you know after taking a look."

When Maya was gone, I showered and changed clothes before going downstairs to see what was worrying Dot. She was waiting when I reached the foot of the stairs.

"I'm in trouble," she said.

"What happened?"

"I can't tell you here in the lobby. My apartment is behind the check-in counter."

I followed Dot through the door into her efficiency apartment. She sat at the kitchen table and put her hands over her face.

"It can't be that bad," I said.

"Worse," she said. "I hacked into the hospital computer and got caught."

"Tell me what happened," I said.

"My computer's at the desk in the corner. I was trying to hack into the system and reached the Louisiana Mental Hospital's login portal. The layers of security would deter most hackers. I was prepared for it.

"After several minutes of navigating firewalls and bypassing encryption protocols, I was in. Patient files, treatment records, and sensitive data. It was all there. I've hacked into systems on other occasions. It doesn't prevent my heart from racing. The weight of what I was about to do overcame the initial thrill of hacking into the hospital's system."

Dot's hands trembled, and she was visibly shaken.

"Are you okay?" I asked.

"I knew the risk I was taking. The Health Insurance Portability and Accountability Act, HIPAA, loomed over my actions like a dark specter. Unauthorized access to hospital information is a federal crime. I almost fainted when an alert popped up on the screen saying Unauthorized Access Detected."

"You backed out of there ASAP, I hope."

"I panicked. The hospital's IT department knows its system has been compromised, and the breach triggers mandatory notifications. I had no time to find what I was looking for and get out before the system locked me out and traced my location."

"The hospital is on to you?" I asked.

"I initiated a secure deletion protocol to cover my tracks. Now, I can't shake the feeling of being watched, and the weight of potential imprisonment is so troubling that I don't even want to think about it."

"It's okay," I said.

"No, it isn't," she said. "I crossed a line. The F.B.I. will show up at my door and arrest me. Who's going to take care of my kids?"

"You didn't access any files or see anything. If the Feds show up, tell them you got into the hospital's system by accident and have no clue how to hack into anything."

"They won't believe me," Dot said.

"Yes, they will. Trust me when I tell you the F.B.I. has bigger fish to fry than you."

"You truly believe that?"

"Just forget about the incident and go on about your business. The F.B.I. won't show up here at the hotel. Tell them what I said if they do, and you'll be fine."

"Thanks. What you say makes sense. I'm sorry I wasn't able to help you."

"You tried, and that's what counts," I said.

Dot was smiling again when I followed her out of the little apartment. I wasn't worried about the Feds arriving to arrest her. What worried me was the incursion into the system alerting Dr. Felix that someone from Pinebridge was nosing around. I called Maya to tell her my concern.

"I think Dot Beaufoy at the hotel is in danger," I said.

I could hear the wind blowing and cars passing on the highway and knew that Maya was on the side of the road, viewing the body of a dead man.

"Why is she in danger?" she asked.

"She tried to hack into the hospital's record system. The surveillance software blocked her and probably recorded the location of her computer."

I waited through a long pause before Maya said, "Hacking into the hospital computer system is a federal crime. You know that, don't you?"

"She didn't penetrate the system, and that's not what worries me."

"Then what does?"

"If the attempted breach spooks the wrong person, they may try to kill Dot," I said. "We don't need another murder on our hands."

"Okay," Maya said. "I'll schedule surveillance of the hotel."

"Thanks," I said.

"Wyatt, will I have to arrest you before we resolve this case?"

"Hope not," I said. "Whatever happens, I won't involve you."

"Good luck on that one," she said. "What's on your agenda?"

"Back to the hospital to talk with Billy Williams," I said.

"Wyatt," Maya said. "Don't get yourself killed."

I'd barely put away my phone and walked out the hotel's front door when it rang. It was Celeste.

"Dr. Felix is in my office and wants to meet you," she said.

"I'm on my way. I'm on foot, so it'll take a while."

"No problem," she said. "Dr. Felix and I are reviewing paperwork and have lots to do until you arrive."

The day was warm, and the sky was sunny as I hiked toward Pinebridge Mental Hospital. Before I was halfway there, my phone rang again. I answered and heard Frankie Castellano's raspy voice.

"My plans changed. I'm at the Hilton on the edge of Pinebridge," he said. "Where are you?"

"On my way to meet the head doctor at the hospital," I said.

"Good," Frankie said. "I'm meeting you and Ms. Gauthier at the Raven's Roost. Harper said you know where it is."

"It's across the street from where I'm staying."

"We're meeting at seven," Frankie said. "You can tell me then what you've learned."

"No, I can't," I said. "Celeste Gauthier is a suspect."

"No way," Frankie said. "Harper told me she is above reproach."

"I have lots to tell you. I won't do it in Celeste's presence. You'll have to trust me on that decision."

After a pause, Frankie said, "Harper isn't involved, is she?"

"I'm ruling no one out," I said.

"I didn't hire you to dig up dirt on the Queen of the Krewe of Illusion," Frankie said. "She's a friend of mine."

"It came with the territory. You can't be a good investigator and begin by excluding possible suspects."

"You can If I say you can. You're my employee and not the government. Tony knows how to follow orders."

"Are you firing me?"

"Let's just say you have lots of explaining to do. I'll defer that explanation until we can speak alone."

"Thanks, Frankie. This case has become far more complicated than I can explain over the phone."

"Tony and Lil are back from their vacation in Italy. Do I need to call him in to assist you?"

"I have things under control," I said.

"Okay," he said. "See you at seven."

I was stung by Frankie's offer to send Tony Nicosia to help me. I stopped beneath a giant elm tree and called Tony to explain the situation to him. He answered on the first ring.

"Can I call you back? I have Frankie on the phone, and he's taking no prisoners," Tony said.

"Sure," I said.

Tony had signed off before I got the word out of my mouth. I was doubly pissed as I finished my short trek to the hospital. It didn't matter, I told myself as I entered the front door and proceeded down the hallway to Celeste's office.

When Celeste introduced me to Dr. Felix, I had to catch my jaw before it bounced off the floor. The man I was shaking hands with wasn't Dr. Felix. He was none other than Axel Devereaux.

Years before, when I was still a lawyer, I had done a legal job for Axel Devereaux. He looked no different than he had then. I hoped he didn't recognize me, though I saw no sign in his eyes that he did.

"Pleased to meet you, Mr. Thomas," he said.

"Likewise," I said. "I'm enjoying the hospital's hospitality since arriving in Pinebridge."

"Happy to hear it," he said. "Celeste said you wanted to meet me. I had business in New Orleans and returned to town earlier than I thought."

Celeste motioned for me to sit facing her desk in one of the leather chairs. My mind continued to reel as I did so.

"Frankie Castellano called me earlier," she said. "He's in town and meeting Wyatt and me for dinner at seven. We'd love to have you join us."

"Nothing I'd like more, though I already have plans," Dr. Felix's imposter said.

Axel Devereaux had to decline the dinner offer. He'd met Frankie many times. It seemed Celeste had no idea that the person she thought was Dr. Felix was her lesbian lover's father.

My battery of questions for Dr. Felix suddenly became moot, and I had to dig deep for an answer when Devereaux asked me a question.

"How exactly can I help you?"

"Mr. Castellano hired me to locate his half-sister, who once was a patient here. Celeste showed me her records, enough for me to conclude my investigation. Mr. Castellano needs a little hand-holding to accept my conclusion, and that's why he's in town."

Dr. Felix, or whoever he was, must have liked my explanation because he got out of his chair to shake my hand.

"Happy to hear you've resolved your investigation. I enjoyed meeting you and must go as I've neglected my duties here at the hospital for too long."

When he was gone, Celeste said," That went well. I was worried you would be confrontational."

"You had nothing to worry about," I said. "Dr. Felix seemed very pleasant."

"He's a wonderful person," she said.

"How long have you known him?" I asked.

"Since I began work here," she said.

"Has Harper ever met him?"

"I've only known Harper for about a year, and she's had no opportunity yet to meet Dr. Felix."

I desperately wanted to blurt out something like, "She's going to be surprised when she does." I managed to keep my mouth shut.

"Are you okay?" she asked.

I forced myself to smile and said, "I didn't sleep much last night. Sorry."

"Return to your hotel room and take a nap. I want you to feel relaxed and rested when you introduce me to the King of the Krewe of Illusion."

"Good idea. I'll let you return to your duties." I stopped before leaving and said, "Thanks, Celeste."

"For what?"

"Introducing me to Dr. Felix."

"You're welcome," she said as I walked out the door.

It was still early as I exited Celeste's office and headed for Billy William's little house, hoping to catch him on a break. He wasn't there, so I sat in his recliner and closed my eyes. It was the last thing I remembered until he woke me. His cat, Noseye, was on my lap.

"What time is it?" I asked.

"Almost seven," he said.

I hurried out of the recliner and said, "Uh oh! I just learned something that changes the whole course of my investigation."

"What?" Billy asked.

"Before coming here, I met Dr. Felix at Celeste's office. The problem is the man she introduced me to wasn't Dr. Felix," I said.

"How do you know?" Billy asked.

"I'd met him before. He was Axel Devereaux, Harper's father, pretending to be Dr. Felix."

"For what reason?"

"They were roommates in college. Their friendship continued after graduation. At least until they got crosswise with one another."

Billy wasn't making the connection as he stared glassy-eyed at me, so I stopped explaining and sat Noseye back in the chair.

"You must have been tired," he said.

"Guess so. I have a dinner engagement at seven. I wondered if you're up for breaking into Dr. Felix's house tonight."

"What time?"

"I should be done with dinner by nine. It'll be dark by then."

"I'm ready," he said.

"Good. Can you pick me up in front of the hotel?"

"Sure," he said.

"I'm going to be late and need to go. See you around nine."

"I'll be there," he said.

I didn't want to be sweaty when I arrived at the Raven's Roost. I also didn't want to be too late. I stopped when I remembered I hadn't checked my phone messages.

Tony Nicosia had called and left me a voicemail. It said Frankie had retained him and that he was on his way to Pinebridge. He would be on the road by now, so I decided not to call him. I found Celeste waiting at the front door of the Raven's Roost.

"Where have you been?" she asked.

"Sorry," I said. "I'm here now. Why didn't you go in?"

"I want you to introduce me to Frankie," she said.

"Then let's do it," I said.

Frankie and Kayla were waiting for us at Celeste and Harper's table. His glare turned into a smile when he saw Celeste.

She grabbed his hand and said, "I'm Celeste. So sorry we're late. I take full responsibility."

Frankie wasn't buying her explanation and glared at me. I was wondering if I needed to excuse myself when Kayla kissed me.

"I've missed you," she said. "Where have you been?"

"I'm here now," I said.

Frankie was already drinking doubles, and Celeste was content to join him.

"I'm so happy to meet you," she said. "Harper has told me so much about you."

"Has she now? What else has she told you?"

"Nothing I'm privy to reveal," she said with a wink.

"Good," Frankie said. "Harper never told me how pretty you are."

"She didn't tell me how handsome you are either," Celeste said.

I glanced at Kayla and shook my head. She grinned and said, "Lemonade?"

"Love it," I said.

By the time Celeste was on her second drink, she was holding Frankie's hand. Frankie didn't seem to mind.

"I wish Harper were here with us," she said.

"Me too," Frankie said.

From how Celeste was fawning all over Frankie, I assumed she would take him home with her, or at least attempt to. She didn't. When we finished dinner, she made her apologies.

"I must go," she said.

"Please stay a while longer," Frankie said.

"I'd love to, but I can't," Celeste said. "I have someone coming in early tomorrow and must be at the office by seven. I'll never make it if I have another drink."

When Celeste was gone, Frankie's smile quickly turned into a frown.

"Tony's on his way here," he said.

"I know. He left a message on my phone."

"I think we're pretty much done. You've found my sister's grandson; he knows where I can find Bella Donna. When Tony arrives, tell him all you know. He'll take over, and you can return to New Orleans."

"Yes, sir," I said.

"What else?" he said.

"That's it," I said. "I'm staying at the hotel across the street. If we're finished, I'll go to my room."

Frankie's smile returned. "Thanks, Wyatt. I appreciate you, and there'll be a sweet bonus when you return to New Orleans."

My face burned as I left the Raven's Roost and walked across the street to the Beaufoy Hotel. I had already decided to break into Dr. Felix's house, and Frankie wouldn't like it when he found out.

I was so upset that I forgot to tell Frankie about Axel Devereaux posing as Dr. Felix. I would tell Tony tomorrow everything he needed to know about the case. By then, I would have the evidence to put all the bad actors at the Pinebridge Mental Hospital in the slammer.

When I arrived at the Beaufoy Hotel and went upstairs, the lobby was empty. The door to my room was ajar. Someone had been there. I pushed open the door and stepped inside. Something hard and heavy smashed into the back of my head, and it was the last thing I remembered for a while.

Chapter 22

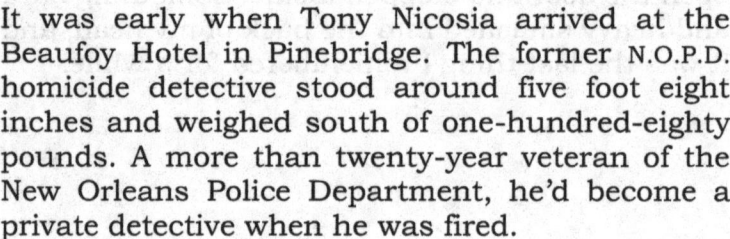

It was early when Tony Nicosia arrived at the Beaufoy Hotel in Pinebridge. The former N.O.P.D. homicide detective stood around five foot eight inches and weighed south of one-hundred-eighty pounds. A more than twenty-year veteran of the New Orleans Police Department, he'd become a private detective when he was fired.

Wyatt Thomas got him his first job as a private investigator. He often worked with Wyatt, though he did many cases independently. He'd become Frankie Castellano's go-to private investigator. Tony had mixed feelings when Frankie called and told him he was hiring him to replace Wyatt.

Wyatt was a pro, and Tony was at the hotel to find out where he was on the case Frankie wanted him to inherit. When he entered the hotel lobby, he found the police trying to calm an older man and woman. Tony bypassed the chaos, going upstairs to Wyatt's room.

The door to Wyatt's hotel room was open, and more police were inside looking for clues. A young woman in a police uniform appeared to be in charge.

"What's going on here?" he asked.

The woman stopped what she was doing and said, "Who are you?"

"Tony Nicosia. Wyatt and I are working for Frankie Castellano. I'm here to replace him and find out where he's at in his investigation."

"I'm Detective Henstooth," the woman said. "We responded to a report about a missing person at the hotel. When we arrived, we realized there were two missing persons. One of them is Wyatt."

"You know Wyatt?" Tony asked.

"There have been two murders since he arrived in Pinebridge, both of them involving the Pinebridge Mental Hospital. Since he and I have parallel interests in the cases, we've worked together."

"I see," Tony said.

"Why are you replacing Wyatt?" Detective Henstooth asked.

"He got crossways with Frankie Castellano, the man who hired him. Frankie sent me to replace him."

"Did he now? Maybe I should talk to Mr. Castellano."

"I'd like to do the same myself. He's not answering his phone."

"Is he in New Orleans?"

"Pinebridge since last night. He had dinner with Wyatt and Celeste Gauthier, the hospital administrator."

"How do you know that?" Detective Henstooth asked.

"Frankie called me last night and explained the situation. He told me he was having dinner with Wyatt and Ms. Gauthier. Something wrong?

"Ms. Gauthier and Mr. Castellano would have been the last two people to see Wyatt before he disappeared. I'll call her."

Tony listened to the one-sided conversation as Detective Henstooth made the call.

"What did she say?" he asked when she put away her phone.

"She said she excused herself after dinner and went home and that it was the last she saw of either Wyatt or Mr. Castellano."

"What time did she leave the restaurant?" he asked.

"Before nine," she said. "Maybe Mr. Castellano returned to New Orleans."

Tony shook his head. "I called his house and talked to his wife. She's also worried because he isn't answering his phone. We need to do something."

"We're in Wyatt's room looking for clues. What else do you suggest we do?"

One of the forensic techs approached them before Tony could answer.

"Found something, Maya," he said.

"What?"

"A bloodspot on the carpet. About five feet inside the door."

"Someone hit Wyatt over the head," Tony said. "He got blood on the carpet when he fell."

Tony started for the door. "Where are you going?" Detective Henstooth asked.

"Downstairs to question the people I saw when I got here."

"Wait," she said. "They're already being questioned."

"Pardon me If I think I can do a better job."

Tony's remark was like a slap in the face to Detective Henstooth. She grasped his shoulder, wheeled him around, and sent him to his knees in pain when she squeezed the pressure point between his thumb and index finger.

"Uncle!" he said. When Detective Henstooth released her grip, Tony sprang to his feet and got in her face. "I'll have your badge for this," he said.

The two beefy forensic techs working in the room witnessed the altercation and grasped Tony's arms, holding him until he stopped struggling.

"What do you want us to do with this crazy son of a bitch?" one of the techs asked.

"Let him go," Detective Henstooth said.

Tony's face was bright red as Detective Henstooth walked out the door and started down the stairs. He followed her. Instead of stopping to talk with the two people still conversing with the police, she exited the hotel.

"Where do you think you're going?" he asked.

"To kick your ass, cuff you and send you to jail if you lay a finger on me," she said.

Tony took a step backward and raised his hands.

"We got off on the wrong foot," he said. "I apologize. You're the boss. I only want to come along for the ride."

"Then let's get one thing straight," she said. "This isn't New Orleans. You're on my turf, and I don't like being disrespected."

Tony grinned and rubbed his sore hand. "I won't make that mistake again, and I said I was sorry. Can't we start over?"

"Fine," she said. "Get in the squad car."

Tony climbed into the passenger seat of the police vehicle.

"What's your name?"

"Detective Henstooth," she said.

"Your first name," he said.

"Maya."

"You're one hell of a police officer, Maya," he said. "I would have been proud to work beside you while on the force."

Tony extended his hand. Maya nodded and shook it. "Just don't get in the way," she said.

Tony smiled again. "It's been a long time since anyone said that to me. Where are we going?"

"Billy Williams's house," Maya said.

"Who is he?"

"The grandson of Mr. Castellano's half-sister. Wyatt spent the night before last at Bella Donna Castellano's cottage in the Kisatchie National Forest. He and Wyatt intended to break into the house of Dr. Felix, the head doctor at the hospital."

"For what reason?" Tony asked.

"Things are happening at the hospital: abuse, unauthorized medical procedures, the list goes on. Billy had helped a patient escape from the hospital. She is non-verbal but told Billy by sign language that Dr. Felix recorded every dirty deed he participated in and that the records are locked in a vault in his bedroom."

"Frankie didn't tell me any of this," Tony said.

"Wyatt didn't tell you?"

"My wife Lil and I just returned from Italy on a second honeymoon. I was unavailable when Frankie learned about his half-sister."

"Why did Mr. Castellano stop trusting Wyatt?" Maya said.

"Frankie doesn't trust anyone," Tony said. "Not even me. That's not the problem."

"Then what is?"

"Wyatt speaks his mind and probably said something that pissed Frankie off. He didn't tell me what had happened between them."

It started raining when Maya pulled into the abandoned parking lot near Billy Williams's house. Tony lagged behind when Maya headed across the vacant field. Maya stopped and waited for him.

"You okay?" she asked.

"I had knee surgery a while back," he said. "It still gets stiff when I sit too much."

Maya waited for him to catch up to her. "It isn't far. Can you make it?"

"I'm slow but right behind you," he said.

The door to Billy's house was open, and his black cat was lying on the bed. Maya and Tony wheeled around when someone came through the door.

"What are you doing here?" Billy Williams asked.

"Have you seen Wyatt?" Maya asked.

"Not since yesterday," Billy said. "Why?"

"He's missing." Billy's head dropped. "You know something, don't you?" Maya said.

"Wyatt was at my house when I got home yesterday. He said he was having dinner with Celeste and Grandmother's half-brother at the Raven's Roost. He wanted me to pick him up at the hotel at nine to check out Dr. Felix's house. I waited outside till I realized he wasn't coming out, and then went to his room and found the door open. Wyatt wasn't there."

Maya glanced at Tony and said, "I think Wyatt has been kidnapped."

"And ditto for Frankie," Tony said.

Maya turned to Billy and said, "Did Wyatt tell you anything else that might be important?"

"He'd come from Celeste's office, where she had introduced him to Dr. Felix. He told me something that didn't seem quite right."

"Like what?" Tony said.

"He said Dr. Felix wasn't really Dr. Felix."

Tony glanced briefly at Maya and said," Then who was he?"

"Wyatt said he was Axel Devereaux, Harper's father."

"Are you sure?" Maya asked.

Billy nodded. "Wyatt said they were roommates in college."

"What else did he tell you?" Tony asked.

"That's all," Billy said. "He could see I wasn't fully understanding what he was telling me."

Tony asked Maya, "What the hell is this supposed to mean?"

"Dr. Felix lives on an estate on the edge of town that can only be described as a castle. Wyatt wondered how Dr. Felix could purchase such an expensive property on a public servant's salary. What Billy just told us could explain things."

"How so?" Tony asked.

"According to Wyatt, the Devereauxs are wealthy and politically connected. Axel was appointed the Louisiana Board of Mental Health Director soon after graduating college."

"No doubt about their wealth. They are possibly the richest family in Louisiana. The Devereauxs are as powerful as they come. He probably got his buddy Felix the job with the Pinebridge Mental Hospital," Tony said.

"And purchased the estate during his frequent visits to the hospital," Maya said. "I'll call headquarters and have them do a record search of the property and find out who the real owner is."

"Celeste Gauthier left the restaurant early last night. By all accounts, she left Wyatt and Frankie alone."

"My guess is Mr. Castellano ended up at Celeste's house," Maya said.

"What makes you think so?" Tony asked.

"Kayla Duhon, a student at Pinebridge College and waitress at the Raven's Roost, is Celeste's main squeeze when Harper Devereaux isn't in town. She probably took Frankie to Celeste's house after Wyatt walked across the street to the Beaufoy Hotel."

"What about the third missing person?" Tony asked.

"Dot Beaufoy," Maya said. "She's the hotel's nighttime desk clerk."

"Why would someone kidnap the nighttime desk clerk of the hotel?" Tony asked.

"Because she hacked into the hospital's database looking for evidence to help Wyatt," Maya said. "The system detected a breach, locked her out, and traced her location."

Maya nodded when Tony said, "Did Wyatt tell you that?"

"He said she was frightened out of her mind and was worried the F.B.I. would arrest her. It wasn't the feds worrying Wyatt. He feared the hospital goons would come looking for her and asked me to post security around the hotel."

"Why didn't you?" Tony asked.

"I did," Maya said. "Don't know why they weren't there when the kidnappings occurred."

"Doesn't matter now," Tony said. "What goons are you talking about?"

"The hospital employs three attendants who aren't part of the medical staff," Maya said.

"What do they do?" Tony asked.

"Muscle the most mentally ill patients when they get out of line. They work directly for Dr. Felix. Wyatt and I suspect they're responsible for at least one of the murders and all of the abuse happening in the hospital."

"Then the hospital is the common denominator tying all the kidnappings together," Tony said.

"And Dr. Felix and his attendants are the bad guys," Maya said.

"Bingo," Tony said.

"And if Wyatt, Dot Beaufoy, and Frankie Castellano aren't already dead, they're probably in a padded cell at the hospital or Dr. Felix's house," Maya said. "I'll get a search warrant."

"No," Tony said. "Wyatt, Frankie, and Dot Beaufoy will be nowhere near either place by the time you get the warrant."

"Where would they be?" Maya asked.

"Alligator bait at the bottom of some bayou. We have to think of another way to rescue them."

"We can't get into either the hospital wards or Felix's house without someone knowing," Maya said. "What do you suggest?"

"Don't know, but time's probably running out, and we need to think of something," Tony said.

"I have an idea that might work," Billy said.

210

Chapter 23

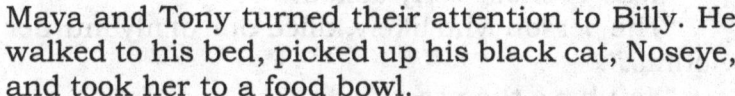

Maya and Tony turned their attention to Billy. He walked to his bed, picked up his black cat, Noseye, and took her to a food bowl.

"Don't keep us in suspense," Maya said.

"You know Wyatt and I helped a patient escape from the hospital," Billy said.

"He told me," Maya said.

"Her name is Lyrica Winter. She is non-verbal and communicates only by signing."

"What about her?" Tony said.

"Rica isn't dangerous, though the attendants kept her in the padded cells where they keep the most dangerous patients. She also spent time at Dr. Felix's house and knows both places."

"Wyatt and the others will be locked down. Even if she finds them, how will they escape?" Tony said.

"Locked doors are no problem for Rica," Billy said. "She can enter and leave any room."

"How does she do that?" Tony asked.

"Don't know, though I know for a fact she has the power," Billy said."

"She already rescued Wyatt once," Maya said. "He was locked in the basement of the hospital. She found him and unlocked the door. That's when he took her to Billy's."

"Where is she now?" Tony asked.

"My grandmother's house."

"Will you take us there?" Maya asked.

"Wyatt rescued Rica. There's nothing I wouldn't do for him," Billy said. "Let's go."

Maya and Tony followed Billy in his old truck out of Pinebridge. They soon drove past Alligator Bayou and Kool Point Landing.

"The bayou is creepy," Tony said. "Looks like a perfect place to get rid of a body."

"Inga Talledaga has a cabin near here," Maya said.

"Who is she?" Tony asked.

"The person who likely killed one of my murder victims."

"You have the proof?"

"Enough to know she probably did it," Maya said. "You like catfish?"

"Love it," Tony said. "I missed breakfast and would like nothing better right about now."

"The best catfish in Louisiana is served at a little restaurant near here."

"Doesn't look like Billy's going to stop. Where is he taking us?"

"Bella Donna Castellano, Billy's grandmother and Frankie Castellano's half-sister, lives in a cottage in the Kisatchie National Forest," Maya said.

"Damn!" Tony said. "Finding his half-sister is why Frankie sent Wyatt here in the first place. How the hell did this get so complicated?"

"He'd accomplished that mission," Maya said.

"Why didn't he tell Frankie? He could have collected his bonus and gone home. Frankie would have been over the moon." Tony asked.

"You don't know Wyatt as well as you think," Maya said.

"He's one of a kind. No doubt about that. Doesn't matter because finding Frankie's sister just got relegated to the back burner."

"That's a fact," Maya said. "Billy's turning off the blacktop. I don't even see a hog trot trail. Where is he taking us?"

"The middle of nowhere," Tony said.

"Amen to that," Maya said.

Maya followed Billy's old truck down a barely visible path through a forest of majestic pine trees. She was beginning to think they were lost when they entered a clearing in the forest. In the middle of a manicured garden set a magical stone cottage that looked more like a house someone might find in England than in Louisiana.

Billy stopped his truck, and Maya parked beside him.

"This must be it," she said.

Several friendly dogs bounded off the porch to greet them, their tails wagging when Billy rubbed their heads. Three smiling women occupied rockers on the anomalous wooden porch.

"Cottages don't have porches," Maya said.

"This one does," Tony said. "Works for me."

Maya and Tony approached the women on the porch. "I'm Maya Henstooth, and this is Tony Nicosia," she said.

"We've been expecting you. I'm Bella Donna. This is my daughter Wanda, and the pretty young thing is Lyrica Winter."

"Did Billy call and tell you we were coming?" Maya asked.

"Didn't have to. We all sensed something bad had happened to Wyatt."

"You know Wyatt?"

"He spent the night with us after rescuing Lyrica from the bad people at the hospital. He's a wonderful person."

"Wyatt has been kidnapped," Billy said. "We think he is either at the hospital or Dr. Felix's house."

"Your half-brother Frankie was also kidnapped," Maya said.

Rica had Billy's attention and was signing frantically.

"We need to wait until after dark," Billy said. "Rica and I will go to the hospital to look for Wyatt and the others."

"I'll go with you," Tony said. "Even if you find them, you'll need some muscle to help get them out."

"Don't leave me out of this," Maya said.

Rica and Billy began signing again. When they finished, Billy said, "Rica will enter the hospital alone. The staff is used to seeing her roaming the halls. No one will question her presence if she's spotted. If she finds Wyatt and the others, she'll lead them out of the hospital to my truck."

"Your truck isn't big enough to bring everyone out," Maya said. "Rica can come with me. I'll intervene if she has a problem getting out of the hospital."

"We can't go until after dark," Billy said. "I'll think about it,"

"It won't be dark for hours," Bella Donna said. "Wanda and Rica have a pot of chicken and dumplings on the stove. Anyone hungry?"

"Don't have to ask me twice," Tony said.

The wonderful aroma from the kitchen was enticing as Tony and Maya sat at a large table waiting to eat. They were soon feasting on bowls of chicken and dumplings.

"Best I've ever tasted," Maya said. "My grandmother couldn't have made them any better."

"Happy to hear it," Bella Donna said.

"Rica and I have decided we don't need help," Billy said. "Your presence might cause more problems than they solve. When it gets dark, we'll go alone."

"Wait just a minute," Maya said. "I'm the police and the one calling the shots. I'm going."

"So am I," Tony said.

"Let Billy and Rica take care of it," Bella Donna said. "There's a reason."

"What reason?" Maya asked.

"Darkness is still hours away," Bella Donna said. "I'm a scotch drinker. What about you, Tony?"

"I could use a scotch," Tony said. "Neat."

Bella Donna smiled. "Just the way I like it. Maya?"

"I don't drink," she said.

"How about a glass of tea?" Bella Donna asked.

"I'm already drinking tea," Maya said.

"Mom makes a chilled herbal tea that's to die for," Wanda said. "Like to try it?"

"Why not?" Maya said.

Wanda soon served drinks, scotch for Tony and Bella Donna, and herbal tea for Maya. Tony was the first to respond.

"You spiked my scotch," he said.

Maya's cheeks were beginning to go numb, psychedelic floaters dancing in her eyeballs.

"And my tea," she said.

"There's a reason," Bella Donna said. "You are both alphas and want to call the shots. Billy and Lyrica need to do this alone. Besides, there are other reasons to stay here after dark."

Tony had dozed off in his chair, the last of his drink spilling on the cottage's wood floor. Maya was numb but fighting it, though without much luck. Time seemed to stand still. Outside the cottage, the wind was gusting through the pines.

"It's time," Billy said. "Rica and I are going."

"Be careful," Wanda said.

Tony and Maya faded in and out of consciousness unable to move from their chairs as the storm outside intensified.

"What's my little brother like?" Bella Donna asked.

"Rich. Powerful. I can tell you're related," Tony said.

"Did you know my dad?" Bella Donna asked.

Tony's words were low and drawn out. "I was with Paco when he died," he said.

"You're making that up," Bella Donna said.

"Your brother is a talented musician. He could have been a famous trumpeter."

"Could have?" Bella Donna said.

"Paco took your brother's horn and hid it because he wanted him to focus on the family business and not on music. When Frankie got old enough to do something about it, he hired me to find his trumpet."

Tony nodded when Bella Donna said, "You found it for him?"

"When Frankie took control of the family business, he had Paco confined to a nightclub in Metairie. Paco was in bad physical condition, on a bed, when I found him. He told me where to find the trumpet and then died in my arms. He had a white cat lying on the bed with him."

"You sure?" Bella Donna asked. He would never allow me to have a pet."

"He mellowed in his old age and sickness," Tony said.

"People tell me he was mean and vindictive. I never saw that side of him," Bella Donna said.

"Keep your fond memories of him," Tony said. "It isn't up to me to tell you something different."

Bella Donna glanced at Wanda, and she brought Tony another scotch.

"Is it drugged?" he asked.

"Only with alcohol," Bella Donna said. "Billy and Lyrica needed to go to the hospital alone. Now that they're gone, it's okay for you to return to normal."

Wanda brought Maya a glass of sweetened iced tea.

"I'm not drinking this," she said.

"The drug I gave you in the first glass of tea was mild and harmless. It will soon leave your system completely. You need to be here and not at the hospital."

"But why?" Maya asked.

"Your last name is Henstooth. This enchanted cottage belonged to Efy Henstooth. Efy was a witch and taught me everything I know. Though I'm not a witch, you are."

"You are full of it," Maya said. "I'm not a witch. I'm a Baptist."

"Despite what you believe, you can't change who you really are," Bella Donna said. "Efy brought you here because she wants to talk to you."

"You said Efy is dead."

"Spirits abound. You only have to look for them," Bella Donna said. "Efy is in this room at this very minute."

Thunder shook the roof, proving the storm outside the cottage was still strong. Bella Donna, and Billy's cats were asleep in the cat bed in front of the massive stone fireplace. Flames crackled in the hearth. A gust of wind blew down the chimney, lighting an explosion of sparkling embers and dull gray smoke. When the smoke disappeared, an old black woman stood before the fireplace. She smiled and approached the chair where Maya was sitting.

"I'm Efy," she said. "Don't be frightened."

"Where did you come from?" Maya asked.

"I live in this house, though my presence isn't always apparent," Efy said.

"Are you a ghost?"

"Spirit of the night," Efy said.

"What do you want from me?" Maya asked.

"To tell you something you haven't heard. Like me, you're a witch with certain powers that will become available to you as you grow older and learn how to employ them."

"You're crazy," Maya said.

"You have powers. Surely, you've felt them," Efy said.

"I have no clue what you're talking about and no special powers."

Efy pointed her hand at a candle burning on the fireplace's mantle. A flame burst from her finger, and the candle melted into molten wax.

"Try it," Efy said.

Maya pointed her finger at the melted wax. Nothing happened.

"I'm not a witch," Maya said. "I have no powers. I've never heard of you. How are you related to me?"

"Baptists don't like witches," Efy said. "I was banished and forgotten by your family long before you were born. I was a slave before the Civil War."

"Like I said. You're crazy. You're a figment of my imagination. A mental remnant of whatever drug Wanda gave me."

"You're wrong, baby. Now, I must go, though we will meet again."

When thunder struck, Efy disappeared in an explosion of smoke. As the smoke cleared, Wanda brought Tony more scotch and Maya another iced tea.

"I hope you haven't signed Billy and Lyrica's death warrants by not allowing Tony and I to accompany them to the hospital," Maya said.

"Destiny isn't a plan," Bella Donna said. "It's what happens. Like it or not, remaining with us is your destiny."

Chapter 24

My head ached when I opened my eyes, and I didn't know where I was. A dim light barely illuminated the small room I occupied. It took me a moment to realize I was in a padded cell, probably in the Louisiana Mental Hospital.

The tiny room smelled like a sewer. There was no window, door, toilet, or sink, only the off-white walls saturated by decades or more of urine, excrement, and blood. Remembering my recent stay in the dark basement of the hospital, I grew increasingly claustrophobic.

A primal scream emanating from a vent at the top of the cell rocked my sanity to the core, and it caused me to remember the haunting sounds I'd heard the first night I'd arrived in Pinebridge and followed Celeste on a shortcut through the psych ward of the hospital.

I spent the next hour feeling the walls, searching for a seam or some way out of the cell from hell. Finding none, I sat on the floor, propping my back against the crusty padded wall, trying to meditate to slow my racing heart.

Hours must have passed as I listened to the screams, wails, and cries for help emanating from the cells in the psych ward. As my senses grew more attuned to the darkness and solitude, I began discerning individual voices from the lone vent. I heard the gentle weeping of a woman as she chanted a Catholic prayer I recognized. It was the voice of a very distressed Dot Beaufoy. I stood below the vent and called to her.

"Dot, can you hear me?"

"Oh my God, Wyatt. Please get me out of here," she said.

"I'm also locked in a cell. Stay calm. Someone will get us out," I said.

Dot's voice trembled when she said, "I'm trying, but it's not working. I'm going to die. I know it."

"Stay strong, Dot. If you can't do it for yourself, do it for your kids and husband. Someone will come for us. I promise."

Another captive patient heard us talking and called out. It was Frankie Castellano.

"Wyatt, is that you?"

"It's me," I said. "How did you get here?"

"I think I've died and gone to hell," he said. "This cell smells like a shithole."

I was upset that Frankie hadn't answered my question, so I asked another.

"Are you hurt?"

"Somebody knocked the hell out of me. I was lying on the floor in this shithole when I came to," he said.

"Did someone take you from your room at the hotel?"

"The pretty little waitress Kayla had drinks with me when you left the restaurant. She convinced me to go with her to Celeste's house."

"Let me guess. They drugged you."

"I feel like an idiot," Frankie said. "Adele will divorce me if she ever finds out."

"She's probably worried sick, and I'm sure she's called the cops," I said. "Stay cool. It's a matter of time before help arrives."

Someone other than the mental patients must have heard our conversation because the door of my padded cell opened. Two people I recognized, and one I didn't, came through the door.

Inga Talledaga was as tall as I was. Grabbing my shoulders and wheeling me around, she pushed me into the hands of Bud Johnson. He backhanded me, breaking my lip and bloodying my nose.

Johnson was six inches taller than me and weighed two hundred pounds of solid muscle. Before falling, I scraped a fingernail across his huge forearm, decorated with crimson tattoos. He had the eyes of a reptile, and I half expected him to hiss at me. A second man, who I didn't recognize, yanked me off the floor.

I caught a fleeting glimpse of the swastikas on Hank Bauer's arms as he worked me over with the back of his hand. I lay in a crumpled mass on the floor of the cell when the three attendants grew tired of hitting and kicking me.

Inga ripped my shirt sleeve and injected me with a hypodermic needle. I grew instantly groggy, though coherent enough to realize the two men were wrapping me in a strait-jacket. I was too out of it to struggle when they lifted me onto a gurney and covered me with a sheet.

They wheeled me out the backdoor, where a hospital van awaited. The ensuing trip took about twenty minutes. Hank Bauer, Inga Talledaga, and Bud Johnson rolled me into a dark garage, empty except for the hospital van. After wheeling me into an elevator and pushing a button, I watched the door close.

They didn't answer when I said, "Where are you taking me?"

After exiting the elevator, I was pushed into a hallway. The wood flooring, carved baseboards, and flocked wallpaper told my drug-altered brain that I was in an eloquent and expensive house. When we reached a door, Hank Bauer knocked and waited for someone to respond.

"Enter," a voice inside the door said.

The attendants wheeled me into a large room with Oriental rugs covering the wood floors, expensive leather furniture, and all the trappings of a men's club's main lounging area. After being lifted off the gurney, I stood before two men smoking cigars and enjoying cocktails. Even in a state of drugged grogginess, I recognized them. At least, I thought I did.

Dr. Felix looked identical to the man beside him except for his beard and mustache. The man I'd thought was Axel Devereaux was Dr. Felix. It meant Dr. Felix was Axel's twin brother.

Dr. Felix looked at the attendants and said, "You're dismissed. Dr. Devereaux and I will handle things from here."

The picture became suddenly clearer. Dr. Felix was Felix Devereaux, which explained why he hadn't recognized me when I met him in Celeste's office. He was also probably Emma Duhon's ex-husband and Kayla Duhon's father. It also pegged both he and Axel Devereaux as child abusers and Harper and Kayla as first cousins.

"You've become quite the pest, Mr. Thomas," Axel Devereaux said. "You should have returned to New Orleans when you had the chance."

He smirked when I said, "I hadn't finished my job."

"Well, it's finished now," he said. "The person we sought is in a cell at the hospital, and you will soon suffer an even worse fate than him."

Axel Devereaux nodded when I said, "Frankie Castellano?"

"Frankie's father caused quite a stir when he interceded with the Governor," he said. "Years have passed since the incident occurred, though we haven't forgotten."

"We had to take extraordinary measures to right the ship," Felix Devereaux said. "Now, Mr. Castellano will pay for his father's indiscretions."

"Frankie is a powerful man. His wife and his staff know he is in Pinebridge. You won't get away with harming him," I said.

Felix Devereaux smiled. "Frankie molested Kayla and Ms. Gauthier."

I looked at him and said, "Don't tell me. You filmed Frankie Castellano having sex with your daughter. How can you live with yourself?"

Axel Devereaux pressed a button on the chair and waited for one of the attendants to reply.

"Yes, sir," Bud Johnson said.

"Return to the study. We have questions."

Hank Bauer, Inga Talledaga, and Bud Johnson soon stood beside me.

Felix Devereaux acted as if they weren't even present when he said, "How I live is no concern of yours."

Axel Devereaux grinned when I asked, "What about you? Your daughter Harper isn't aware of what's happening at the hospital. How do you intend to keep her silent?"

"Harper is a beautiful woman," he said. "It would be a necessary shame if I had to silence her voice. Doesn't matter because her gorgeous body would still belong to me."

"You're sick," I said.

I recoiled when Inga Talledaga backhanded me. "You can't talk to Dr. Devereaux like that," she said.

"It's okay," Axel said. "Seems as if Mr. Thomas has too much testosterone. I look forward to putting him under the scalpel tonight to remedy his condition."

"Can't wait," Felix said. "We haven't performed in the amphitheater in ages."

"And there's no better time than tonight," Axel said.

"I'm excited," Felix said. "Inga has worked hard arranging the banquet."

"My pleasure," Inga said.

"Frankie Castellano will be the show's star and Mr. Thomas the best supporting actor," Felix said.

"And our admiring community will be here to watch our performance," Axel said. "How is your R.S.V.P. list?"

"Everyone is excited about the banquet and performance as you are," Inga said.

Plans for my imminent demise weren't what I was prepared to hear.

"Frankie is as powerful as you are," I said. "It won't stop him from coming after you, even if you successfully send him to prison."

"Mr. Castellano will never leave the hospital, and the only prison in his future will be in his own mind," Axel said.

"How do you intend to get away with that?" I asked.

"After committing the heinous acts on Ms. Gauthier and my defenseless daughter, Mr. Castellano lost his mind," he said. "Back in the day, we'd have said went insane."

"Frankie isn't insane," I said.

"He will be when we notify the authorities," Axel said.

"We used to do lobotomies," Felix said. "Now, there are chemicals that provide the same results."

"You're crazy," I said. "You'll never get away with it."

I felt the blood trickle down my face when Bud Johnson slapped me again.

"You won't be so lucky," Felix Devereaux said. "a full-frontal lobotomy is in your future, and you'll live out your days in one of the stinking cells you just came from and minus your family jewels."

"No one's going to believe Frankie lost his mind," I said.

"Au contraire, Mr. Thomas. When it's aired, the video of his attack will convince everyone. Even his loving wife will have no compunction about locking him in a padded cell for life."

"The Castellano's will get their just reward, and Axel and I will have our revenge," Felix Devereaux said. "And we'll have some fun along the way."

"I'm not Frankie Castellano, though someone will report me missing if I don't return to New Orleans," I said.

"Bertram Picou?" Axel Devereaux said. "He's as expendable as you are."

"Bertram isn't the only person who'll know I'm missing. Frankie hired Tony Nicosia to take my place in the investigation."

"Mr. Nicosia and his wife, Lil, are both expendable," Felix said.

"Maybe so, though you won't find him as easily as you found me," I said.

Axel glanced at Bud Johnson and asked, "What's the story on Tony Nicosia?"

"Another private dick Castellano hired," Bud Johnson said.

"Go get him and bring him here," Axel said.

"We can't find him," Hank Bauer said.

"How can that be?" asked.

"We located his car in the parking lot of one of the hotels on the edge of town. The attendant said he missed his reservation and never checked in. We've checked with people everywhere, and no one has seen him."

"Impossible. People don't just disappear," Felix said. "Pinebridge is a small town. Find him and bring him to us."

"Tony isn't simply a private investigator," I said. "He was the former chief N.O.P.D. homicide detective, and he'll soon see right through your deception."

"Not if we find him first," Axel said.

Devereaux's reply was forceful, though even in my grogginess, I detected the concern in his voice.

"Too many people know what's going on at the hospital," I said. "What's to stop your own employees from turning on you?"

Axel glanced at Inga and said, "You like women more than men, don't you?"

"Yes, sir," she said.

"Remove your blouse," he said.

We watched as the big woman unbuttoned and removed her denim blouse.

"And your bra," Felix said.

Inga's bra dropped to the floor.

"Come here," Axel said.

Inga stood before Axel and Felix Devereaux and remained stoic as the two fondled her large breasts.

"If I asked you to perform a particular sex act on my brother, what would you do?" Felix asked.

"Whatever you desire, I'm your servant," she said.

Axel tossed Inga's blouse and bra at her. "Put your clothes back on. As you can see, Mr. Thomas, our people are ready to die for us."

"Stop your madness," I said. "You have enough political clout to wriggle out of this situation without making matters worse."

"You're right about that," Axel said. "I could shoot someone in broad daylight on Canal Street and wouldn't be convicted of any crime. You and Mr. Nicosia are little more than human mosquitoes that must be swatted. We have you and will soon have your partner in our custody."

"Louisiana mosquitoes aren't always dealt with so simply," I said.

Neither Felix nor Axel responded to my feeble attempt at humor.

"You have less than a few hours to contemplate your situation," Felix said.

Inga, Bud, and Hank returned me to the gurney and started away down the hall when Inga's cell phone rang.

"Nicosia was spotted near the hospital. Let's return this asshole to his cell."

Chapter 25

My eyes opened to someone calling my name, and I immediately sensed a foul stench. The three attendants had returned me to the same stinking cell I had last occupied, and Dot Beaufoy's voice called through the vent.

"Wyatt, please answer me."

I struggled to move, leaning against the wall beneath the vent.

"Dot, I'm okay."

"I listened to the beating I heard you taking. Then you disappeared. I thought you were dead."

"I'm alive," I said. "How are you doing?"

"I haven't stopped praying since those people abducted me from the hotel and brought me here. Someone took your friend."

"Frankie?" I asked.

"The same people who beat you took him. I tried calling him. He doesn't answer."

"I have no clue how long we've been here, but I do know that by now, Maya knows we're missing and has the police looking for us."

"What about your friend?"

"Frankie is important, and his disappearance won't go unnoticed. Whoever's responsible will be sorry they abducted him. I promise you."

After meeting with Felix and Axel Devereaux, I wasn't sure about my claim. It seemed to positively affect Dot because when she spoke, I could almost hear the renewed hope in her voice. Neither Felix nor Axel had mentioned her, which could only mean they weren't worried about her telling anyone what was occurring at the hospital.

It probably meant her parents, husband, and children were safe, although her death sentence had probably already been signed. The thought discouraged me because there was absolutely nothing that I could do about it.

She must have fallen asleep from exhaustion because she stopped talking. In the darkness of my cell, I couldn't tell if it was daylight or dark. When the other patients in the ward began their nightly cacophony, I realized they somehow knew it was night. I fell asleep to their moans, groans, and unearthly wails. When Dot Beaufoy's cries resounded over the other noises, I awoke with a start.

"Wyatt, are you there?"

"I'm here," I said.

"Oh, my God!" My door is opening. They're coming for me!"

"Stay strong, Dot. They have no reason to harm you. You'll be okay."

I kept my ear to the wall, hearing the struggle as Inga Talledaga and her two cohorts took Dot. One thing gave me hope: the inevitable wasn't yet due. There was still time for something positive to happen.

If Axel and Felix planned to castrate me before an adoring crowd, Dot and Frankie would probably be chemically lobotomized at the same event, and hours remained for something or someone to save us. The thought managed to give me a measure of hope while scaring the hell out of me.

Sliding down the wall, I covered my eyes with my hands, feeling helpless and worried that my situation was hopeless. The horrible stench of the padded cell did nothing to relieve my anxiety as I awaited the arrival of the three attendants to take me to the van.

I fell asleep sometime after closing my eyes. I was still in the same cell when I awoke, which left me wondering why Inga and her crew hadn't come for me. They weren't there, though I wasn't alone. Rica was kneeling beside me and shaking my shoulder. I smiled when I saw her, and she returned my smile.

The door to the cell was open. I gathered myself off the padded cell floor, clutched Rica's hand, and allowed her to pull me into the dark hallway. I was still wondering about Dot and Frankie. Maybe I was mistaken about Inga and the others taking them.

"Dot Beaufoy and Frankie Castellano may be in one of the cells," I said. "We have to open them and find out."

Rica was ecstatic as she began opening the doors to the padded cells. The mental patients began moving into the hall. They followed Rica to the door leading to the hospital reception area and began filing out of the hallway and into the hospital reception area as a disorganized unit. Rica put up her hand, stopping me from following them. She started in the opposite direction and motioned for me to follow her instead.

The backdoor to the cemetery was the same one I had taken with Celeste when we discovered Oliver Marshall's murder. The sky was dark, with thick clouds covering the moon and the stars. The air was humid, and I sensed it was about to rain. It would be a relief after hours of sweating in the hot cell.

Billy was waiting outside the door for us, and his embrace with Rica lasted over a minute. When Rica pulled away, she began signing frantically.

"All hell's about to break loose," he said.

"What?" I asked.

"Prison break. I heard a commotion and looked around the front to see what was happening. Someone opened the doors to the padded cells and let the patients loose." Rica smiled and nodded when he said, "Was it you?"

I could only imagine the shock of the people in the hospital waiting room as fifty mental patients, some of them naked and coated with their own excrement and urine, burst through the door. They probably reacted to the appearance of the disturbed patients as if they were suddenly participants in a horror movie.

The people waiting in the reception area were horrified when the wild mob filled the lobby. The receptionist frantically called Celeste, who couldn't believe her eyes when she hurried from her office to see what was happening. She quickly punched a number into her cell phone.

"Inga, we have an emergency on our hands. Where the hell are you?"

Inga's phone went directly to her voicemail. Some patients were already out the front door and headed toward Pinebridge.

"Oh, my God!" the receptionist said. "What'll we do?"

"Call the police," Celeste said. "They are going to wreak havoc if they reach Pinebridge."

Celeste got back on the phone and called Dr. Felix.

"What is it?" he asked.

"Someone let the most mentally disturbed patients out of their cells. They've escaped the building and are on their way to Pinebridge."

"Holy Hell!" Dr. Felix said.

"I can't find Inga, Bud, or Hank," Celeste said. "They aren't answering their phones."

"They are on their way here with our three captives," Dr. Felix said. "They are all participating in tonight's surgical extravaganza."

"Looks as if I'm going to be late," Celeste said.

"As soon as Inga and the others arrive, I'll head them toward Pinebridge," Dr. Felix said.

"Tell them to hurry," Celeste said. "Sirens are blaring and already moving in that direction."

Billy led us to his pickup and cranked the big V8 engine.

"What now?" he asked.

"Is there a television station in Alexandria?" I asked.

"Yes," he said.

"Do you have a phone?"

Billy handed me his phone, and I called for information. I was soon speaking with a television station's news department.

"How can I help you?" the voice on the line asked.

"A mass escape from the Pinebridge Mental Hospital. Fifty severely incapacitated patients are headed toward downtown Pinebridge."

"Can you give me more information," the person who answered my phone call said.

"It's mass chaos in town. You need to get a film crew there right away."

"What else can you tell me?"

"Sorry," I said. "That's all I have."

Billy was laughing when I tried handing him his cell phone.

"Maybe you should call a few radio stations," he said.

"Good idea," I said.

When I finally returned the phone to Billy, he said, "That'll shake things up."

"Big time," I said. "Let Celeste and Dr. Felix try to explain this one."

We soon heard sirens in the distance. Rica and Billy were grinning.

"Someone is going to catch hell over this," he said.

"Let's just hope it isn't us," I said. "Get us the hell out of here."

Billy peeled out of the abandoned parking lot near his house. If the police weren't already dealing with a major issue, they would have arrested us. They had bigger fish to fry and no time to deal with a speeding motorist.

We were soon on the main highway out of town, Billy's truck going eighty miles per hour. He barely slowed when he reached the rural blacktop. He was laughing.

"What?" I asked.

"I wish I were in town to see what panic the escaped patients are causing."

"I was thinking the same thing," I said. "Hopefully, the news stations are arriving to cover it live. Where are you going?"

"To Grandmother's cottage," he said.

"No time. Take me to Dr. Felix's house."

"Too dangerous," Billy said.

"Dot Beaufoy and your mother's half-brother were also prisoners in the psych ward. Inga Talledaga and the other two attendants took them. A banquet is going on, and I suspect all forms of debauchery are taking place. Dr. Felix was going to castrate and lobotomize me and lobotomize Dot and Frankie chemically. They need our help."

"What do you intend to do?" Billy asked.

"Enter the house. Find Dot and Frankie and free them," I said.

"You have a plan to do that?"

I shook my head. "There should be lots of confusion with the banquet going on. Maybe I can get in and out without being noticed."

Billy wheeled the truck around on the blacktop and stepped on the gas, the back wheels spinning wildly before gaining traction and moving us forward in a chaotic burst of speed.

"We can't get to the back fence in the truck. We'll have to hike the rest of the way."

"Is that a problem?" I asked.

"Only if we're chased," he said.

"I need to talk to Maya," I said.

"She and Tony Nicosia are at Grandmother's house," Billy said.

"How do you know?" I asked.

"They followed me there."

Billy nodded when I said, "They're together? After you take me to Dr. Felix's, go to Bella Donna's cottage and get Tony and Maya."

"What can they do?" Billy asked.

"I may need help. Tony will think of something."

"Sure about that?"

"Hell no, but we have to do something," I said.

Billy followed the main highway back to town, finally turning onto a barely discernible trail in the thick clump of hardwood trees growing behind Dr. Felix's estate.

After parking the truck, he said, "It's about a mile from here. This is as close as we can get in the truck. I'll lead you to the fence."

Billy signed for Rica to wait on him. She didn't follow his directions. He fumed as she accompanied us through the thick vegetation to the back of Dr. Felix's estate. Billy lifted me to the top of the fence enclosing the compound. Rica demanded he do the same for her.

"I don't like this," he said.

I grabbed Rica's hand and pulled her to the top of the enclosure when Billy lifted her off the ground. When I turned, I saw the thick hedges, walking paths, and flower gardens that covered the estate.

The large house had lights on, and I heard the muted sound of orchestral music. Dozens of cars were parked in the large drive, the banquet in full swing. I wondered how the doctors intended to explain to participants that the main object of the surgery wasn't going to be there.

"How long will it take you to travel to Bella Donna's and back?" I asked.

"About an hour, more or less," Billy said.

"Rica and I will stay hidden in the hedge until you return with Tony and Maya. Blow your horn three times when you're in place. After that, we're going in."

"I'll do it, but I don't like it," he said.

When Rica blew him a kiss, he nodded and started through the trees to his truck. We found a comfortable spot between the hedges and the fence. As I waited, it became apparent to me that it may already be too late to save Dot and Frankie from being chemically lobotomized. I wished Rica could speak or that I knew sign language so I could discuss it with her. Worrying about the situation served no purpose, so I leaned back against the fence and closed my eyes.

Chapter 26

An unsettling silence, broken only by the faint whisper of the wind through the trees, draped Dr. Felix's estate. The gigantic banquet hall, opulently decorated yet shrouded in darkness, awaited its guests. One by one, they arrived, each clad in an identical deep crimson hooded cowl that draped over their shoulders and obscured their faces.

The cowls bore an intricate emblem: a twisted serpent coiled around a staff, symbolizing their perverse power over Pinebridge Mental Hospital. Without their disguises, Dot Beaufoy would have recognized every guest. Beneath the hoods, their faces were hidden by masks—some blank and expressionless, others carved into grotesque visages. Their identities were hidden, and they liked it that way.

This eerie uniformity created a chilling sense of unity among them as if they were not individuals but parts of a greater, malevolent whole. As they took their seats, the flickering candlelight cast long shadows, turning the hall into a theater of ominous silhouettes.

Standing at the head of the table, Doctors Felix and Axel welcomed them with smiles that didn't reach their eyes. The room buzzed with palpable tension, anticipation mingled with fear, as the guests prepared for the night's forbidden entertainment. Felix and Axel knew the upcoming grotesque spectacle would seal their complicity and bind them even closer to the dark heart of Pinebridge.

The cowled guests and two wealthy doctors weren't the only ones in the large house. Felix had cooks and servants who had worked for him for years. Each of his employees had been indoctrinated into the cult.

The servants were clad in white togas with nothing on underneath, and all were used to being groped while never expressing any emotion or ever speaking a word. Dr. Felix paid his servants well, but any infraction was dealt with harsh punishment. Dr. Felix was drinking wine from a silver chalice when a gorgeous young woman in a toga whispered something in his ear.

The people at the crowded banquet table reacted with applause when he shouted, "Eat, drink, and revel. I have business to attend to but will return shortly."

Dr. Axel followed his brother out of the banquet hall into a small study where Celeste Gauthier was waiting, her expression morose.

"Where have you been?" Dr. Felix said. "The guests are already at the banquet table and excited to witness the impending medical procedures."

"Frankie Castellano and the hotel woman?" Celeste said.

"And Wyatt Thomas," Dr. Axel said.

"Inga didn't take him when she and the others took Castellano and Beaufoy from the hospital," Celeste said. "He isn't here."

"Impossible," Dr. Felix said. "He's in a cell in the basement along with the other two."

"No, he isn't. He escaped with the other patients when someone unlocked their cells."

Dr. Felix yanked his cell phone from his pocket and dialed it. "Inga," he said. "Come to my study."

Someone soon knocked on the door. It was a cowed Inga Talledaga. "Yes, sir," she said.

"Are all three patients ready for the performance?" Dr. Felix asked.

"We don't have Wyatt Thomas," she said.

"Why not?" Dr. Felix asked.

"Castellano is stronger and meaner than he looks and fought us when we took him from his cell. When I tried to inject him with a sedative, he kicked the needle out of my hand and then head-butted Hank and kicked Bud in the shin, practically breaking it. He fought like a demon. Bud and Hank tried to restrain him, and I returned for Dot Beaufoy."

"And?"

"Castellano was still fighting us when we got him into the back of the van. We decided to bring him and Beaufoy here and return for Thomas later. We were heading to the hospital when you called and told us about the patients breaking out of their cells."

"Is it possible you somehow unlocked the cells and forgot to secure them when you left with Mr. Castellano?" Dr. Felix asked.

"No way," Inga said.

"Then how did they get out?" Dr. Axel asked.

Inga was visibly shaken when she said, "I don't know."

Inga's head bobbled when Dr. Felix slapped her. "Unacceptable!" he said.

Besides the handprint on her face, Inga didn't respond except to say she was sorry.

"The guests are all assembled," Dr. Axel said. "What now?"

Dr. Felix frowned and said, "We castrate Castellano and perform a hysterectomy on the woman before lobotomizing them. Celeste, don your cowl and join the party."

"Can't do that," she said. "The hospital is swarming with police and film crews. I must return to make excuses and secure the patients in their cells."

"Do you need Inga, Hank, and Bud?"

"Yes," Celeste said. "I've already had two staff members resign when they saw the escaped patient's condition. The news people are demanding a tour of the facility."

"Do it," Dr. Felix said. "Just don't show them the padded cells."

"That's the first thing they want to see," Celeste said. "We even made the national news."

"Holy hell!" Dr. Felix said.

"That isn't all," Celeste said. "Harper called and is panicking. The Governor's phone is blowing up, and he wants to know what the hell's going on in Pinebridge."

"And?" Axel Devereaux asked.

"She smoothed things over, though I don't know what will happen if she starts nosing around."

"You told us she was under your control," Axel Devereaux said.

"She is, though I've never told her everything we do here," Celeste said. "She's damaged goods, though not stupid."

"You need to do something about your daughter," Dr. Felix said. "She's a Devereaux, just like us. If she's implicated in a scandal, it could prove messy for all of us."

"I'll call and have her meet me here," Dr. Axel said. "It's probably best she disappears for a while."

"This is so unnerving," Dr. Felix said.

"Return to the banquet and have fun," Celeste said. "I'll clean up as much of this mess as possible. There's no smoking gun here. We should be okay."

"Hope you're right," Dr. Felix said.

"The surgeries will put you back in the right state of mind," Celeste said. "I only wish I could be here to witness your brilliance."

"You're right. We'll perform the procedures without anesthetics. Seeing Castellano strapped to the operating table and hearing him screaming his lungs out is what I need right now," Dr. Axel said.

"And our adoring audience will love it," Dr. Felix said.

Billy wasn't happy leaving Rica inside Dr. Felix's compound and exceeded all speed limits on his way to his grandmother's cottage. When he pulled into the clearing where the cottage was located, he found everyone sitting on rockers on the front porch. Maya and Tony reached the door of the truck before Billy exited.

"Where's Lyrica?" Maya asked.

"With Wyatt," Billy said.

"Are they okay?"

"Rica broke Wyatt out of the hospital. I was coming here when he insisted I take him to the back of Dr. Felix's compound."

"Because?"

"The hotel lady and great-uncle Frankie were also prisoners at the psych ward. The attendants took them to Dr. Felix's estate."

"For what reason?" Maya asked.

"There's a party going on with every wealthy and powerful person in the parish present," Billy said. "The doctors intend to perform surgery on Dot Beaufoy and Uncle Frankie."

"How do you know?" Maya said.

"Wyatt told me. We watched some of the guests arriving. They were all dressed the same, in crimson-colored hooded cowls. Their faces were even covered with grotesque masks."

"What makes you think the guests were wealthy and powerful?" Maya asked.

"They were driving cars that are too expensive for most people in the parish to look at, much less to own."

"The cowls make it sound like a cult," Tony said.

"Or a secret society," Maya said. "What else?"

"There was an emblem on their cowls: a snake wrapped around a staff."

"Any cults in Rapides Parish that wear outfits like Billy described?" Tony asked.

"Not that I've heard of," Maya said. "Cults can be dangerous. Secret societies are even more so. Wyatt's going to get killed if he goes in there alone."

"He isn't alone. Rica is with him, and they need your help," Billy said. "Wyatt sent me to get you."

Tony grasped Maya's forearm when she reached for her phone and said, "I'm calling in reinforcements."

"You have no warrant. Remember?" Tony said.

"I don't need a warrant if I believe some innocent person is in imminent danger," Maya said.

"I'm telling you, Maya, the Devereauxs have all their bases covered. Calling in the police will only get you fired. We need to help Wyatt some other way."

"What other way?" she asked.

"Don't know," he said.

"Papa Paco was the most powerful man in Jefferson Parish," Bella Donna said. "He had to call in all his chits to get any action, and it still didn't change how things are done at that God-forsaken hospital."

Billy squeezed his grandmother's hand, a smile creeping across his face.

"I know that look," Wanda said. "What are you grinning about, Billy Williams?"

"Rica wasn't satisfied with letting Wyatt out of his cell. She opened the doors and released all the severely disabled patients."

"You mean the patients in the padded cells?" Bella Donna asked. "Good for her."

"They went out the front door and headed toward Pinebridge," Billy said. "Wyatt called the TV and radio stations to ensure they had film crews to cover the event."

"I'd better call the station and find out what happened," Maya said.

Everyone waited as Maya participated in a mostly one-sided conversation. She was grinning when she put away the phone.

"What?" Tony said.

"Like Billy said, the escaped patients paraded down the main street of Pinebridge with cops, reporters, and the public all getting an eyeful. Glad I was off duty. The police returned them to the hospital, though not before a major PR catastrophe."

"Too bad Grandmother doesn't have a television," Billy said. "Ms. Celeste is probably up to her eyeballs in reporters demanding answers."

"Couldn't have happened to a nicer bunch of people," Bella Donna said.

Billy kissed his mother and grandmother and said, "I'm going to help Wyatt and Rica."

"Please, son, don't get yourself killed," Wanda said.

Billy glanced at Tony and Maya and said, "Coming with me or not?"

"I'm in," Tony said.

"Me too," Maya said.

Maya and Tony followed Billy off of the porch. When Maya climbed behind the wheel of her police cruiser, Tony motioned for her to lower the window.

"I'll ride with Billy and find out more of what Wyatt wants us to do. I'll call you."

"Good idea," Maya said.

Billy's old truck powered out of the yard; Maya followed as Tony held on to the passenger strap.

"What's Wyatt's plan?" he asked.

"Bang on the front door and create a diversion to give him and Rica time to find Dot and my great-uncle to escape the house and get over the back fence. I'll be waiting for them in the trees behind the compound. If we can get on the road before they catch us, they'll never find the cottage in the forest. Wyatt said you and Maya would know what to do."

"We'll make it work," Tony said.

Maya struggled to keep up with Billy as he raced down the main highway toward town. He stopped on the road when he neared the front of Dr. Felix's estate.

"Good luck," Billy said as Tony exited the truck.

"That goes for all of us," Tony said.

"Wyatt and Rica are waiting for me to blow my horn as a signal. When I do, they'll enter the house from the back and search for Dot Beaufoy and my great-uncle. After hearing my horn, enter the compound and make something happen. Good luck, and don't get yourselves killed."

"Same goes for you," Maya said.

When Billy had driven away, Tony said, "What now?"

Maya's determined countenance explained her resolve even before she said, "We wait."

Chapter 27

Rica and I waited in the bushes for what seemed an eternity. I got off the ground when we heard three honks in the distance. We were holding hands, and I squeezed hers.

I knew Rica was non-verbal. I didn't know if she was also deaf. I looked directly at her so she could read my lips if she were.

"It's time," I said. "Ready?"

Dark clouds had begun covering the moon and stars, and I could see that it was only a matter of time before the rain started. Dr. Felix's yard was beautifully manicured, and floodlights illuminated every inch of the compound. I didn't doubt that security cameras were positioned to detect illegal entry. Rica was attuned to the compound's security measures and signaled me to follow her.

Rica was amazing, a human chameleon who could blend with any background. Felix's castle wasn't just big; it was huge, and it took us ten long minutes to reach the backdoor of the estate. There was no door I couldn't open, though I was an amateur compared to Rica. She had only to turn the knob of any door to open it. I don't know how she did it, but I followed her through the backdoor of Dr. Felix's castle.

The back hallway was dark. Rica took my hand and pulled me forward. I couldn't see a thing, and I had no clue how she navigated the darkness. We soon reached a stairway. Rica started up the stairs, and I grabbed the rails for support and followed her. Halfway up, she stopped and turned around, tugging my hand. Since I couldn't ask her what she was doing, I followed her.

Outside, thunder rumbled, shaking the roof. I couldn't remember a spring in Louisiana with as many storms. Rica sensed I was paying attention to something other than her and tugged my hand again. We found a door on the ground floor. Rica passed her hand over the knob, and it opened.

We entered a darkened hallway, and a heavy wooden door with a small window peered into the basement's main room. Dim light flooded the hall from the other side of the door, and I wasn't prepared for what we saw when we stared through it.

The old Charity Hospital in New Orleans had a sunken operating room with several tiers of seats so medical students could observe operations in progress. Axel and Felix Devereaux had recreated the operating room in the gigantic basement. This one lay hauntingly silent like the abandoned operating room in the Charity Hospital.

The basement of Dr. Felix Devereaux's mansion was a nightmare conjured from the darkest corners of the human mind. Cold steel and sterile white walls gleamed under harsh fluorescent lights, casting long shadows that danced like malevolent spirits. Rows of surgical instruments lay on gleaming trays, ready for use in the twisted rituals of the Devereaux twins.

Something else was present on the operating floor: twin movie cameras. New Orleans is a mecca for the motion picture industry, and I'd witnessed many crews filming on the streets of the French Quarter. Devereaux's equipment was fully professional and poised for action, like the French Quarter movie set cameras.

As we followed the hallway past the operating floor, I wondered how many illicit operations Devereaux and Felix had performed there. I also wondered who had witnessed the operations, possibly applauding when the doctor in attendance performed unspeakable medical procedures, and who knows what abominable acts of horror. The thought made my skin crawl.

"The operations haven't started. Maybe we can find Frankie and Dot and get out of here before Dr. Felix and his people arrive," I said.

The hallway led to cells, their doors open, revealing metal O-rings in the walls that must have provided physical restraints for the prisoners awaiting their time on the operating table. I wondered if anesthetics were used or if the operations were part of the physical torture the prisoners were forced to endure.

The hallway led past rows of cells that seemed more dungeon-like and medieval than even the padded cells at the hospital. Rica opened one, casting a pale blue light on the stone wall so I could see the two skeletons, their arm bones still in the grip of the iron restraints lifting them off the floor.

"Holy Hell!" I said.

All the cells were empty, and Frankie and Dot were nowhere to be found.

"They've taken them," I said.

Down the hall, we began to hear sounds coming from the direction of the amphitheater. Someone was chanting. The words, spoken in unison, were slow, rhythmic, and chilling:

By the light of the moon, in the dead of night, we gather here, veiled from sight. In shadows deep, where secrets sleep, the veil will part, and blood shall seep.

Flesh and bone, blood and stone. Our voices rise, a chilling drone. In sacred rites, we seek tonight a glimpse of terror and pure delight.

O darkened lords, hear our plea. Unveil the horrors meant to be. In this hallowed place, we seal our fate, to witness pain, to desecrate.

Sounds of torment, whispers of fear. The time has come; the end is near. With hands that cut and eyes that see, we offer this sacrifice, so let it be.

"Someone is chanting as they fill the seats in the amphitheater," I said. "We may be too late."

We returned toward the amphitheater, creeping silently through the dimly lit corridor. Rica's mental sirens sounded, and she communicated with me through rapid hand signals. Her eyes were wide with fear, though also determination.

"Almost there," I said.

Rica nodded, her fingers flying in response. Ahead, the muffled sound of chanting grew louder, my heart pounding as we reached the door to the amphitheater.

Through the window in the door, we could see the cult members in their crimson cloaks sitting in the amphitheater's tiered seating. Frankie Castellano and Dot Beaufoy lay on operating tables, and for a moment, I feared we were too late. Camera operators dressed in white togas had manned the cameras, and Doctors Felix and Axel, dressed in flowing black robes, were taking their bows and playing to the adoring crowd.

Frankie Castellano lay naked on an operating gurney and appeared unconscious. He was lying on his stomach, and from the swollen whelps on his back, he had endured a brutal flogging.

Dot Beaufoy was beneath a rubber sheet on the gurney beside Frankie's. It seemed to mean Frankie's impending operation was first in line.

Rica and I needed to do something. When I saw the three attendants on the operating room floor, any action on our part seemed hopeless, as they were armed with handguns and what looked like automatic weapons.

～〜✕〜〜

Tony and Maya waited in her squad car, in the shadows, outside Dr. Devereaux's compound. An armed guard controlled the front gate and continued opening the door for late arrivals.

When they heard Billy's honking in the distance, Tony said, "How are we going to get into the compound?"

"The guard will open the door for the police," Maya said.

"Don't bet on it," Tony said.

When a late arrival drove up to the gate, the storm had intensified, and rain practically obscured the entrance to the compound. Without turning on the lights of her car, Maya pulled in behind the late arrival. When the gate opened, and the vehicle passed through, Maya followed it. Realizing what had happened, the angry guard rushed out of the control booth.

"What now?" Tony asked.

Maya handed him a pair of handcuffs. "We restrain him."

When the guard banged on the window of Maya's squad car, she lowered it, grabbed his collar, and banged his head against the doorframe. Tony hurried out of the passenger seat and cuffed the man while he was still groggy. He and Maya dragged him to the control booth.

"Remove the cuffs," Maya said.

Tony did a doubletake and said, "You crazy?"

"I can't go in there in a police uniform. Get his shirt and jacket off," Maya said.

Maya stripped off her shirt and donned the guard's uniform. The man was still unconscious when Tony cuffed him, stuffed a rag in his mouth, and covered him with a blanket.

"What about me?" Tony said.

"You'll be my prisoner."

"Good idea. Let's do it," Tony said.

Maya banged on the front door of Dr. Felix's house until a man dressed in a toga opened it. Seeing Maya's security guard uniform, he allowed them to enter.

"I caught someone nosing around outside. I need to lock him up somewhere," Maya said.

Maya and Tony were drenched from the rain falling in waves outside the door. The doorman looked shocked as they dripped water on the floor, and Maya's pistol was stuffed into Tony's back.

"The cells are in the basement," the man said.

"How do I get there?" Maya asked.

"Down the hall to the stairs. The door to the basement is at the foot of the stairs, though the performance has begun, and you can't take him there."

"Why not?" Maya asked.

"Dr. Felix doesn't like his performances disturbed."

"Then where can we put him?"

"Follow me," the man said. "We can lock him in a closet until the performance ends."

The man in the toga had a set of keys and used them to open a closet near the kitchen. When he walked inside, Maya knocked him cold with her revolver, took his keys, and shut the door on him."

Maya and Tony found the stairs and hurried down them to the door the man in the toga had described. Even through the closed door, they could hear the chants from the basement.

"You ready?" Tony asked.

"Now or never," Maya said.

❧

Doctors Felix and Axel had stoked the audience's passions, and their chants echoed against the bare walls. The Devereaux twins were happy to oblige and flipped Frankie onto his back to the roaring approval of the gallery.

Olga Talledaga, Hank Bauer, and Bud Johnson set their machine guns aside and hurried to help secure Frankie. As Rica and I watched through the window in the door, they strapped his hands and feet to the gurney to immobilize him during the operation.

Dr. Felix and Dr. Axel, identical in their malevolent intent, hovered over their victims, surgical tools in hand. Frankie's eyes opened when Dr. Axel placed smelling salts under his nose. Whatever was about to happen, I had to do something.

"Stay here. If I get hurt, run."

Rica shook her head, frowning and signaling frantically that she was coming with me.

I took a deep breath and said, "Okay then, One... two... three!"

The doctors, Inga, the other attendants, and everyone else in the amphitheater turned when I kicked the door open with a resounding crash. The cultist's chants faltered as we burst into the room.

"Move away from the gurneys!" I shouted.

Dr. Felix sneered, his eyes narrowing. "You're too late, Mr. Thomas," he said. "The ritual is already underway, and you'll die attempting to stop it."

Dr. Felix and Dr. Axel turned in surprise when Tony and Maya followed us into the amphitheater. The three attendants reached for their pistols, but it was too late as Maya hurried to the gurney and grabbed the back of Dr. Felix's operating smock. His scalpel bounced on the floor when Maya pointed her gun at his head.

Rica moved swiftly, racing to one of the movie cameras and pushing the cameraman in a toga aside. Maya shot at the ceiling, the crack echoing through the amphitheater. The cultists and the attendants froze as I unstrapped Frankie's arms and legs.

"Stay where you are, or I'll blow the good doctor's head off," Maya looked at the three attendants and said, "Unbuckle your holsters and drop them to the floor."

Tony retrieved the holsters when Inga, Hank Bauer, and Bud Johnson obeyed Maya's order.

Axel's scalpel was still in his hand. After he and Felix exchanged a glance, he lunged for Tony, slashing him with the surgical instrument. When Tony dropped the holsters, all hell broke loose.

Dr. Felix grabbed Maya's hand and began wrestling her for her pistol. Inga hurried across the amphitheater to where the automatic weapons lay but quickly realized she couldn't use them without causing collateral damage.

Hank Bauer grabbed Maya's pistol when it clanked to the floor. Bud Johnson wrapped his hands around her ankles and wrestled her into a prone position. The situation looked bleak when a vivid blue flame burst from Maya's index finger, catching Johnson and Bauer's clothes on fire. The black robes of Doctors Axel and Felix were also aflame, smoke rising from the burning fabric as they rolled on the floor to extinguish them.

Flames continued to shoot from Maya's index finger, and cultists began scattering as she strafed the tiers of the amphitheater. Before she figured out how to stop the flame, the wooden beams in the basement roof had caught fire.

Chapter 28

A sudden explosion rocked the house, and my eyes widened as the ceiling above us cracked, plaster raining down on our heads. Frankie was standing alone but bracing his unsteady legs as he leaned against the gurney.

The wooden parts of the roof were aflame, and thick smoke had begun filling the amphitheater. I looked around for Rica but didn't see her. Maya's shoulder was beneath Tony's arm as she helped him to the door.

Felix staggered to his feet. He'd managed to rip away his burning robe, but his clothes continued to smoke. He grabbed a syringe from the tray and lunged at Frankie.

"You'll pay for this," he said.

Frankie grabbed Felix's arm. For a moment, it was a question of who was the strongest. Frankie prevailed, driving the needle into the mad doctor's own neck. Felix's eyes widened in shock as he collapsed. Axel was kneeling over his brother's lifeless body when a ceiling timber came crashing down on him. I yanked Dot off the gurney and began slapping her until her eyes opened.

"Wyatt, is that you?"

"It's me, Dot. I'm busting you out of here. Can you walk?"

Dot struggled off the gurney. "I'm tough," she said.

"That you are," I said.

The ceiling continued to fall all around us as Frankie clutched Dot's arm and said, "Get us out of here."

"Yes, sir," I said.

A siren began wailing as if we had set off an alarm. Maya had ascended the stairs with Tony. When she got him outside, she returned to help, grabbing Dot's arm and pulling her to the door, Frankie and I following. When we reached the front door, we saw the flashing lights of cop cars and fire trucks. Cultists in crimson robes and servants in togas piled out of the burning building, the police arresting them as soon as they did.

There were also ambulances, and I watched paramedics load Frankie, Dot, and Tony. They squealed from the parking lot amid screaming sirens.

Rica was nowhere to be found. Opening the front door, I reentered the burning building. Billy appeared from the rain and followed me.

"Where's Rica?" he said.

"Don't know," I said. "I'm going to look for her."

"Me too," he said.

"I'm coming," Maya said. "Let's hurry."

We encountered Inga Talledaga, Hank Bauer, and Bud Johnson emerging from the smoke. Maya had recovered her pistol. She drew it and pointed it at them.

"Hands in the air. You're under arrest for the murder of Oliver Marshall."

Billy and I continued into the smoke as Maya escorted the three attendants to the front door. We hadn't gone far when Rica appeared carrying a paper sack. She handed the sack to Billy and began signing.

"What?" I said.

"Dr. Felix's film records," Billy said. "Enough evidence to end the reign of terror here in Pinebridge."

When we reached the front door and hurried outside, the rain was falling in torrents. The fire department was on location, but there was no fire to extinguish—the rain had already done it. A police officer grabbed Maya's shoulders.

"Are you okay, Detective Henstooth?"

"Couldn't be better, Officer Santos," she said. "Thanks for getting here so fast."

"Where's your uniform?" he asked.

"Long story," she said.

Officer Santos smiled and said, "Got to go. See you back at the station."

I glanced at Billy and asked, "Where did you come from?"

"I heard the alarms and got worried," he said.

I handed the sack of evidence to Maya as death investigators removed the bodies of the Devereaux twins.

"Rica collected all the evidence we'll need to put this case to rest," I said. "What now?"

"Get out of this security worker's uniform," she said. "Wait on me, and we'll go to the hospital and check on Tony."

"You got it," I said.

"What about Rica and me?" Billy asked.

"Return Rica to Bella Donna's," Maya said. "She's still an escaped patient until we get things sorted out."

Maya changed into her uniform and then joined me in her police cruiser.

"Feel better?" I asked.

"Much better," she said.

"I knew you and Tony would figure a way to help us rescue Frankie and Dot. The way you did it amazed me."

"Me too," Maya said. "Efy Henstooth was correct. I do have the power."

Maya smiled when I asked, "How will you explain to your family and friends that you're a witch?"

"I'm not explaining anything," she said. "This is between you, me, and Tony, and I expect both of you to keep it to yourselves."

"You have no problem with me, and I'm sure Tony will feel the same."

The rain had finally stopped when we pulled into Alexandria's hospital's parking lot. In the wee hours of the morning, people were moving in the reception area and hallways as we received directions. Frankie was in bed, awake and smiling, as we entered his room.

"What did the doctor say?" I asked.

"Except for a few bruises, I'm good to go, though they decided to keep me overnight."

"Glad to hear it," I said.

"When I'm released, I want to meet my sister and her grandson," Frankie said.

"I'll arrange it," I said.

Frankie became introspective and said, "Wyatt, I'm sorry."

"For what?" I asked.

"Doubting you."

"No problem," I said. "I'm a pro and can handle constructive criticism."

"My criticism wasn't constructive, and my lack of good sense almost got me killed."

"Everything worked out," I said. "Axel and Felix Devereaux didn't survive the fire, and the evidence Rica collected will thwart any complaints their family may have."

"What about Harper?" he asked.

"Best as I can tell, she wasn't involved in the corruption and malpractice at the hospital. She was a pawn of her father and Celeste Gauthier. She'll have lots of mental healing to do."

"I'm relieved," Frankie said.

"You still have feelings for her?" I asked.

"What I had was a middle-age crisis. Harper made me feel I was truly the King of the Krewe of Illusion. In the end, an illusion was all it was."

"What about Adele?" I asked.

"When I return to New Orleans, I'm going to get on my knees, confess what I did, and beg her to forgive me," Frankie said.

We turned to the door when someone said, "Forgive you for what?"

Frankie's wife, Adele, and her daughter, Toni Bergamo, stood in the doorway. Adele hugged me before turning her attention to Frankie.

Adele was a gorgeous middle-aged woman with dark hair and eyes. Her daughter Toni was equally gorgeous and had the same dark eyes, but her hair was short and ash blond. Both were wearing stylish black dresses.

Toni looked at Maya and asked, "Is Frankie in trouble with the police?"

"No trouble at all," Maya said. "I'm here with Wyatt to see his partner, Tony."

After introducing her to Maya, Toni said, "Tony's in the hospital? How is he?"

"Don't know yet. We'll see him soon as we leave here," I said.

Though engaged in an intense conversation, Adele was holding Frankie's hand. Maya glanced at me and then at the door.

"Nice meeting you, Ms. Bergamo," she said. "Looks as if it's time to go."

"Mom and Frankie need some space. I'll come with you," Toni said.

Dot Beaufoy's room was down the hall, and we found it filled with her parents, husband, and children. I smiled and waved and then pointed to the door.

"Wyatt," she said. "Don't go yet."

Dot was crying as she hugged me. "Are you okay?" I asked.

"I'm fine. They're keeping me overnight and releasing me tomorrow. Thank you for saving me."

"I didn't do it alone," I said.

Dot introduced me to her family. As we prepared to leave, Father Piastri appeared, smiling when he saw me and Maya.

"Still singing, I hope," he said.

"Thanks to you, Father," Maya said. "I have my first professional gig next month in New Orleans."

"Wonderful," he said. "You know I'm retired now. Any chance of me scoring a ticket."

Maya nodded. "You'll have the best seat in the house."

Maya smiled as we walked down the hall to Tony's room. He was awake, and a nurse was checking his vitals as we entered.

"Toni," he said. "What are you doing here?"

"Mom couldn't wait another minute. She wanted me to drive but would have taken a bus if I had refused. You okay?"

"Another incision mark on my belly," he said. "None of my vital organs were affected, and thanks to Maya, I didn't bleed to death. I'll be here a few more days."

"What about Lil?" I asked.

"She panicked when I called her. I convinced her I was okay, and it was too dangerous to drive here."

"Who is Lil?" Maya asked.

"Tony's better half," I said. "I was worried. When I asked for your help, I wasn't expecting you to get stabbed."

"Neither was Lil. She's talking retirement again."

"Are you listening this time?" I asked.

"Hell no!" he said. "Thanks for saving my life."

"Anytime," Maya said.

"Something you want to tell me about the fire shooting from your hand?" he asked.

"When we have a minute alone," Maya said. "I'll tell you all about it."

"I can wait," he said. "How's Frankie and Dot?"

"None the worse for wear. Both will be released later today," I said.

"Is Frankie happy?"

"He will be once he meets his sister and nephew," I said. "The Devereaux brothers were the only casualties of the fire, and Rica retrieved enough evidence from the house to prove all the abuse and corruption at the Pinebridge Mental Hospital. If I have anything to say about it, the padded cells will become a thing of the past."

"If you stick around until the doctors release me, I'll give you a ride home," he said.

"Sounds like a deal," I said. "I wasn't relishing having to hitchhike or take the bus."

"When are you going to break down and buy a car?" Toni asked.

"Never," I said.

"You look beat," Toni said. "I'll stay with Tony if you two want to leave and get some rest."

"Good idea," I said. "I suppose I still have a room at the Beaufoy Hotel."

"One more thing before you go," Tony said. "Who murdered Oliver Marshall?"

"Inga Talledaga," Maya said. "She even had the switchblade that she used to kill Marshall when we arrested her."

"Why did she kill him?" Tony asked.

"She and Marshall both had a crush on Lyrica Winter. When Marshall took Rica to the cemetery to molest her, Inga followed them. She killed Marshall and then returned to his body later and worked it over with a panther claw."

"Panther claw?" Tony said.

"One of the things we found when searching her cabin on the bayou," Maya said. "The coroner realized the scratches occurred long after the murder because there was no blood involved."

"And the barman? Who murdered him?"

"Don't know yet. My guess is we'll tie it to a contract hit by Dr. Felix Devereaux."

"And Ms. Gauthier?" Tony asked.

"Up to her neck in everything except the murders," Maya said. "There's definitely prison time in her future."

"What about Kayla Duhon?" I asked.

"We have no proof she had anything to do with the hospital," Maya said. "Celeste liked younger women and had the means to attract them. Kayla was a victim, just like Harper Devereaux."

"I'm happy it's you tying all the loose ends in this case and not me," I said.

"I'll probably need your help before it's all put to bed," she said.

I smiled and said, "You can count on me."

The sun was rising as Maya stopped her police cruiser on the street in front of the Beaufoy.

"How much longer will you be in town?" she asked.

"At least until Frankie and Bella Donna are introduced. The family has some problems to resolve and kinks to sort out."

"Leo's is a good place to strengthen old bonds and create new ones," she said.

"Great idea," I said. "Any chance we'll hear you sing?"

Maya waved and said, "Never know. Sleep tight."

"You too," I said as she rolled up the window and drove away down Main Street.

Chapter 29

By the time I checked out of the Beaufoy Hotel and said goodbye to Dot Beaufoy and her family, I had managed to catch up on my sleep. I waited in the covered driveway with my suitcase. Before returning to New Orleans with Tony Nicosia, I'd promised to accompany Frankie Castellano to his sister Bella Donna's cottage and introduce them. The trip to the cottage proved more stressful than I had anticipated.

Frankie and his crew arrived in a gray Mercedes SUV that had probably cost more than I had ever made in a year. Adele, Frankie's wife, was driving, Frankie in the front passenger seat. Tony Nicosia and Toni Bergamo, the two tees as I'd come to call them, were in the back seat, and I joined them after stowing my suitcase in the back of the SUV. Adele and Frankie were engaged in conversation and barely greeted me before driving away from the hotel.

Maya had provided Adele with GPS coordinates to Bella Donna's house, and she was driving with one hand, gesturing with the other, and barely noticing the shops and churches of Pinebridge we passed.

"I glanced at Toni and said, "Is Frankie in trouble?"

"He's fritzing out about meeting his sister," Toni said. "Mom's trying to calm his nerves without much success."

Catching Toni's comment, Frankie said, "I'm not fritzing out about anything."

"You've all but drummed a hole in the dashboard," Adele said. "You're not just nervous, you are frightened beyond belief."

"Nervous, maybe; frightened, never," he said. "I just can't stop thinking that Papa loved her more than me, even though she's half black."

"We've been married for almost seven years, and I've never heard you mention your father," Adele said. "And what difference does it make if Bella Donna is half black? You don't have a racist bone in your body, so why does it make a difference now?"

"Paco, my dad, was the meanest old bastard who ever walked the face of the earth. I can't even begin to tell you everything he did to me when I was a boy."

"Name one," Adele said.

"He took my horn and hid it from me," Frankie said.

"Because he wanted you to concentrate on the family business. It didn't mean he didn't love you."

"He had an illicit affair, sharing his affections with someone other than his family," Frankie said.

"Better watch it, Mr. Castellano," Adele said. "Your dad isn't the only person guilty of indiscretion."

"Paco never confessed to my mom," Frankie said.

"Because your mother had already passed away by then," Adele said. "Who was he supposed to tell?"

"He could have told me," Frankie said.

"Wyatt," Adele said. "You've met Frankie's sister. What's your opinion of her."

"She's attractive, highly intelligent, and a caring human being. She's definitely Frankie's sister, and you'll see the resemblance the moment you meet her," I said.

"What about Billy?" Frankie said. "He's autistic."

"I never knew you when you were young," I said. "If I had, I imagine you were probably much like Billy is now."

"I'm not autistic," he said.

"Autism isn't a death sentence, and it takes many forms. Albert Einstein was autistic. So is Elon Musk and Bill Gates. Shall I continue?"

I nodded when Frankie said, "Albert Einstein?"

"Billy is working on a degree in business online and will soon be a college graduate. My guess is he'll make you proud someday."

"Okay," Frankie said. "I'll quit being an asshole. What about my niece?"

"Your niece Wanda and grand-nephew Billy are extraordinary people. Paco wasn't the best papa in the world, though he probably had an extraordinary mind. You and Bella Donna are recipients of his intelligence. One thing I know for sure: she's dying to meet her little brother."

"Paco did more harm than good," Frankie said.

"To a degree, we're all guilty of that," I said.

Frankie turned in his seat, looking at me, and asked, "What would you do if you were in my situation?"

"If I suddenly learned I had an older sister, I would embrace her and learn everything she could tell me. I promise you're going to love her."

"Will Bella Donna accept me for who I am?" Frankie asked.

I laughed and said, "Hell, Frankie. That's a tall order."

Frankie didn't take offense and smiled. "I'm doing my best to remain positive."

Adele reached across the console and squeezed his hand.

"Whatever happens, we're here for you," she said.

"And that comforts me," he said.

"Does everyone like barbecue?" I asked.

"Love it," Tony said.

"My favorite," Toni said.

"Maya's brother has a barbecue joint with a chopped beef sandwich to die for," I said. "There's a band, and Maya will be singing tonight. She's invited us to go there after you meet your sis," I said.

"Do they have scotch?" Frankie asked.

"Lots of it," I said.

Tony removed a flask from his shirt pocket and handed it to Frankie.

"Guess I'm going to have to buy you one of these," he said.

Tony's scotch somewhat calmed Frankie, though he was still nervous when Adele pulled in front of the rustic cottage. Bella Donna, Wanda, Billy, and Rica waited on the porch. When Frankie exited the Mercedes, Bella Donna got to her feet and left the porch to meet him.

They stared at one another for what seemed like an eternity. Bella Donna began to weep as she embraced her little brother. We watched Frankie put his arms around her, tears rolling down his cheeks. Not a word was spoken between the two. Their embrace said it all.

Chapter 30

The morning was sunny and humid as a man in an excavator dug a large hole on the grounds of the Pinebridge Mental Hospital. Maya, Tony, Billy, Rica, and I watched as the machine operator cut the engine and waved to Maya.

"Bones," he said. "Lots of them."

Forensic anthropologists and workers armed with shovels and spades climbed into the hole and began digging.

"Found it," Tony said. "How did you know where to start?" he asked.

"Ground Penetrating Radar," Maya said. "The data indicates more than a thousand bodies are buried in that hole. Many families will finally get closure and learn what happened to their loved ones."

"I wonder if Enrique Navarro's body is there?" Billy asked.

"His parents will be proud when the documentary created from his exposé airs," I said. "I predict your friend will receive a posthumous Pulitzer."

"Thanks to Rica. So sad he was so young," Billy said.

"This place ended dreams and shortened many young lives," Maya said.

Billy and Rica smiled when I said, "It brought you two together. What now?"

"Uncle Frankie hired me. Rica and I are moving to New Orleans after we're married."

"Wonderful," I said.

Rica had a rose in her hand. She stepped forward and tossed it into the excavation.

"That's for Enrique and all the others who lost their lives here," Billy said.

He smiled when I asked, "What about your mom and Bella Donna?"

"They'll visit us in New Orleans, though they're never going to leave the cottage in the forest."

"Neither would I if it were me," Maya said. "The place is truly enchanted."

"Thanks again for everything," Billy said.

After warm embraces, Billy and Rica followed the pathway back to his house on the hospital grounds.

"We're done here," Maya said. "The job of sorting and identifying the remains will take months if not years."

"The French Quarter Fest is next month," I said. "Will you be singing?"

"Wouldn't miss it for the world," she said. "Father Piastri was right. Singing is such an integral part of my life, I couldn't suppress it forever."

"Tony and I will be there when you hit town. I'll show you around. When your concert ends, you'll be a French Quarter insider."

"And if you ever decide to leave the force here in Rapides Parish, you can join Wyatt and me in New Orleans," Tony said.

"You think I'm a good detective?"

Tony nodded and said, "As good as they come."

I laughed when Maya asked, "Are there Baptists in New Orleans?"

"Every religion you can imagine," I said.

"When are you and Tony returning to New Orleans?" Maya asked.

"We're packed and ready," Tony said.

"It's almost lunch and not that far to Leo's," she said. "Can you eat some barbecue before you leave?"

"Count me in," Tony said. "New Orleans has wonderful food, but no better barbecue in the world than Leo's."

"You Wyatt?" Maya said.

I grinned and said, "Like I told you once before, you had me at hello."

End

Book Notes

Krewe of Illusion draws heavily on conjecture and local rumors about the Central Louisiana State Hospital in Pineville, Louisiana. The psychiatric hospital, built in 1906, is still in operation.

Established many years before the dawn of modern psychiatric medicine, it housed thousands of patients at a time and has just as many buried among its grounds.

Shrouded in decades of mystery, the hospital was the perfect model for a fictional tale of government and medicine gone horribly wrong.

I hope you enjoyed reading *Krewe of Illusion* as much as I enjoyed writing it and that you liked all the eccentric characters. I hope you'll read all my French Quarter Mystery Series books featuring moody private detective Wyatt Thomas.

The *Paranormal Cowboy Series* features Buck McDivit, my modern-day cowboy detective who likes horses, cowgirls, and Australian sheepdogs. My *Oyster Bay Mystery*, set on a Louisiana island near New Orleans, shares many French Quarter Mystery characters. Thanks for being a fan. My stories would be little more than morning fog wafting across a forgotten lawn without beautiful readers like you.

About the Author

Eric Wilder is an American author known for his gripping mystery novels set in New Orleans. He was born and raised in Louisiana, where he discovered his love for storytelling at a young age. After completing his education, Wilder spent several years in the oil and gas industry before pursuing a career as a writer.

Wilder's breakthrough came with the publication of Big Easy, which introduced readers to his signature blend of suspense, action, and local color. The book instantly succeeded, drawing critical acclaim and a devoted following. Wilder followed up with a collection of thrillers set in the heart of New Orleans.

Wilder's writing is characterized by his deep knowledge of the city and its unique culture and his skillful use of suspense and plot twists to keep readers on the edge of their seats. His books have been praised for their authenticity, vivid descriptions, and compelling characters.

Today, Eric Wilder is a respected author with a loyal fan base and a reputation for delivering top-notch thrillers that transport readers to the heart of New Orleans.

Wilder is the author of twenty novels, several cookbooks, many short stories, and Murder Etouffee, a book that defies classification. His series features characters who often find themselves involved in the paranormal.

Eric Wilder lives in Oklahoma near historic Route 66 with his wife, Marilyn, a gorgeous pit bull named Moebius, and two remarkable cats, Buttercup and Blanco.